Property of Bridge Water
Please Return to
Landmark Lodge

Walking Shoes

A Mt. Hope Southern Adventure

Book One

Lynne Gentry

TRAVEL LIGHT PRESS
FANTASY   DRAMA   ADVENTURE

Walking Shoes (Mt. Hope Southern Adventures, Book One)
Revised Edition of *Reinventing Leona*
(Tyndale House Publishers 2011)
Copyright © 2016 by Lynne Gentry
November 2016 Edition. All rights reserved.

No part of this publication may be reproduced, stored in a retrieval system or transmitted in any form or by any means, electronic or mechanical, including photocopying, recording, or otherwise, without written permission from the publisher.

For information visit: www.lynnegentry.com

This is a work of fiction. Names, characters, organizations, places, events, and incidents are either products of the author's imagination or are used factiously.

Cover photo Shutterstock
Edited by Gina Calvert
Cover by Travel Light Press

ISBN: 978-0-9986412-0-1
ISBN: 0998641200

Summary

When stepping out is the only way forward…

When Leona Harper crashes into tragedy,
the shocked pastor's wife
is forced to summon her estranged children home.
But parenting young adults in a nosy, small southern town
may prove more difficult than reinventing herself.
Determined to give her broken family a shot at a second chance,
Leona begins to put one foot in front of the other.
Reconciliation and healing won't come easy
in this zany, trouble-filled, walk-through-grief adventure.

Humor. Heart. Hope.

Escape into this delicious southern adventure.

Subscribe to Lynne's **JOIN THE ADVENTURE** Newsletter.
Subscribers receive a FREE download of bonus material.

www.lynnegentry.com

Next in the MT. HOPE SOUTHERN
ADVENTURES

Shoes to Fill
Dancing Shoes
Baby Shoes

WOMEN OF FOSSIL RIDGE SERIES

Flying Fossils
Finally Free
First Frost

Check out Lynne Gentry's
Nail-Biting Medical Thrillers
Ghost Heart
Port of Origin
Lethal Outbreak
Death Triangle

Have you checked out Lynne Gentry's
Sci-Fi/Time Travel Adventures?

The Carthage Chronicles
Healer of Carthage
Return to Exile
Valley of Decision
A Perfect Fit
Shades of Surrender

For My Mother
Who is finally free to dance in red high heels.

Walking Shoes

Chapter One

"Living in the parsonage is not for sissies." Leona Harper's husband planted a kiss on the top of her head. "If you want to wear fancy red shoes, wear 'em, darlin'."

"Maybe I'll wait until Christmas."

"It's almost Thanksgiving. Why don't you go ahead and break them in?"

"I was fixin' to, but ..." Leona twisted her ankle in front of the mirror, imagining herself brave enough to wear trendy shoes whenever she wanted. "You don't think they might be a bit much?" She reached for the shipping box. "The bows didn't look this big on my computer screen."

"So what if they are?"

"I wouldn't dare fuel Maxine's fire."

J.D. tucked his Bible under one arm and pulled Leona to

him with the other. "If Sister Maxine wants to talk, let's give her somethin' real juicy to say."

Leona loved the way this bear of a man nuzzled her neck every Sunday morning. J.D. Harper was as handsome as the day they met some thirty years ago, even with the silver streaks traipsing across his well-trained waves. Folks often guessed him a successful CEO of some major corporation rather than the pastor of a dying church in a small west Texas town.

"I can hear her now. 'Anyone who can buy new shoes doesn't need a raise.'" Leona pushed J.D. away and undid the ankle straps. "Eighteen years and we haven't even had a cost of living adjustment."

"The church provides our house."

"You know I adore living in this old parsonage, but we're not accruing a dime of equity." She buried the shoes in the box and closed the lid. "How are we ever going to be able to afford to retire?" She stashed the box next to her forgotten dreams.

"We've got equity where it counts—"

"Don't say heaven." Leona rolled her eyes at J.D.'s ability to remain slow to anger. "As long as the Board believes we're living on easy street, I don't know how we're going to make ends meet here on earth."

"The Board? Or Maxine?"

"Same thing."

"Live your life worrying about what Maxine Davis thinks, she wins." He had her, and he knew it. "Is that what you want?"

Ignoring the righteous twinkle in his eye, Leona slipped on the sensible brown flats she'd worn for the past ten years. "I hate it when you preach at me, J.D. Harper." She threaded her hand through the crook in his suit-clad arm.

"So many worries. So little time." He kissed her temple. "If it weren't for guilt trips, you wouldn't go anywhere."

"It's all we can afford." Leona scooped up the Tupperware caddie that contained her famous chicken pot pie. What good did it do to dream of exotic cruises or expensive adventures? She'd given up those dreams, along with her dreams of writing, years ago. But she'd never give up on wanting her family whole, "Let's get the Storys and go."

Sitting on the parsonage living room couch were the blue-haired twins and founding members of Mt. Hope Community Church. They waited where they waited every Sunday morning. Today, instead of their regular offering of homemade pickles, they each had a large relish tray on their lap.

"Etta May. Nola Gay. I'm fixin' to preach the Word. You girls got your amens ready?" J.D. offered Nola Gay his arm.

Nola Gay blushed, "Reverend Harper, you're such a tease."

"It's my turn to hold his arm, Sister," Etta May complained.

"Lucky for you lovely ladies, I've got two arms."

Arm-in-arm J.D. and his fan club crossed the church parking lot, trailed by the lowly pastor's wife.

J.D. opened the door to the fellowship hall. The familiar aroma of coffee and green bean casseroles assaulted Leona's nose. If only she had a nickel for every meal she'd eaten in this dingy room, maybe they could pay all their bills, save a little for retirement, and even afford the mini vacation J.D. had reluctantly agreed to take when the kids came home for Thanksgiving.

"Y'all need help with those trays?" Leona asked Nola Gay.

"We may be slow, but we can still handle a few pickles," Nola Gay assured her.

"Holler if y'all need me." Leona headed for the kitchen, weaving through the scattered tables. Crock-Pots brimming with roast and carrots or pinto beans and ham lined the counter.

While J.D. checked the overloaded power strip, Leona deposited her contribution for the monthly potluck scheduled to follow the morning service. She glanced at the dessert table. Maxine's coconut cake was not in its usual place. "I'm going to my seat."

"You can't avoid her forever," J.D. whispered.

It wasn't that she was afraid of the sour elder's wife; she just hadn't figured out the best way to address Maxine's latest attack on J.D.'s attempt to make the worship service a little bit more relevant, something that would help an outsider feel welcome.

Truth be known, Maxine and Howard didn't want outsiders to get comfortable on the pews of Mt. Hope Community Church. Especially anyone they considered to be "the less fortunate." With the addition of the highway bypass, the community had experienced an influx of vagrants. Most of them needed help. Howard and Maxine preferred these interlopers to just keep walking.

Why God had seen fit to park a generous man like J.D. Harper at a church where the chairman of the elder board's wife loved only two things—having the last word and adding to her list of complaints against the Harpers—was first in a list of pressing questions Leona intended to ask when she did get to heaven.

"I don't want to start a fight before church," Leona said. "It would ruin my worship and I'll be hanged if I'll let her take that too."

"That's my girl." J.D.'s eyes lighted on something behind her. "Better put your game face on, Maxine's fixin' to test your resolve."

Leona turned to see Maxine prancing through the door with her coconut cake seated on a throne of beautiful cut glass and her heavy purse dangling from the crook of her arm.

"Morning, Leona!" Maxine crowed.

Leona plastered on a smile and maneuvered through the chairs. "Can I give you a hand?"

"I don't think so." Maxine pulled her cake out of reach. "Unlike that cheap Pyrex stuff you bring your little casserole in, this is an extremely expensive piece of antique glass. This pedestal has been in our family for years."

Leona knew all about the Davis glass. Every Christmas, Leona had to practically beg Maxine to let the hospitality committee use the crystal punchbowl the Davis family had donated to the church on the condition the church insure it. The job of washing the slippery thing was one Leona tried to avoid.

Leona nipped the reply coiling on her tongue and offered her best platitude, "Your cake and platter are as beautiful as ever. Oh, I forgot I promised the Storys I'd give them a hand." She smiled and quickly moved on to help the twins fussing over how many dill or sweet pickles they should put on their trays.

Leona regretted that from behind her retreat could leave the impression of her tail securely tucked between her legs. She waited until Maxine exited the fellowship hall before she headed to the sanctuary and her regular front row pew.

J.D. slid in just as Wilma Wilkerson blasted out the first note on the organ. He winked at her and began to sing.

Still stinging from her failure at repairing her relationship with Maxine, Leona inched along the wooden pew that vibrated from the force of her husband's resonant bass. Clutching the worn hymnal, she filled her lungs to capacity, tightened her diaphragm, and joined him in praise. Music always carried her past any earthly troubles.

Behind the large oak pulpit, song leader, Parker Kemp brought the organist and sparse crowd to a synchronized close. Blue from holding on to the last note, Leona glanced across the sanctuary aisle. Maxine Davis eyed her back with her nose wrinkled in disapproval. Leona quickly diverted her gaze.

"And the church said?" Parker flipped to his next selection.

"Amen," the Storys chimed in unison.

"Before the sermon, we'll be singing all five verses of page 156. Please stand, if it's convenient."

Solid oak pews groaned as the congregation lumbered to their feet.

Parker gave a quick nod to the organist, readying his hand for the beat. His expression morphed into that dazzling smile sure to land him the perfect wife someday.

Leona loved the Sundays this radiant young fellow led. Unlike the steady diet of first-and-third-versers, the county extension agent sang every word of every verse. Hymns that once plodded the narrow aisles danced before the Lord under Parker's direction. His ability to stir in a little spirit always gave

Leona the distinct feeling rain had fallen upon her parched lawn, offering a smidgen of hope that if this congregation had a shot at resurrection, maybe she did too.

Naturally, Maxine claimed allowing such unrestrained expressions of joy during the song service might lead to who-knows-what in the sanctuary. It had cost J.D. popularity points with the elder board, but in the end none of them had been willing to remove Parker's name from the volunteer rotation. Thank God.

The congregation fidgeted as Wilma Wilkerson attempted to prod some heft into the organ's double row of yellowed keys and squeaky pedals.

Leona used the extra time to beseech the Lord on Parker's behalf. She'd always hoped their daughter Maddie would one day consider Parker more than an irritation, but Maddie was insisting on going another direction.

Perhaps the recent arrival of Bette Bob's adorable niece was God's plan for Parker. Unlike J.D., who never did anything without praying it through for weeks, she was flexible. To prove it, she made a quick promise to the Lord that she'd do her best to connect Parker and Bette Bob's niece at today's potluck.

J.D. reached for Leona's hand and gave it a squeeze, same as he did every Sunday before he took the pulpit. Some pastors prayed. Most checked their fly. Mt. Hope's preacher always held his wife's hand during the song preceding his sermon.

Relishing her role as coworker in the Kingdom, Leona wiggled closer, her upper thigh pressed tight against her husband's. Nestled securely against J.D.'s charcoal pinstripes, Leona could hear the throaty warble of the Story sisters parked three pews back.

The blue-haired-saint sandwich had a crush on her husband, but to begrudge these seniors a little window shopping bordered on heresy.

The old girls had suffered a series of setbacks the last few months, burying several of their shriveled ranks. What would it hurt if staring at her handsome husband gave them a reason to get out of bed on Sunday mornings? Besides, Widow's Row vacancies were increasing at an alarming rate, and replacing these committed congregants seemed unlikely, given the current trend of their small town's decline.

J.D.'s familiar grip throttled Leona's errant thoughts.

She patted his hand. Her husband felt unusually clammy this chilly fall morning. Was this a new development, or something she'd missed earlier because she'd been in such a twit?

J.D. had been dragging lately. She'd just written off his exhaustion as the discouragement that hounded a man with the weight of a dying congregation on his shoulders.

What if something else was wrong? What if the elders had voted to let them go and J.D. hadn't told her? She felt her keen senses kick into overdrive. Out of the corner of her eye, she checked his coloring.

"Are you okay, J.D.?" Leona whispered.

He kept his eyes on Parker, but Leona knew he wasn't just waiting for his cue to take the stage. He slipped his arm around her trim waist, drawing her close. He whispered, "Who by worrying can add a single hour to her life?" His breath warmed the top of her color-treated head. A tingle raced through her body.

J.D. had promised her he'd take off for the entire week of Thanksgiving. He needed a break and they both needed the time to reconnect their family.

Both kids had finally agreed to come home from their universities. Leona wanted to believe David's and Maddie's hearts were softening, but she knew they'd only consented to a family gathering because it was their father's fiftieth birthday. For him, they would do anything. For her? Well, that was a prayer the Lord had yet to answer.

The song ended, but the glow lighting Parker's dark eyes did not. "You may be seated." He gathered his list and songbook and left the podium.

J.D. ascended the stage steps as if taking some faith

mountain.

He removed the sermon notes tucked inside a leather-bound Bible and surveyed the crowd's upturned faces.

Leona recognized the tallying look in her husband's eyes. He would know the dismal attendance count before Deacon Tucker posted the numbers on the wooden board in the back of the sanctuary.

J.D. unbuttoned his coat, ran his hand down his tie. "Mornin', y'all." He greeted his congregation of eighteen years with the same determined expression he had his first Sunday in this pulpit. Filleting the worn pages of his Bible with a satin ribbon, he opened to the day's chosen text.

The rustle of people settling into their favorite pews rippled across the sanctuary.

The Smoots' tiny addition fussed in the back row. Newborn cries were rare here. Leona was grateful the Smoots had decided to stay in Mt. Hope. Other than Parker, most of the young people, including her own children, left after high school and never came back.

The sound of children was something Leona missed. She'd loved the days of diapers, sleepless nights, and planting kisses on the exquisite soft spot right below tiny earlobes.

If only dispensing love could remain that simple and teething remain a mother's biggest worry.

Leona offered a quick prayer for the fertile mother of four. Maybe the Lord would spare that young woman the mistakes of her pastor's wife.

Leona reined in her wandering focus and aimed it on the man standing before the congregation. No matter what became of her relationship with her children, she could always take comfort in the fact that at least she had J.D.

Uneasiness suddenly intruded upon her admiration. Something wasn't right. A shimmering halo circled her husband's head. Surely the unnerving effect was the result of the flickering fluorescent stage lighting. J.D. would surely lampoon her overactive imagination, but Leona couldn't resist scanning the platform.

Four dusty ficus trees and two tall-backed elders' chairs were right where Noah left them when he exited the ark.

Leona smoothed the Peter Pan collar tightening around her neck. Her hand froze at her throat, her breath trapped below her panicked grasp.

Glistening beads of sweat dripped from J.D.'s brow. He removed a monogrammed handkerchief from his pocket and mopped his notes. With a labored swipe, he dried his forehead and returned the soaked linen to his breast pocket. As he clasped the lip of the pulpit, his knuckles whitened.

Leona stood, ready to call out no matter how inappropriate,

but her husband's warning gaze urged her to stay put.

J.D. cleared his throat. "There was one who was willing to die—" the pastor paused—"that you might live." A pleased smile lit his face. He placed a hand over his heart and dropped.

* * * * *

J.D. Harper had always been the spontaneous one. Dying in the middle of his sermon was so like him.

The weight of the crocheted afghan anchored Leona's body to the wingback chair in the corner of her bedroom. Her mind bobbed in a cloudy soup. She didn't remember walking across the parking lot, climbing the steps to the parsonage, or stumbling to her bedroom. Nor did she recall shivering uncontrollably.

For some reason Roxie's reassuring words—"Let's bundle her like a burrito and stave off the shock"—kept colliding with the apologetic image of Charlie Copeland saying, "I'm so sorry, Leona," as he closed the ambulance door.

"How about I turn on your music?" Roxie didn't wait for an answer. She flipped a switch on the small boom box on top of the dresser, activating the croon of the Gaither Vocal Band.

A spectator in her own bedroom, Leona puffed at the blue yarn irritating her nose. She watched her best friend flit around the shade-darkened space, turning on the lamps and barking orders as if tragedy came boxed in the parts shipments arriving daily at her auto parts store.

How Roxanne Brewer peddled everything from carburetors to windshield wipers wearing those above-the-knee skirts and stilettos had vexed men far and wide for years. But this mother of four could put her finger on replacement valves in record speed, and she'd give a person the shirt off her Marilyn Monroe figure if she thought it would get them on the road again.

Roxie wedged herself like a tire jack between Leona and the big-boned elder's wife hovering nearby. "Maxine, you're going to have to back up and give the woman some air."

"Roxanne, our pastor's wife does not need a tune-up." Maxine peered over the edge of the half-glasses perched on the end of her pointed nose. "She needs spiritual comfort."

"From you?"

"I *am* the Chairman of the Board's wife."

"My point exactly!"

"Roxie," Leona's voice sounded more pathetic than usual.

"I'm sorry, Leona." Sparks flashed in Roxie's sapphire eyes, igniting the static in her fly-away red hair. She turned to Maxine. "How about we take this discussion outside?"

"J.D. Harper's passing is not a matter for the Episcopalians." Maxine's spine straightened to its full five-foot-ten height. Leona recognized the familiar battle stances and braced for the worst. Hardly a chamber of commerce meeting passed that the

Cadillac Queen and the Parts Princess didn't mix it up over competitive practices, business, and religion. "The saints at Mt. Hope will tend to their own," she finished in a huff.

"I've seen how your husband herds the sheep at Mt. Hope." Roxie rested her hand on Leona's shoulder, her voice turning sugary sweet. "If you don't mind, I think my friend here will pass on your offer."

"A true friend would not let her own bitterness over losing a major customer interfere with her friend's best interests." Maxine's voice dripped saccharine.

Roxie's focus zeroed in on Maxine's smug grin, her restrained temper flushing her cheeks crimson. "I don't care where Davis Cadillac gets their auto parts these days. Can't you understand this poor woman needs a minute to herself?"

"We will see." Maxine approached Leona. Slicing the air in front of Leona's face with her flattened palm, she fished for support. "Sister Harper, do you want *me* or this chop-shop hussy to stay with you?"

Judging from the elder's wife's planted size-eleven feet, Leona suspected Maxine had no intention of leaving without a fight, let alone going peacefully. Much as she'd dreamed of the day she could give Maxine what for, right now she didn't have an ounce of fight left in her.

"Ladies, please. I know we're all upset, but I need to call the kids."

Roxie placed her hands on Maxine's shoulders, ratcheting her sideways. "In private."

Maxine's head swiveled, neck bones popping, her face demanding a reprieve. But Leona nodded, relieved she had not had to say the words she dreaded. Telling her children their father had just died would be difficult enough without the prying eyes of those who deemed her incompetent listening in. She didn't have it in her to smile at their critique of her coping methods.

Roxie pointed at Leona's silent face. "There you have it, Maxine." Roxie smiled. Don't let the door hit you in the butt on the way out."

"Episcopalians." Maxine stomped toward the exit. She turned and waggled her finger in Leona's direction. "Don't think for a moment this liberal heathen is interested in caring for the widows and orphans, Leona Harper." The door clicked shut with a decisive disgust.

Widows? Orphans? The ugly words ricocheted off the floral wallpaper, bounced around with Gloria Gaither's chorus of "Something Worth Living For," pierced the blue afghan, and slammed directly into Leona's heart.

"Thank goodness she's gone." Roxie peeled back a corner of the blanket and Leona felt her emotions hemorrhage. "You ready, girlfriend?"

Leona nodded but her body had joined forces with her ebbing resolve in a conspiracy to shut her down.

Roxie reduced the stereo volume. "I'll be right here." She drew her phone out of her bra and pressed a number on her favorites list. "Here you go."

Leona searched the liquid pools of Roxie's eyes, finding that familiar island of support. Fingers trembling, she took the phone and brought it to her ear. Trepidation rang loud and clear on her end. No one answered on the other.

Chapter Two

David Harper fiddled with the volume control then yanked out his disposable earphones. It was no use. He couldn't concentrate on a movie. Digging his fingers into the armrests of his first-class seat, he returned to an upright position. He stared out the window at the vast darkness, feeling separated from home by more than an ocean. Surprised he'd been able to catch an international flight on such short notice, he wasn't surprised he'd been unable to sleep as the plane hurtled him toward Momma. His normally sharp edge dulled with each tick of his expensive watch. He ripped out the in-flight wish catalog, flipped through a few pages, then stuffed it into the pocket. Shoe-shine kits and tie organizers were useless to a man headed home to bury his father.

He pressed the call button.

A uniformed woman appeared in the aisle. "May I help you?"

"A cup of coffee, please."

The flight attendant smiled. "Cream and sugar?"

Arriving exhausted and cranky to face Momma would not serve him well. "Black. The stronger, the better."

Tossing the tiny airline pillow onto the empty seat beside

him, he wondered why his mother thought he could preach his father's funeral sermon. *What makes her think I'd want to?* Hadn't he made it clear when he left the States to get his graduate degree in history that he had no intention of ever stepping into a pulpit, especially the one his father occupied? Had occupied.

David lowered his tray table. He raked his straight brown hair off his forehead, rested his head against the leather seat, and closed his eyes. He rubbed the place at his temples where Momma's words pounded out a haunting rhythm. Dad's dead. Dad's dead. Dad's dead.

David shifted in his seat, drumming his fingers on the makeshift table as he waited for his coffee. But he could not get comfortable. Nor could he shake the guilty feeling that disappointment had ruined his father's health, and his announcement would break his mother's heart.

* * * * *

A mountain storm had hit Denver during the night. Sleet pelted the window of Madison Harper's loft apartment. Sitting up in bed, she pushed mussed blonde curls away from her eyes, and checked the time on her cell phone. Eleven a.m. Apprehension fluttered in her growling stomach as she noticed she'd missed a call from Aunt Roxie at ten Central time and another from her mother not five minutes later.

"Why would Momma call during church?" Maddie rubbed her eyes, checking the screen again. "Pickings must have been slim at the church potluck for the attendance police to call before two."

Pressing Momma's number, Maddie braced for her mother's weekly grilling. *Did she go to church? Then where? Tell me about it.* Maddie reached for the fast food cup that had left a ring on the hand-me-down nightstand and wet her throat with the watery Diet Coke. What excuse could she offer Momma today? Last week it was that-time-of-the-month. This week she would have to claim late-night surgery rotations again. Risky, but even if Momma had her suspicions, she'd never fault attention to excellence.

"Maddie?" Her mother rarely answered on the first ring.

"Hey, Momma." Maddie doubted her sleepy voice would get past those keen ears, but hoped they could continue the pretense: Leona Harper didn't know her daughter spent Sunday mornings at the church of the sacred pillow, and Maddie didn't know her backsliding ways drove her mother crazy.

"I tried calling Katie Beth so you wouldn't be alone when I tell you . . . but Katie Beth didn't answer her phone. I went ahead and called your brother since England is several hours ahead of us."

Maddie's heart skipped a beat at the unusual sound of panic in Momma's voice. "K.B. must be at church." She'd regret admitting that her roommate was a better Christian than the preacher's daughter, but it was too late now. "What's so tragic that you spent the money to call David?"

"Sweetheart, maybe you should sit down." Why did her mother have to make a production out of every little thing? Maddie jabbed a pillow between her back and the wrought-iron headboard. "I am sitting down." Nobody exited the stage of Momma's show until she gave the cue so she might as well get comfortable.

"Sweetheart, I hate telling you this over the phone, but . . ." Momma's voice cracked. "Daddy's..." the hitch in Momma's voice stopped Maddie's heart. "Your father ... is ... dead."

Silence, heavy as the sinkers her father used to tie on the end of her fishing line, weighted the airwaves. Maddie yanked the phone away from her ear and stared at the blank screen. They hadn't been disconnected. If this new tactic was supposed to guilt her back to church, Momma had sunk to an all-time low.

"What do you mean?" Maddie didn't hide the edge of irritation creeping into her voice.

"He was in the middle of his first sermon point when suddenly he collapsed behind the pulpit. By the time I got to him . . ." Momma paused. "He was gone."

A loud buzzing crackled through the thick hush on the other end of the line, swelling to a roar inside Maddie's head. She'd not heard correctly. The seriousness of the words matched her mother's tone, but like a fever that had no obvious explanation, they did not make sense. Ask questions. Get the facts straight before you make a diagnosis. "What are you saying?"

"Maddie, I know you're shocked but we need to make a plan—"

"This isn't funny, Momma."

"Sweetheart, is there someone who can take you—"

"Daddy can't be dead." Suffocating beneath the unbelievable words, Maddie threw back the heavy quilt. She could hear muffled crying. "Momma!" The scream had come from somewhere deep within her body cavity, ripping a gash through every major organ as it exited.

"Maddie?" A smooth Southern alto flowed across the line. "Calm down, baby."

"Aunt Roxie?" Maddie adored her momma's best friend. The flaming-haired rebel was more fun than any of their stodgy flesh-and-blood relatives. Every time Roxie pried open the straitlaced parsonage lid sheltering the preacher's kids, Maddie sucked in the breath of fresh air as if it were her last.

"Baby, you need to catch the next plane home. Charge it to

my credit card."

A million unanswered questions raced through her mind, but only one thing mattered. "Aunt Roxie, did my daddy suffer?"

"Hell's bells, you know God wouldn't do that to your daddy."

"Tell Momma I'm on my way." Maddie closed her phone, her hands trembling. She swung her feet to the floor, but could find no solid footing on the cold wooden surface. Without the rock that had been her father, there was no place safe to stand.

* * * * *

Maddie dragged her finger through the thick layer of dust settled upon the darkened oak desk her father hauled up three flights of stairs the day he moved her to Denver.

If the family car goes over the rail, save Momma.

Why had Maddie's jumbled gray matter landed on her mother's ironclad rule? Maybe it was because the woman hated water deeper than a puddle, and this frightening development would be worse than the time they went to Memphis and had to cross that huge arched bridge spanning the Mississippi. Momma rolled down the windows, gripped the door handle, and made us promise we'd save her first since we could all swim.

For the most part, Daddy, the Maypole around whom Momma fluttered, humored his wife's irrational fear of drowning. But Maddie remembered feeling grateful when her father drew the line at Momma's determination to have the handy saying cross-stitched into the bands of the family's underwear.

As for rescuing Momma from a raging river, Maddie had yet to witness the need for such a heroic action. In truth, it was a well-known fact that most everybody in Mt. Hope believed Leona Harper walked on water. Maddie thought she'd seen her do it one time at the beach, but turns out Momma had found footing on a hidden sandbar.

Ratcheting up the heavy roll-top cover, Maddie cringed at the familiar squeak. She gathered the stack of blank residency applications and jammed them into a worn backpack. How had Daddy ever gotten Momma's head beneath the surface of the baptismal waters? The woman would rather take her chances with the devil than submit to a dunking. Either he tranquilized her or she must have really loved him.

Forcing the latch on the door of the secret cubby, Maddie found the tattered Bible her mother said she would want someday. Hands trembling, she opened the cover and read the words her father had written in his firm scrawl: *May the Word of the Lord always be a lamp unto your feet, Princess.*

Maddie slid the satin ribbon over tissue-thin pages and opened to the marked passage. While her father's exhortation took her aback, she was not surprised her mother had marked this particular passage, the twentieth chapter of Exodus.

Daddy believed in living the commandments, but Momma made sure that disobey and die had been encoded into her children's DNA.

To behave outside the boundaries of the preacher's wife's tidy little box demanded a round of punishment more memorable than Leona Harper's savory chicken pot pie. Taking a moment, Maddie looked over the rules God chiseled in stone.

Thou shalt not do this. Thou shalt not do that. Blah, blah, blah. Maddie couldn't help feeling sorry for the children of Israel living under the weight of the law.

She closed her daddy's Bible and stuck it in on top of the residency forms. She zipped her backpack.

Maybe the save-Momma commandment was another one of her mother's leadings of the Spirit. She had to admit Momma had the sixth sense of a psychic when she accurately predicted Deacon Hornbuckle's disappearance with his blonde secretary. I bet Momma knew Daddy would drop dead. Shame at her wicked thoughts washed over Maddie.

Despite any celestial forewarning, Momma would be scared to death. What would the woman do? How would she support herself? Leona Harper had been a preacher's wife for thirty years, having never worked a day outside the home since giving birth to David, the golden child.

The reason for her years of intense childhood training became crystal clear and jerked Maddie's head with a start. In her typical plan-ahead fashion, Momma had foreseen the possibility of this day and reared her children accordingly. She would expect her children to come home the same way she expected them to rescue her if the family car plunged through a guardrail.

David and Maddie Harper were Momma's catastrophic-event insurance policy.

Visions of her own plans disappearing below the churning surface of this tragedy flashed through Maddie's mind. Bile rose in her throat. How could she become a doctor if she dropped everything and dove in after Momma? How could her parents do this to her? Even more galling—how could God do this to her?

Maddie brushed away hot tears. She dug the point of a pen into the scratch pad and scribbled a note for Katie Beth. She hoisted the backpack to her shoulder, yanked the handle of the wheeled carry-on bag. The apartment door slammed behind her.

A sleety mix glazed the streets surrounding Colorado's best med school. Maddie pulled her jacket hood over her head and waited for the taxi to the airport. She scrolled to the med school number. The message she left on a secretary's voice mail claimed a family emergency.

Next, she scrolled to her boyfriend's number. Maddie hesitated before pushing Send. Maybe she should wait, call Justin after it was too late for him to insist on coming. Finding the right time to introduce the aspiring Olympic snowboarder was . . . dicey. Choosing this moment to spring the announcement that she planned to move in with him when her current lease expired was . . . suicidal. Snow had better survival odds in the eternal lake of fire.

This wasn't her father's fault. Unlike Momma, the good pastor never expected someone to jump in and rescue him. Maddie's breath hitched in her chest. Without Daddy, who would quiet the storm of her exasperating mother in cahoots with a rule-chiseling God?

Chapter Three

Surrounded by a circle of stunned church members, Leona sank onto the threadbare couch in the parsonage living room. A plate of food appeared under her nose. She shook her head and waved it away. A wave of concern rippled through the onlookers.

She didn't know how to release them from their culpability in adding to J.D.'s stress any more than she knew how to alleviate her own guilt.

Maybe if she had made a sign years ago that said, "Don't feed the preacher," J.D.'s arteries would not have been clogged by the abundance of cholesterol-laden casseroles that appeared every time two or more Christians gathered in one spot.

Roxie broke through Leona's raw and irrational thoughts, her face a billboard of concern. "Girlfriend, the Storys are here."

Leona eyed the Mason jar Roxie held as if the pickled contents were radioactive. "We're gonna need more chairs."

"You stay put," Roxie said. "I know just where to put these. I'll send someone to the church for a few folding chairs." Roxie marched the quart of homegrown baby gherkins to the kitchen, and Leona allowed her body to fall back against the green and gold plaid upholstery.

"Yoo-hoo." Nola Gay Story pressed through the crowd like a World War II bomber plane looking for Hiroshima. The elderly woman gave her a pitying look and offered a veined hand. "Sister and I are so sorry about the passing of Brother Harper."

"Thank you." Why was she thanking people? Shouldn't they be thanking her for sacrificing her husband for the good of the cause? Leona released Nola's calloused hand, shirking her too-little, too-late benevolence.

Etta May wiggled in close. "Sister and I never figured J.D. Harper to be the dramatic type, but he certainly went home with a glorious flair."

Nola Gay turned to Etta May. "That we could all meet our Maker with the words of the Lord upon our lips. Almost makes you wish women could preach, doesn't it, Sister?" Her jowls jiggled agreement.

The swaying motion gave Leona a touch of seasickness, or was her nausea a normal characteristic of grief? She diverted her eyes and let her mind drift back eighteen years to the day the Harper U-Haul arrived at the two-story yellow brick parsonage.

Leona had imagined a shady wraparound porch, an anxious

welcoming committee, and a tall glass of lemonade. What she got: a flat, crusty yard with a fire ant mound the size of a small child and two elderly bookends waving the first place ribbon the last pastor's wife had won for her pickled peaches and apparently left behind.

"Do you can, dear?" Nola Gay had asked as she charged down the sidewalk.

"No," Leona reluctantly admitted, ashamed she was making such a poor first impression on what must surely be two of the charter members of their new congregation.

"For crisp pickles, you must pick the short, chunkier cucumbers." Etta May pointed to the dark green specimens stuffed inside a glass jar.

"But not bloated, Sister," Nola Gay clarified.

Etta May nodded agreement. "Pick an overripe cucumber, and you will have mushy pickles for certain."

A sudden whiff of apple cider and cloves, the Storys' trademark fragrance, acted as smelling salts, reviving Leona from her catatonic disconnect. How quickly the last eighteen years had passed. Where had the time gone?

Life was short. Way . . . too . . . short. She remembered thinking these very thoughts the day she took her oldest to college and again two years later when she dropped off her youngest. Children growing up is a transition a person knows will come, a pain that can be prepared for. But becoming a widow before the closing prayer had never crossed her mind. Not ever.

Blinking back tears, Leona focused on the matching weathered faces hovering over her.

Etta May's stout finger poked Leona's shoulder. "Aren't the children coming home?"

Leona bristled. Surely it was the shock of J.D.'s death that made her want to claw everyone's eyes. She clamped her hand over her mouth, refusing to even entertain the possibility that this was who she really was without J.D. She reminded herself that despite the irritations she often felt for this body of folks, when it came to her darkest hour, most of them would be there for her in the best way they knew how. Especially these two women.

"Sister, that Brewer woman told you that David and Maddie are on their way. I just hope they beat the threatening weather. According to the Almanac it's going to be the roughest winter we've ever had." Nola Gay leaned in close, her breath smelling of denture cream. She dropped her voice. "Do you think it wise to fraternize with an Episcopalian?"

Cucumber beetles had better survival odds in the old girls' garden than she had of adjusting their conviction on who would or would not populate heaven. "Nola Gay, why don't you and

Etta May help yourselves to the Coca-Cola cake Bette Bob brought over? I know how you both love chocolate. I think the ladies have set up the food in the dining room."

Nola Gay patted Leona's hand. "Always thinking of others." Etta May's blue-tinged head bobbed in pleased admiration.

Simultaneously the sisters squeezed Leona's shoulders, linked arms, and shuffled through the congested living room. "Bette Bob, where's that chocolate?"

Slumping on the couch, Leona chided herself. Why hadn't she told these misguided sisters what they could do with their opinion of her best friend's salvation, and their infuriating implication that the preacher's children were anything less than perfect?

J.D. always said, "Leona, the day will come when you will have to choose between caring what other people think and trusting yourself."

Leona felt her insides tumble together and sink. She never expected today would be the day.

Chapter Four

The front door of the parsonage flew open and the woman Leona had been dreading swept in with the cold north wind.

"Mother?" Freeing herself from Roxie's protective grip, Leona rose from the couch. "How'd you get here so fast?"

Roberta Worthington could part a crowded room faster than Moses holding a staff over the Red Sea. "This dusty spot in the road is only two hour's drive from the city, Leona. If you came home more often you'd—"

"Bertie." Roxie flew to Leona's side, her russet hair raised like the ruff of a riled guard dog. "Nice to see you again. Can I take your coat? Get you something hot to drink?"

Fire flared in her mother's eyes, and Leona doubted if there was enough sweet tea in all of Mt. Hope to douse the flame.

"Mother, I'm sure you remember some of the folks from the church." Leona started the introductions with the wide-eyed Maxine parked on the far end of the couch, working her way around the room. As she neared the Storys, her mother held up a flattened hand.

"I'm an agnostic, Leona, not an Alzheimer's invalid. What I remember is that I never liked any of these country do-gooders."

Leona would be the first to admit the members of Mt. Hope Community Church had the uncanny ability to try the limits of brotherly love, but trashing these people who'd become like extended family crossed the line. "Mother!"

Roxie clamped an arm around Roberta's shoulder. "How about I help Bertie find a cup of coffee and a few kind words?" She flashed her don't-mess-with-me smile, the one she reserved for crotchety old geezers who complained about the scourge of foreign cars upon the American automobile industry while frequenting her store.

Roberta planted her feet and raised a perfectly stenciled brow at Roxie. "A cup of coffee would be nice."

Roxie mumbled something better not repeated and stomped off to the kitchen, where Leona suspected her next-door neighbor would regroup and return with a vengeance.

Squirming under her mother's sizing gaze, Leona prayed that Roxie would not dally. She hoped this desperate petition got better results than her pleas to change her mother.

Concentrating on each Italian-leathered tip of her gloved fingers, Leona's mother seemed to relish the mental stress her restrained quiet added to the room's general discomfort. "After my driver deposited me here, I sent him to the airport to pick up the children." She extracted a manicured hand from the cashmere lining and repeated the process on the other hand.

"You mean Melvin?"

"Whatever his name is."

"Mother, I wish you had asked before you made poor Melvin drive back to the city. Cotton has gone to fetch Maddie. And David plans to take a taxi because his flight is getting in so late." Leona pinched the throbbing place between her eyes. Any moment she expected the pain to explode into a full-fledged migraine.

"Well, as usual, you have everything under control. Obviously, you don't need your mother." She paired the gloves and dropped them into her oversized Gucci handbag.

"That's not true." Leona put her arms around the stiff woman and gave her a quick hug. "I'm glad you're here. Really I am." Surely the Lord would forgive this tiny fib considering the dire circumstances.

Her mother took a small step back. "It's just that I hate to think of my granddaughter climbing in some rattletrap vehicle with a church janitor. But you've always allowed Madison more freedom than I would have."

Leona felt everyone's eyes. "Mother, this is not the time—"

Her mother flashed a flattened palm, the unarguable signal that nothing Leona said would penetrate that rigid wall of the woman's made-up mind. "No matter our differences on child-rearing, it's ridiculous for you to spend what little money you have on taxi fare. I can ring my chauffeur, tell him to pull into the airport parking garage, and wait for David."

"Mother, you don't need to inconvenience Melvin."

"Nonsense." She slipped out of her fur coat. "My driver can sleep in the limo. He does anyway. He thinks I don't know his habits, but I can tell when someone's been dozing on my nickel."

Leona's mother dropped her coat and purse in Maxine's lap. The weight of full-length ermine nearly knocked the elder's wife off the couch. Sinful thoughts of Maxine flat on her back and smothered in weasel momentarily relieved the pressure building between Leona's eyes.

Parker Kemp cleared his throat. "Okay, people. Nothing to see here." Everyone politely returned to their conversations and pretended not to listen.

Leona's mother turned her coiffed head. "Do I know you?"

"Uh . . . we met once."

"I think I'd remember someone as awkward as you."

"Mother!"

"No worries, Mrs. Worthington. It was years ago." Parker

reached around the prickly woman and offered Leona his hand. "Mrs. Harper, I'm fixin' to go. I'm so sorry about Reverend Harper. He was a good man."

"Thank you, Parker." Leona smiled at the formerly scrawny teenager who'd grown into a strapping young man on their watch. She blinked back the sudden wave of tears threatening to spill over and ruin her mascara. "He thought the world of you. Said the Lord's church would be just fine if there were more young men like Parker Kemp."

Parker's Adam's apple bobbed up and down. "How about I come over first thing in the morning and run my leaf blower over your sidewalks?"

Leona started to shake her head. Good preacher's wives didn't need help. Catching Parker's helpless look, she realized yard work was his way of easing her burden. Reconsidering would comfort him. She could almost see J.D. smiling. "That would be real nice, Parker. Thank you."

He gave a pleased nod and strode through the crowd, his dark unruly curls head and shoulders above every concerned caller in the room.

"Isn't that the boy who had a crush on Maddie?" Her mother's narrowed eyes followed Parker to the door.

"I thought you said you didn't remember him."

"Well, I'm glad Madison did not allow herself to fall for that.

Can you imagine what would have happened to the girl if she'd ended up stuck here? She would have dried up and blown away just like …" Leona's mother let her sentence hang in the tense air.

"Like me, Mother?" Leona sat on the couch, trying to breathe, but once again Roberta Worthington had managed to suck the oxygen right out of the room. "Parker is not stuck here. The man has a master's degree in agriculture. We are lucky to have him as our county extension agent."

"Our tax dollars at work."

"Mother, everything is not about money."

"Isn't it? We'll see how you feel once you realize that no-account husband of yours has died and left you penniless, without even a home to call your own."

Leona felt as if her mother's jeweled hand had slapped her across the face. Except for the sound of Nola Gay's fork attacking a dessert plate, silence fell over the packed living room. Leona struggled to recover, locating her voice in the process. "How could you say such a cruel thing?"

Her mother's gaze panned the church members who'd maintained the tiled roof over Harper heads for years. Roberta lifted her chin. "When you realize what a pickle you're in, Leona, don't come crying to me."

"Pickles?" Nola Gay spit the word out around a mouthful of

chocolate cake.

Etta May's face flashed pleasure. "Leona's mother must garden too, Sister."

"Bertie!" Roxie appeared at the living room doorway, hands on her hips, fire leaping from her eyes. "Let's take this conversation to the kitchen." She bulldozed her way through the crowd, took Leona's mother by the elbow, and marched her past the swelling murmurings.

Roxie had threatened to put Leona's mother in her place for years, and secretly Leona prayed she'd do it tonight. But what good would it do, really? Roxie could point out all sorts of things Leona could never say, even toss in a few expletives, but it wouldn't change the fact that her mother was right.

No matter what kind of brave face she put on in front of the curious onlookers, Leona knew one daunting question remained: what would the dried-up preacher's wife do without her preacher?

Leona's head drooped into her hands. She was unable to stop the tears that had been dammed up since Charlie Copeland closed his silver paramedic case and exited Mt. Hope's small stage with the love of her life.

* * * * *

"Hey, Cotton." Maddie released her luggage handle and made a beeline across the baggage claim area. She threw her arms around the janitor's thick neck. "Thanks for coming."

She loved how Cotton's starched and pressed denim shirts always smelled of Lysol and furniture polish. Everything about this dear man was clean, no dirty little secrets waiting to be unearthed and trashed by nosy congregants.

Cotton's sky-blue eyes twinkled under an awning of snow-white brows. "Wouldn't have had it any other way, Monkey-shine."

Maddie smiled at the nickname Cotton had given her when she was six and David was eight, and he'd caught them swimming in the sanctuary baptistry.

They had just moved to Mt. Hope. The parsonage didn't have a pool, and Momma didn't allow mixed bathing at the public pool. So when David suggested they spend the hot summer afternoon swimming in the baptistry, Maddie peeled down to her underwear and jumped in with her big brother.

After Cotton fished them out and delivered their dripping bodies to the parsonage door, Momma scolded, "Stay away from the water until you learn how to swim."

Maddie remembered pondering the preposterous contradiction of that statement. It made no more sense than her famous "Stay away from the piano until you can play." Or "Stay out of the kitchen until you can cook." Now that she thought about it, the private swimming lessons Momma insisted they take after the baptistry episode were just one more safeguard for Momma's future.

Cotton pressed his trademark peppermint candy into Maddie's hand and brought her back to the somber present. "That all your luggage?"

"Didn't exactly have time to pack like I normally do." Maddie popped the peppermint in her mouth. She watched a relieved expression cross Cotton's weathered face.

No doubt he remembered all the times her inability to make a decision had caused her to bring excessive baggage. The tendency had forced Cotton to repack the U-Haul trailer before the youth group could set out for camp.

A girl could never be certain which shoes would be needed until after her outfit decisions were finalized. "Shoes make the outfit," Momma always said.

But how would she know?

Momma had worn the same brown flats for years. Only once had Maddie seen her mother dare to wear heels. It had been for the wedding of one of the Davis children. Maxine had made such a big deal about Momma's one-inch sensible heels, Momma had slipped them into a clothing drive box and they were never seen again.

Maddie glanced at the expensive birthday boots she had on her own feet. When they came in the mail, why hadn't she realized Momma must have done without all these years so she wouldn't have to?

Maddie swallowed her shame. She would never be accomplished in doing without. Financial security was one of the prime motivators driving her through the grueling work of becoming a doctor. It had never occurred to her that no matter how much money she made, one day she might have to do without her father.

"You wait here." Cotton crossed to the moving turnstile and took the handle of the abandoned wheeled carry-on. He pulled it to where she stood.

She put her hand on his sturdy arm to steady herself. "Did Daddy suffer?"

"J.D. Harper went home rejoicing." His eyes glistened as he told Maddie of the congregation rising to their feet when the good pastor dropped on the stage. "While we waited on the ambulance, Wilma Wilkerson fired up the organ and led the choir in several verses of 'It Is Well with My Soul.' It was as if the angels themselves had swooped in to escort that fine man to his heavenly reward."

The simplicity of Cotton's faith tugged at Maddie's knotted insides, but made no headway in untangling the mess. Any man who could see the face of God in toilet bowl rings had a grasp on something she didn't think she'd ever embrace again.

The medical mission trip she'd taken to Central America while she was in college exposed a side of God she didn't understand. How could a caring God allow so much suffering?

Either he wasn't so caring, or this God who'd enslaved her parents did not exist. This conflict had bolstered her determination to become a doctor. She would put a stop to pain, with or without the help of the Almighty.

"And Momma?" The words grated Maddie's throat.

"Leona is . . . Leona." He gave Maddie a knowing wink. "A tower of strength."

Momma was a tower all right. A buttoned-down, impenetrable fortress where no emotions ever got in and, even more importantly, no emotions ever got out.

* * * * *

David rapped his knuckles on the limo window, startling Melvin and nearly sending him through the closed sunroof.

Melvin scrambled out of the car. "Glad to see that you got the page. I'm to take you to Mt. Hope straightaway."

"Thanks, Melvin. Sorry to make you wait half the night."

The chauffeur opened the backseat passenger door. "No problem. I should have you home in time for a hot breakfast. Climb in, Mr. Harper, and I'll get your bags."

Being referred to as Mr. Harper stopped David cold. His full name was James David or J.D., like his father. Momma had agreed to the repeat because David, her favorite Old Testament hero, was not only a man after God's own heart, but a decent songwriter. Momma had always been a sucker for tear-jerking lyrics.

Who could possibly fail the Lord with such solid biblical credentials bestowed upon them at birth?

David tossed his briefcase on the backseat. He ducked his head and slid across the supple leather.

Hands gliding along the limo's expensive interior, an anxious tingle traveled through his extended limb. He was tired of telling himself that the feel of expensive buckskin was not why he'd originally attended law school. Hadn't he pursued a history degree to escape the desire to be comfortable? A history degree would allow him to teach. To make a difference in the world. To prove to Momma he wasn't all about the money.

But, dang it, he wanted more than a dilapidated house on the plains of Texas and a dying church.

Grandmother had been right in her prediction that one day he would want the helm of the law firm his grandfather had left him, along with all the perks that accompanied the position.

That day had come.

Wrestling with his decision had grown wearisome, and he was finished with the struggle. When this current term was completed, he was putting aside his interest in first century history and coming to Texas to finally put his law degree to work.

It felt good to know he had a plan. A direction.

By this time next year, if all went according to his projections, he would be well on his way to claiming a rich heritage in one of the city's most prestigious firms. Soon he would take his place in the nicest neighborhoods, drive the newest cars, and garner more respect before he was thirty than a pastor could in a lifetime.

Grandmother would be thrilled. Momma would be another story.

Melvin closed the trunk and slid into the driver's seat.

David waited until the immaculately-packaged man was buckled up. "I take it Grandmother's already in Mt. Hope?"

"Dropped her off last night, right before I came for you."

"Bet the parsonage was crawling with people."

"There were a considerable number of cars along Church Street. Every light was on in the house."

"That was fireworks, Melvin."

The driver cast a confused glance in the mirror. "Fireworks, sir?"

"You know, after Grandmother waltzed in and told Momma this was the best day of her life."

"I wouldn't know, sir." Melvin returned his focus to the road.

"I left Mrs. Worthington's bags at the door."

"Smartest move you ever made, Melvin."

David stretched his legs, resting his head against the plush leather. Blinding rays of sun broke over the horizon and pierced the tinted windows. He squinted, trying to block the image of his grandmother's face, smug in the knowledge that she had been right all along.

Maybe he was selling his soul to the devil, but he was going to need the seasoned battle-axe on his side if he had any hope of fending off the guilt churning in his gut.

Chapter Five

Leona sat at the table of her darkened kitchen. She closed her Bible. The Lord wasn't speaking to her and she didn't feel much like talking to him. She rested her chin on one cupped hand and swirled a spoon through a mug of cold coffee with the other.

The parsonage's antiquated heater clattered to a halt. The racket did not disturb the dog snoring under her feet.

Leona ran her roughened soles over Tater Tot's silky coat. She burrowed her toes deep into the furry warmth of her faithful companion.

Once the children left home, she'd filled the emptiness by turning her energies on the dog. She'd discontinued giving the cocker a buzz cut and allowed his feathers to grow long and curly. Tater loved the extra attention of brushing and treats.

But now, Tater's treat-thickened torso appeared to be twice its actual size. Leona dismissed J.D.'s complaints of wooly bear hair all over his favorite recliner. Maintaining Tater's tangled skirt seemed to make the Harper nest less empty. Now she realized her efforts were merely a trick that lulled her into believing she was still needed.

The steady rise and fall of the old pooch's barrel chest vibrated under her feet, but did not quell the panic that had made it impossible for Leona to sleep. Tater was loyal, but she doubted his presence would fill the huge crater her husband's sudden departure had created in her heart.

And that was J.D.'s fault as well. After all, acquiring the buff-colored cocker had been his idea.

All of the Harper pets had been named after the kids' favorite candy bar.

The trend started when the kids named the Easter bunny Reeses, followed by Peanut the gerbil, and capped off by the faithful yard dog, Buttercup. Put them all together, and David and Maddie had been the proud owners of a Reese's Peanut Butter Cup.

Repeating the clever combination to their friends garnered the Harper children a great deal of respect among their peers.

Thus, when Peanut died, leaving a hole in the renowned empty-calorie lineup, J.D. felt an obligation to replace the gerbil.

But when he surprised the kids with a puppy, they thought the blond cocker looked more like a Tater Tot than a Peanut.

The name stuck, thus ending the enviable chocolate streak. Relieved her tenderhearted husband would not feel compelled to purchase another mouth to feed when the rest of the candy bar died off, Leona set to work housebreaking Tater.

Early on, the dog had taken up with her. Leona figured this honor was due to the fact that she was the one who fed the animal and taught him tricks.

The grandfather clock in the hallway chimed. Leona picked up her cup and rose, careful not to disturb Tater. She went to the sink and poured the untouched coffee down the drain. Rinsing away the brown splatters, she thought about how smoothly her daughter's homecoming had gone.

Around midnight, Cotton had delivered Maddie. For the first time in months, Leona had finally been able to wrap her arms around her wayward daughter. While they clung to each other, Leona had not detected any of the animosity she expected.

In fact, Maddie fell into her arms the way she had as a child when she needed her mother to fix yet another boo-boo. If only a Band-Aid would make this nasty gash better.

Leona stashed her rinsed cup in the dishwasher. She caught a glimpse of her haggard reflection in the darkened window. "Okay, so you were right, J.D. All things do work together for good, but this is not how I would have worked things out." She closed the dishwasher and returned to her deserted chair, the chill of the linoleum numbing her feet and beginning to register with her despondent brain.

Truth was, tragedy could go either way.

After years in the ministry, she had witnessed adversity's ability to mend broken fences or completely destroy any hope of reconciliation. She gathered her robe and lowered onto the seat. What would this disaster do to her family? Would their differences be forgiven and forgotten? Much as that would thrill her, she knew it was far too early to tell.

Tater stretched. As if he sensed her worry, he pressed a hairy paw against her leg.

Maybe the tears had blurred her ability to see clearly into Maddie's heart. Maybe she had been so wrapped up in the overwhelming emotion of the moment that she had seen what she wanted to see . . . a daughter who wanted her mother's comfort.

Maddie hadn't needed her mother in years. *What if my self-sufficient daughter never does?*

Leona rubbed Tater's paw. She should try again to get some sleep, but she could not make herself climb into that empty king-sized bed.

Dog and master paced the floors listening to the comforting settlings of the eighty-year-old parsonage.

Leona knew every sound of this old house as well as she knew her own body. From the rattle of the rusty pipes to the rumble of the ancient furnace waking from its slumber in the basement, she could predict their next major repair with amazing accuracy.

The work and personal expense had not deterred her love affair with making the parsonage their home. From her first step onto the large wraparound porch, she felt as if she'd been called to Abraham's bosom. While J.D. had been excited about the church, when he saw all the work the parsonage would require, he shook his head and groaned like God had sent him to Canaan.

Together, they'd spent their years in Mt. Hope restoring all the baseboards and moldings, patching every crack in the plaster, dealing with temperamental plumbing, and learning to replace fuses each time someone plugged in a hair dryer while the portable dishwasher gyrated across the kitchen floor.

J.D. balked at each improvement project Leona proposed, but combining his handyman skills with her decorating sense had saved the church thousands of dollars and turned the embarrassment of Church Street into a home anyone could be proud of.

Suddenly, the kitchen light flipped on, startling Leona from her recollections.

"I'll be lucky if I don't break a hip or blow a knee on those blasted stairs." Leona's mother hobbled over to the counter and thumped the glass coffee carafe. "How old is this stuff?"

"I was fixin' to make a fresh pot, Mother."

"Fixin' to? Listen to yourself, Leona. You even sound like these hicks now."

Arguing was useless. She'd have to be more careful. Leona held her tongue and scurried to the coffeemaker, lifted the pot, and poured the darkened contents down the drain. "Sleep well?" How many more years would it take before her mother's presence would not tangle her tongue into meaningless babble?

"On that lumpy mattress?" Using the toe of her pointed slipper, Roberta prodded Tater Tot from his repose in front of her chair.

"You gave us that mattress."

"Thirty years ago. It's a shame you could never afford to replace things." Her mother brushed crumbs from the rickety chair, shaking her head in disapproval at Tater Tot's enthusiasm over his domestic chore of licking them up. "David home?"

Weariness settled on Leona's shoulders. "Not yet. Melvin called. They should be here soon."

Eyeing the seat, Mother lowered herself. She drummed her manicured nails on the Formica tabletop. "So have you made any plans, Leona?"

What was it about her mother that reminded Leona of a recurring nightmare in which she was the only one who showed up at church wearing pajamas while everyone else was dressed to the nines? "I thought I'd wait for David. I think he and Maddie should have some say about the funeral."

"I'm not talking about the funeral. I mean, have you made plans for your life?"

Leona raised her eyebrows. "What do you mean?"

"For one, where are you going to live?" Her mother's voice was void of compassion.

"Here. This is my home."

"No, it's not. This hovel belongs to the church. Now that J.D. is dead, I can't imagine the Christians letting you squat here for free. That can't be good for business."

The blunt proclamation waylaid Leona, as if the icy hand of truth had just slapped her across the face.

Her mother was right; this wasn't her house. Hadn't she said that very thing to J.D. this morning? She'd lived in the parsonage so long, it felt like her home. J.D.'s promise that the Lord had and would provide had been fulfilled with this house. How else could she make a borrowed house a home for her family?

Forbidding any exposure of the host of dawning fears clawing her insides, Leona struggled to maintain her composure. "Mother, I—"

"Secondly, how are you going to support yourself, Leona?"

Her mother seemed oblivious to the interruption— and the panic brimming on the edge of Leona's lashes. She picked up the newspaper lying on the table and rolled the rubber band down the cylinder. "Surely you're not counting on cashing in all those make-believe stars the pastor was adding to his heavenly crown to buy your groceries."

"Mother, that's enough. God will provide." Leona hoped her voice possessed the conviction she'd relied upon for the past thirty years, because her doubtful knees were about to drop her on the floor.

Her mother aimed a shiny red nail in her direction. "He'd better, Leona, because I doubt that loser husband of yours had a cent of life insurance to his name, let alone a decent investment portfolio."

Tater Tot's ears pricked. At the squeak of the front door hinges, he went ballistic.

"That's David." Leona came and stood in front of her mother, feeling like a child asking for permission to play outside. "For your grandson's sake, could you please keep your opinions of J.D. to yourself? David loved his father."

Leona allowed her mind a moment to pause on the kaleidoscope of memories of her two guys huddled together at this very table, poring over adventure magazines and plotting their next backpacking trip into the wilderness.

Her mother gave a noncommittal shrug. "My lips are sealed." She drew an airy line across her smug lips, twisted an imaginary key, and tossed it over her shoulder.

Despite her mother's placating country club smile, Leona thought hell had a better chance of freezing over.

* * * * *

The roar of lawn equipment outside Maddie's window woke her with a start. Who does yard work in November? She snatched her pillow and held it tight against her head, but she couldn't drown out the buzz.

Maddie rolled over. Gray light peered through the cracks of the yellowed roller shade.

Her gritty eyes skimmed the room's flowered wallpaper. A row of faded homecoming mums lined one wall. Tarnished Bible Bowl trophies filled the shelves of an old bookcase.

Home.

How could one word raise two opposing emotions?

The smell of coffee and bacon wafted up from the kitchen, reminding Maddie of Daddy's day off. While other fathers dashed out the door on Monday morning to start their workweek, the pastor took his day of rest. Momma always marked the importance of the sacred time with pancakes and crispy bacon.

Maddie closed her eyes and breathed in deeply of the

comforting scent, awaiting her father's delivery of Momma's special brew: milk and sugar, with a hint of coffee for color.

Reality pounced hard. Daddy wouldn't be tapping on her door. Ever again.

Throwing back the quilt the Story sisters had pieced together for her high school graduation present, Maddie stomped to the window and yanked on the bottom of the shade. The brittle vinyl zipped out of her hands and wrapped around the roller. Dust settled on her hair and face.

She pounded the glass, but the stocking-cap-clad man with his back to her continued blowing leaves off the sidewalk.

"Hell's bells . . ." Maddie let her Aunt Roxie's favorite curse fly, brushed at her face, grabbed the ratty terry cloth robe hanging on the back of her bedroom door, and stormed down the stairs. She burst into the kitchen, determined to swat the mosquito buzzing outside her window.

"David!" Maddie's anger melted immediately. She ran and fell into the open arms of her big brother. "When did you get here?"

Tater Tot barked and circled their legs, demanding to be part of the reunion.

"A few minutes ago." David pulled back and gave her a perusing look. "So, *doctor* Harper, love how you're rockin' the mountain woman look." He crossed his arms and leaned against the counter, a teasing disapproval lighting his tired face.

Maddie gathered her robe closed, belted the sash, shook out her hair. "Starving med students must sacrifice the luxuries." She kissed her brother's cheek. "How's the Queen?"

Momma cleared her throat and handed her a cup of steaming coffee. "I was just making David *and* your grandmother an omelet." Brows raised, she motioned for Maddie to look behind her. "Care to join them?"

Heat blazed up Maddie's neck. She swallowed and turned. "Grandmother. You're up early."

Her grandmother peered over the edge of the paper. "Sorry the Queen missed your arrival last night, Madison."

Sure she was.

Roberta Worthington had made it clear years ago that the limited space in her heart was reserved for only one grandchild. David had been declared the lucky winner simply because he was born first and looked like their mother. The enviable position came with a paid education and exotic graduation trips after each degree.

Maddie, who resembled her father, had received a down comforter, snow tires, and Grandmother's declaration that doctors make plenty of money to pay off their med school loans.

Momma had tried to soften the old witch's inequities by reminding Maddie how much her grandfather adored her when he was alive. Leona Harper could sell wind in a bag, but she could not lessen the sting of Grandmother's ugly slight.

"I'm not really hungry." Maddie sipped coffee Momma had sugared and creamed to perfection. "Where's Melvin?" She leaned against the counter and ran a bare foot over Tater's bouncing back, hoping the extra attention would calm him.

"I sent him to the motel." Grandmother snapped the paper up in front of her face. "Leona, do something with that yapping dog."

"Tater." Momma snagged the worn collar with one hand and Maddie with the other. "We've got a lot to decide today. The sooner we get started, the sooner we'll have the worst of it behind us."

"I can't believe you're in such a hurry to get Daddy behind us."

Momma's face looked as if she'd been hit with a cup of cold water. "Maddie, I didn't mean—"

Maddie regretted the pain she'd just inflicted, knowing full well Momma dreaded this day as much as she. She hadn't come home to fight. Really. But if she gave in now, how long before Momma would want to control her life. She'd worked too hard to set her own course. And she wasn't in the clear yet.

The back door opened and the blustery breeze swirled the hem of Maddie's robe. Tater Tot broke free of Momma's hold and charged the intruder swiping his boots on the mat.

"Hey, Tater." The man with the leaf blower ruffled the dog's head then stepped into the kitchen. "Mrs. Harper." He removed his stocking cap. Static popped from his thick, black hair. "Anything else I can do for you before I head to work?"

"Parker Kemp?" Maddie stared at the impressive broad-shouldered, six-foot-four frame of what had once been the youth group's resident gangly geek.

"Hey, Maddie." Parker flashed a braces-free smile that lit up his tanned face. "You look great—I mean, when did you get in?"

Maddie wished she could swipe at the cobweb dangling from her hair, but her hands were full. "Last night." She held the top of her robe closed with one hand, balancing her coffee cup with the other. "What are you doing here?"

"Parker lives in Mt. Hope." Momma reached behind the transfixed young man and shut the kitchen door, her face a picture of balance restored. "He is our county extension agent." She retrieved Tater Tot from Parker's leg. An awkward silence fell over the kitchen. Momma remained uncharacteristically quiet, not jumping in with her usual conversation rescue tactics.

It was David who stepped in, hand extended. "Good to see you, man."

Parker jerked with surprise and shifted the leaf blower. "You too." He pumped David's hand with astounding vigor. "How's

Oxford?"

"Great." David broke free, flexing his fingers as if his circulation needed restoring.

Her brother's avoidance of Momma's eyes at the mention of his studies did not get past Maddie. While she envied his perpetual-student status, she had to give David credit for dodging Momma's ideas for his life, even if he was having trouble finding his way in the world.

"How about some breakfast, Parker?" Momma returned to the bacon sizzling on the stove.

Parker glanced at Maddie, swallowing as if his oversized Adam's apple clogged his throat. "Thank you, but I best be on my way." He gave a retiring wave with his stocking cap. In a move reminiscent of his clumsy four-step basketball layup, he turned for the door. The leaf blower caught the edge of a silver tray loaded with pieces of Bette Bob's Coca-Cola cake. The whole thing flew off the counter and landed on the yellowed linoleum.

Maddie released her hold on her robe and put her hand to her mouth to stifle a laugh.

"Here, turn the bacon." Momma passed the fork to Maddie. "Don't you worry, Parker. I'll get that."

Flipping strips of bacon, Maddie watched Tater Tot and Momma clean up the mess while a red-faced Parker apologized over and over.

Maybe some things never change. But the absence of her father's hearty laugh to relieve the tension was proof the Harpers' future was not one of them.

Chapter Six

Dressed in black, Leona sat alone in the backseat of her mother's limo. Snatches of the funeral hymn, "Going Down the Valley," ran through her mind.

She inhaled through her nose and held it, making use of the controlled-breathing technique J.D. taught her the summer he and David suckered her into hiking a fourteen-footer in Colorado. Each rocky step to the top of the mountain required tremendous effort, but deep breaths had lessened her muscle cramps and lightheadedness.

Reaching the count of ten, Leona exhaled through puckered lips at the same moment her son opened the car door. The biting wind filled the fancy interior. She needed more air than her crushed lungs would hold if she expected to complete today's climb.

Grief had backed up like a cement truck and dumped its load on her chest and kicked her irrational fear of overloaded vehicles into overdrive.

When everyone had piled into the limo to go to the church,

the thought of the added weight elevated her blood pressure to the point of detonation. While her mother's chauffeur circled the block, she'd sat on both hands to keep from clawing through the special-order leather or popping the sunroof to climb out over Melvin's head.

Fear and despair loomed like a mountain. For her children's sake, she could not give in.

David stuck his head inside. "Ready, Momma?"

Lord, help me.

Taking her son's offered hand, Leona stepped out.

Sleet stung her face. From the corner of her eye, she could see that the church parking lot was packed as if today were Easter morning and all the backsliders had clocked in early for their yearly attendance credit.

Leona swallowed and blinked back tears. No matter the reason for the crowd, J.D. would have loved having a full house for a change.

Roxie, who'd insisted she be seated with the family, stepped up and smoothed the wrinkles from Leona's skirt. She gave a tug, and buttoned her friend's coat against the cutting wind. "You can do this, girlfriend."

"I don't know how without J.D." Leona reached for the hands of her children. "Y'all ready?"

David and Maddie offered tentative smiles, their

encouragement rippling through the pressure of their simultaneous squeezes against her cold hands. No doubt about it. The Harper children were made of stern stuff. Thank goodness. This dark tunnel would be impossible to navigate alone.

Ducking her head against the wind, Leona allowed her children to lead her up the sidewalk.

Wayne Darling, director of Darling's Funeral Home, met the little party at the double doors. "Right this way, Mrs. Harper." The pasty little man jockeyed them through the horde of people crammed into the foyer.

A single-file line snaked from the guest book podium and into the hall like the return lane at the Walmart counter the day after Christmas. Had someone promised these folks a refund for eighteen years of contributions if they showed up for the preacher's funeral?

Clutching tight to David and Maddie, Leona summoned a determined smile. She averted her gaze from the commiserating and picked up her pace, sticking close to the mortician.

Wayne herded their grieving party through the large crowd and down the administrative hall. He opened an unlocked door and ushered them into a modest, dimly lit room.

The faint scent of bay lime stung Leona's nose. "Wayne,

what are you doing?"

"Sorry, Leona. But when we have a funeral at this building, J.D.'s office is the nicest place to hold the family until the processional."

Leona stood in the center of her husband's treasured commentaries and concordances. "Can't we wait in the nursery or something? I don't think I can . . ." She looked at the large, empty desk chair half expecting J.D. to straighten the desk pad, stick his sermon notes in his Bible, and escort her to the sanctuary.

Apprehension swept over her. If she couldn't stand being in his office, how could she step into that auditorium and take her place on the second pew for a service her husband would not be conducting?

Roxie wrapped a protective arm around Leona's waist, firmly bringing her close. "Wayne Darling, you've got two minutes to get that processional hymn started and get her out of here, or I'll see to it that you never get another part for that old hearse of yours."

Understanding flashed across Mr. Darling's waxen face. "I'll be right back." He wheeled and darted from the room. His hasty exit spun Leona's mother against the door frame just as she was entering.

Righting herself, Roberta brushed off her tweed jacket.

"Where's the fire?"

"This is Dad's office." David's forced cough failed to veil the crack in his voice.

Surveying the immaculate desk, Leona's mother said, "At least he was neat." She crossed the room and read aloud the inscriptions on the three plaques hanging on the wall commending J.D. Harper for five, ten, and fifteen years of service. "Two more years and he would have had twenty and, no doubt, another plaque to show for his efforts."

Glaring at her mother's cold-blooded eyes and reptilian tongue, Leona made herself a promise. The minute the funeral lunch was over, she'd pack the devil woman into her limo and send her back to the hole from which she had slithered. The Lord would just have to forgive her lack of Christian charity in this undeniably desperate instance.

Elder Davis poked his shiny bald head inside the door. "Wayne says they're ready to start."

J.D. was right. The Cadillac dealership owner's head did look like a Volkswagen Beetle with the doors open. Leona stifled an inappropriate urge to laugh. "Howard, thank you for taking over the service." She gripped the hand of the strong-armed board chairman who turned every board meeting into a wrestling match. "J.D. would have expected no less."

Howard gave a quick nod, ears flapping back and forth. "On

behalf of the board, I want to assure you that it's our Christian duty to care for the widows and orphans, and that's what you can count on us to do."

Roxie snorted. "That's the least you can do, Howard Davis. The Harpers gave you eighteen of the best years of their lives." She nudged Leona. "Get your kids, girlfriend, and let's do this right."

Glancing over her shoulder, Leona shot a smug smile toward her mother. "The Lord provides."

Leona walked the sanctuary aisle supported by her children on either side, her best friend behind her, her Lord leading the way, and his good people surrounding her. Tempting as it was, she mustered restraint and did not check on her mother's ability to negotiate a church aisle for the first time in years.

Only a fool would press the limit of the Lord's forgiving spirit.

* * * * *

David followed his mother, chafing with each offered condolence gushing from the teary-eyed ladies in the funeral-lunch serving line. Smells of brewing coffee, musty hymnals stacked in the corner of the fellowship hall, and baked ham washed over him with an uncomfortable familiarity. He held out his Styrofoam plate and waited.

Maxine Davis spooned up a corner of scalloped potatoes. She plopped the skimpy helping next to a dollop of lime-green congealed salad. "Did you come all the way from London, Davy?" She stabbed a thin slice of sugar-cured ham. Using a long bony finger, she freed it from the fork and dropped the meat beside the crusty potatoes.

"Yes, ma'am." David tugged at the knotted tie pressing against the lump in his throat.

"I told Howard we won't have to look for a new pastor if Davy comes home." Maxine licked ham juice from her fingers. "You're every bit as good as your father." A sly twinkle sparkled in her half-glasses. "Maybe even better."

To his right, David could sense that Momma's intense gaze did not rest on her lanky thorn in the flesh, but rather bore a hole through him, awaiting his reply. Certain his face had turned the color of the Story sisters' tomato relish, David did not risk making eye contact with Momma. "Thank you, Mrs. Davis. But I intend to go into law."

David braced for his mother's weeping, wailing, and gnashing of teeth, but Momma turned quietly and moved on to the desserts without comment. Why did he wish she had thrown a fit? He wanted to punch somebody, but not his recently widowed mother. The fight was coming. He'd been a fool and a jerk to start it today.

"A doctor and a lawyer in the family. Isn't Leona Harper the luckiest woman in the world?" The elder's wife leaned across the folding table, her voice dropping to a raspy whisper. "Well, except for J.D. dying, and her being so young and all."

"Except for that."

"Well, higher education has certainly not improved your manners." Maxine snatched up the empty casserole dish, and made for the kitchen sink.

Landing a verbal blow on the woman he and Maddie had always called 'the Grinch" hadn't given him the perverse pleasure he'd always imagined it would. Nor had it made him feel better for hurting Momma's feelings. He blamed the prick to his conscience on his surroundings, grabbed a roll, and strode toward the head table.

Laughter echoed in the packed fellowship hall. David shifted on the metal folding chair wedged between his mother and grandmother. Insides warring, he tried to focus on the piece of ham floating in a melting puddle of green Jell-O and not on the conversations rolling about in the sea of suits and Sunday dresses.

The entire community of Mt. Hope had turned out to pay their respects to his father. Everyone from the mayor to the Story sisters' brother, Ray, their trash man, stopped by the head table to speak their praise for the Reverend Harper. If these folks loved the guy so much, why didn't they say so when he was alive? David's soul recoiled. Unwilling to absorb any more, his offended spirit slipped back into the hollow place in David's chest.

David swirled the curling meat, creating a tidal wave that turned the scalloped potatoes green. How many meals had he eaten in this cavernous room? Hundreds. Maybe even thousands. And they all tasted the same, whether the menu was ham, fried chicken, or finger foods.

He watched his grandmother daintily picking through a helping of green bean casserole.

Roberta Worthington was a woman who didn't have to depend upon the leftovers from a church potluck to tide her family over for the next week.

David scooted his chair back from the table. Once he was bringing down the big bucks, he'd never eat potluck again. He excused himself and headed for the dessert counter.

Bette Bob McDonald smiled from the other side of the table laden with pies and cakes, wiping her hands on the checked apron covering her from neck to knee. "How about some of my famous bread pudding?"

"Sure." David didn't recognize the petite blonde standing beside Mrs. McDonald and dragging a knife through a pan of nutty fudge.

"We are sure going to miss Reverend Harper." Bette Bob scooped a mound of vanilla ice cream and heaped it upon a bowl of the steaming delicacy. "If I recall correctly, you pick out the raisins and only eat the ice cream." She winked at him.

"Have to get up pretty early in the morning to pull one over on you, Mrs. McDonald." David realized he had instinctively handled his irritation the way Momma had taught him. Paste on the perfect-preacher's-kid smile, keep the voice respectful, but the gaze direct. That he had resorted to this trick of the trade chafed him. He was a grown man, for Pete's sake.

"Aunt Bette, where do you want these?" The curvy candy assistant pointed at the squares of chocolate she'd placed on plates. She smiled at David.

An impish grin spread across Mrs. McDonald's face. "David, why don't you show my niece how we serve dessert around here?"

"Your niece?" David ignored the creamy rivulet trickling over the edge of Bette Bob's bowl of warm pudding.

"Amy Maxwell. She's my youngest sister's girl. Been living with us since she got a job at Mt. Hope's little hospital."

David felt the collar of his white dress shirt tighten as the azure blue eyes examined him. "Are you a doctor?"

"A nurse." Amy's perfect smile warmed the fellowship hall to an uncomfortable temperature.

"David's sister is almost a doctor." Bette Bob's face looked like she had just solved the mystery of gravity or something equally daunting. "Amy, with your medical background you'd fit right in the Harper family." Bette Bob smiled, waving a sticky hand in front of her niece as if she were presenting the prize behind door number one on Let's Make a Deal. "David, why don't you give this *single* lady a little assistance?" She thrust the bowl into David's hand, along with a plate of fudge.

Juggling chocolate, David's blood boiled, which seemed to increase the drip rate of the melting ice cream. He led the attractive blonde to the dessert station. If he was a grown man, why had he allowed himself to be pushed around like a kid? "Just put them there."

Amy slid the plates into place. "Sorry about my aunt. She means well."

David wasn't sure what angered him more, the becoming pink blush on Amy's high cheekbones or being backed into another awkward corner by a meddlesome parishioner. He'd had a bellyful of mystery-meat casseroles, well-intentioned matchmakers, and people making it their business whether or not he ate his raisins.

"They always do," he snapped.

"Excuse me?"

"Everybody believes it's their job to manage the affairs of my family."

Disenchantment washed over Amy's flawless complexion.

"Sorry about your father." A quick spin on heels and the little bombshell was headed in the direction of the kitchen.

Instead of patting himself on the back for his ability to go for the jugular, his conscience ignited with shame. If he was going to make it in the law profession, he needed thicker skin. He couldn't be worried about hurting someone's feelings. So why did he feel like such a jerk?

It was the curse of this blasted church building.

Standing alone at the dessert altar, he glanced around the quiet room. All eyes were upon the perfect pastor's son who'd just lost his cool with an innocent woman.

David abandoned his pudding and seized his exit opportunity . . . a skill Momma promised could be honed to perfection if practiced on a regular basis.

* * * * *

Maddie tried to slip her sweaty palms free of Wilma Wilkerson's vise grip. How the woman made those arthritic mitts tickle the ivories was nothing short of miraculous.

Wilma lifted a gnarled hand and stroked Maddie's. "With fingers like yours, it's a shame you gave up the organ."

The church organist would have made Elton John feel like he could've been something if he'd only practiced his scales a bit more.

Music lessons with Mrs. Wilkerson came flooding back.

Every Thursday after school, Maddie would drag herself into the darkened sanctuary, her untouched practice book tucked under her arm. In the glow of the reading lamp she could see Mrs. Wilkerson's short, stubby legs stomping the pedals while her hands ran up and down the stacked keyboards. Mrs. Wilkerson would make a sliver of room for Maddie on the bench.

It was a miracle the croaking scales Maddie pecked out didn't shatter the stained glass above the baptistery. Mrs. Wilkerson suffered through every one of them. She'd offer words of encouragement and faithfully assign more pages for the next week.

Maddie squirmed under the pressure. "Momma was disappointed."

Mrs. Wilkerson smiled up at Maddie. "I've been praying the Lord uses your hands to his glory." She brought Maddie's hand to her lips and kissed it lightly. "And he will. Practice and these hands will make the music of healing."

The glimpse of understanding Maddie saw in her teacher's eyes sent a sudden surge of warmth to a part of her heart she thought she'd effectively sealed off. "Cotton told me what you did for my father. Thank you."

"I'm just the Lord's instrument." Wilma patted Maddie's hand. "As are you." She chose the plate with the biggest slice of apple pie and lumbered off.

Maddie picked up a dessert and scanned the crowded fellowship hall. She'd had enough of the icy tension between Grandmother and Momma at the head table. And watching David's discomfort wasn't doing anything to ease her own. She spotted Cotton across the room and eased her way through well-wishers to reach the empty seat beside him.

"Did you get some of Bette Bob's pudding?" Cotton dragged a plastic spoon around his empty bowl.

"I don't eat sweets."

One bushy brow rose. "Does banana cream pie count as a fruit at Denver med school?" Cotton's ribbing covered Maddie like hot fudge melting cold ice cream.

She slid the plate onto the table, pulled out a chair, and sat down. "Okay, I don't eat as many as I used to. Gotta watch my figure, you know."

"Your figure seems fine to me." The rich baritone voice came from behind.

Maddie twisted in the gray metal folding chair. Parker Kemp grinned, his puppy-dog eyes twinkling. He was handsomely dressed in a dark suit, tasteful tie, and holding a bowl of pudding.

"This seat taken?" Parker pointed to the chair beside Maddie.

"Do you see anyone sitting there?" Cotton licked the back of his empty spoon. "Have a seat, boy."

Parker looked at Maddie. "May I?"

Maddie shrugged. She scooted her chair closer to Cotton's, but when Parker sat his arm brushed hers. She didn't remember Parker's shoulders being so broad, or the confident air he seemed to possess, like he was comfortable in his tanned skin. Even when she protested his offer of chocolate cake to Tater after he and Momma got all but a few crumbs off the kitchen floor, his smile and the way he ignored her threats said Parker Kemp was no longer the youth group nerd.

What had happened? Had some secret substance changed his entire body chemistry? Maddie shifted in her seat so she could get a better view—purely for scientific investigation, she assured herself.

Parker placed his dessert on the table and sat down. "I thought the service for your father was real nice."

Unnerved by his directness, Maddie swallowed. "Daddy would have preferred to do it himself."

Parker nodded. "And, no doubt, he would have done a better job."

Across the room a group of men laughed. Maddie swiveled in her chair to locate her father's booming bass in the mix. Her daddy loved a joke more than anyone she knew. But he was nowhere to be found. Was that the joke? David, Maddie, and Momma trapped together without Pastor Harper's humor to lighten the tension. It wasn't funny.

Something was off-kilter in this place where she'd eaten more than her share of potluck fare. She'd had this same dizzy sensation while seated in the Harper pew listening to Howard Davis speak from her father's pulpit. Either Mr. Davis was in the wrong place or she was.

This day was a bad dream. Any minute she would wake up in her loft apartment, yell at Katie Beth for letting her oversleep, throw on some clothes, and rush out the door. She'd phone her dad on the way to the hospital, and the ripple of his laughter would make everything that had been wrong about this nightmare right for his princess.

"So, are you about finished with med school?" Parker touched Maddie's arm and she jumped.

"I'm sorry. What did you say?"

Parker chewed the large bite he'd popped in his mouth and swallowed. "When do you finish school?"

"In the spring. Then I'll start my residency."

"Coming back to this part of the country to do that?" Parker asked.

"I hadn't planned to, but now that Momma is . . ." Maddie felt flush under Parker's gaze. She diverted her eyes and noticed the Story sisters aiming their pointed noses in their direction. Their creaky bodies would not be far behind. Maddie hurried to change the subject. "So, what about you? I bet the stimulating work of an extension agent is never done."

Parker smiled. "On call round the clock."

Nola Gay tapped Parker's shoulder. "What are you going to do about our wilt?"

"See what I mean?" Parker winked at Maddie.

"Stem rot." Etta May steadied herself by placing a shaky hand on Maddie's shoulder. "Just about did in our cucumber crop last year."

"It's those blasted striped beetles. They chew into the leaves and the next thing you know, the wilt has spread up and down the runner." Nola Gay pursed her lips and shook her head.

The unruffled extension agent put down his spoon and rubbed his chin. "I've been studying on your problem, ladies." The way he focused his attention reminded Maddie of a doctor contemplating the best way to break the news of a fatal diagnosis. "Why don't y'all have a seat, and we'll see if we can't come up with a plan to shut down those hard-shelled hooligans before they taste another bite of Mt. Hope's best cucumbers. Would you mind making room, Maddie?"

Where did this guy get off thinking she'd want dibs on his

attention? "Of course not." Tamping her irritation, Maddie nudged Cotton and they slid over a couple of chairs. "It's not every day a person gets to see a real live extension agent in action."

Parker seemed to ignore the sarcastic edge in her voice. "Prepare to be amazed." He jumped up, repositioned the abandoned seats in a semicircle around him, and situated his troubled clients on either side. "If we happen to get a big snow cover, and end up with a warm spring, we'll have to take aggressive action."

Nola Gay and Etta May leaned in close, their serious faces awaiting the plan.

"So, I figure we'll put cheesecloth tents over the new shoots and plant several rows of corn on the windward side of your patch."

The sisters frowned, obviously skeptical of the elaborate plan.

Undeterred by their expressions of doubt, Parker continued, "I promise, those thieving scoundrels will be so distracted they'll forget all about your cucumbers."

Nola Gay thought a minute, her eyes gleaming as one plotting evil. "Outsmart the little buggers."

"Beat them at their own game." Etta May glowed, rubbing her hands together.

Maddie watched Parker pick up his spoon and polish off his pudding under the admiring gaze of the Storys. The guy must be secretly nipping on the fertilizer because somewhere along the line, Mt. Hope's extension agent's way with the ladies had blossomed tenfold, no question about it.

Chapter Seven

David sat on the front pew in the empty sanctuary listening to the baptistry heater kick on and off. Leaves that had fallen from the jungle of funeral wreaths littered the space between the preacher's son and the large wooden pulpit towering over him.

In the glow of the afternoon light, David studied the golden rays framing the stained-glass ruby cross. The hopeful scene reminded him of the sun rising over the private pond he and Dad fished when the bass took to their spawning beds.

Upon closer examination of the glass depiction, David realized he took issue with the jeweled path that started wide at the base, curved around, and disappeared into a tiny point beneath the cross. It didn't take a scholar to figure out that in real life, the road to redemption was much longer and not nearly as inviting. He slumped forward, resting his forearms on his thighs.

"Your stepstool is still there." David jumped. "Cotton. You scared me to death."

"Sorry." The janitor squatted, his knees creaking. Leaf by

leaf, he gathered the curling foliage. "Came in to set the thermostats. Can't afford to heat an empty room."

"Momma go home?"

"I saw her loadin' dirty tablecloths into your grandmother's limo trunk."

"The woman took home the laundry?" The urge to hit somebody balled David's hand into a tight fist. How could church members, people who claimed to be her friends, be so inconsiderate? A better question was, why did his mother continue to let them take advantage of her? Didn't she know she owed these ingrates nothing? "I'm surprised the food committee didn't ask her to make a green bean casserole and a couple of desserts for her husband's funeral as well."

"Your momma is a strong woman."

David shuddered, visions of his mother's disappointed face in the lunch line haunting his thoughts. "I hope you're right."

Cotton's X-ray vision cut through the wall David had built around his secrets. The old man could smell guilt as surely as he smelled cigarette smoke behind the parsonage when the preacher's son was twelve.

"Talk to her, boy." The faint odor of chlorine emanated from the pool of water swirling behind the stage.

David dropped his head into his hands, too weary to hide his struggles from his old friend. "And say what?"

Cotton's hand cupped his shoulder. "The truth, son."

Truth? In his experience, Christians had a hard time with truth. He'd seen them turn a blind eye to keep from coming face-to-face with the tricky virtue.

How many Christians really wanted to know the truth about their preacher's finances? Who among them could sympathize with his mother's heartbreak without judging? Would any of them be willing to admit they weren't perfect?

Facing the fine lines of truth was risky—because once you knew the truth, you were bound to pay a price, not the least of which was to take action to right the wrongs. Crossing the dangerously fine line of truth could cost a person all sorts of privileges…all sorts of dreams.

Until now, he'd never kept the truth from Momma. Despite the risks. No matter how dire the punishment was sure to be.

David's stomach twisted, as if his emotions had emerged from their darkened corners and come out swinging. He could struggle all he wanted; a camel had better odds of getting through the eye of a needle than he did of finding the loophole that would spare him the impending scene with his mother. Before it was all said and done, he would have to tell her the truth.

He shifted under Cotton's watchful eye. "Momma may be a pro at swallowing injustice, but I don't know if I can stand to watch her choke down the news I intend to serve her when we get home."

* * * * *

Snow fell in big wet flakes. The weather had worsened considerably since the graveside and funeral lunch. The least little bit of frozen precipitation shut down the roads in this part of the country. Come morning they could all be snowed in.

Leona handed Maddie a butter tub filled with baked beans. "You two go on to the car while I find my keys to lock up." She stacked another foil-covered casserole tin upon the two her mother had already balanced across her outstretched arms.

"Sure you don't need to mop the place too?" Roberta made certain Leona caught the peeved roll of her eyes.

Here it comes.

Leona knew her mother would have something ugly to say about the way things went today. But she didn't care. She'd been warmed and filled by the outpouring of love, and if her mother hadn't bothered to drink in a drop, she had no one but herself to blame when her withered-up soul crumbled and blew away.

"Maxine had a doctor's appointment. Bette Bob had to pick up a sick grandchild from school. I couldn't very well leave all that clean-up to the Story twins."

"Why pay that relic you call a janitor?"

"Everybody pitches in." Maddie had always been first in line when it came to Cotton's defense.

"It's what family does." Leona jammed her key into the lock, cranking her wrist against the contrary resistance. "And like it or not, Mother, these folks at Mt. Hope are family."

"Family doesn't leave you to clean up after your own husband's funeral lunch."

Leona trained her eyes on her mother. "Worthingtons have left worse."

"I'm going to the car," Maddie said.

A familiar ache throttled Leona's heart as she watched her daughter put her head down against the wind and set off for the limo in the far corner of the deserted parking lot.

The Harpers had been the first ones to arrive at the church building and the last ones to leave for so many years that the sight of a lone car seemed natural. Leona couldn't have identified the kind of car anyone drove, except for Howard and Maxine Davis. And she only knew their car because years ago, the Cadillac dealer had insisted on parking his current demo model right next to the spot marked **Visitor Parking Only**.

It had galled J.D. that the chairman of the elder board believed having the visitor spot filled with such an impressive ride would entice those of considerable means inside the church doors. Although J.D. was one to turn the other cheek, he felt making people feel unwelcome was an issue he could not ignore.

Rather than pick a fight, J.D. had employed a brilliant tactic. He sandwiched the visitor space with Howard's Caddy on one side and the Harpers' rusted-out minivan on the other. His non-confrontational approach had pricked Howard's conscience; proof the Lord had known what he was doing when he summoned the extraordinary J.D. Harper to the pulpit in the first place.

Now, as the wind whipped the Visitor Parking Only sign, tears stung Leona's eyes. Who would pick up the Lord's standard and carry on this difficult battle in J.D.'s absence?

"I'm going to the car before my hair is ruined." Roberta wheeled, leaving Leona alone in her battle with the stubborn lock.

Maddie stuck her head out the door of the limo. "Momma, David's not in the car."

"I'll find him." Leona removed the keys and slipped them into her pocket. She jerked open the heavy foyer door. Making her way through the quiet building without flipping on a light, Leona savored the secluded respite from her mother's needling.

If they had driven off, it would not have been the first time they left a child at the church. Once she and J.D. even sat down at Luby's Cafeteria and said the prayer for their Sunday lunch before realizing David wasn't with them.

Leona hurried past the secretary's office. She could swing in and use the phone to call David's cell, but the thought of putting a receiver next to her face that was caked with layers of Shirley's bombastic beige foundation kept her moving. The silver-haired church artifact had seen many a preacher come and go at Mt. Hope and would most likely outlive the next one as well.

The groaning sounds of an overloaded and overworked dishwasher escaped the deserted church kitchen and traveled down the long, empty corridor.

Leona stepped inside the darkened fellowship hall, where the smell of stout coffee still lingered, but David wasn't there.

She retraced her steps, stopping outside her husband's office door. Still locked. Thank you, Lord. She wasn't up to seeing shelves of books awaiting the return of their master. Leona returned to the large lobby.

She stood for a moment, thinking. Where could David be?

The sanctuary baptistry heater rattled to a stop, and she knew.

She cracked open the swinging doors to the place her son used to hide as a kid. Bingo.

Late-afternoon light filtered through the baptistry stained glass and cast a glow upon David seated on the front pew of the auditorium, his head hanging between slumped shoulders.

Lord, help me know what to say. Leona drew in a heavy breath as she eased up the aisle. She laid a gentle hand on his shoulder. "David?"

Her son raised his head, liquid escaping the pools of his dark eyes. "I knew you wouldn't leave me."

"Even if I had—" the desolation in his beseeching look cut to her heart— "I would have missed you come suppertime." Leona nudged her son.

David scooted over, making room for his momma the way he used to when he was younger and wanted her close until he fell asleep.

Shoulder to shoulder, they sat in the cavernous silence, David quietly shedding the tears he'd held back all day. Leona put an arm around this boy who'd grown into a man and gathered him to her, secretly begging God to give her the strength to comfort her son.

He snuffed and sat up straight, drying his cheeks with the back of his hand. "Cotton says my stepstool is still behind the pulpit."

Leona nodded, withdrawing her arm. "I think he's right."

"Would you check?"

She hadn't been back up on that stage since Sunday. If she closed her eyes, she was certain the haunting image of J.D.'s lifeless body sprawled behind the podium would vividly come to mind.

Leona looked into David's anxious eyes. He needed his momma. She'd never let him down before, and she was not about to start now. She swallowed the lump in her throat. "Sure." Summoning strength she didn't know she had Leona rose.

Slowly, she climbed the center steps, one at a time, until she reached the top of the stage. She ran a trembling hand over the cool grain of the massive oak pulpit, yearning for a trace of J.D.'s warmth. She moved behind the hollow lectern. Hanging on to the worn lip, she squatted. Tucked into the far corner was the tiny wooden stool David and his father built together one Sunday afternoon in the garage.

Leona scooped it up. Many coats of lacquer obscured the feel of the grain. Blinking back tears, she pressed the stool to her chest and came down the center steps. "Here you go."

"I haven't seen this in years." David ran a finger over the outline of his name carved in the shiny flat surface. "Remember my first sermon?"

Pride surged through Leona's grief-constricted veins. "How could I forget? Your father said you had to have an attention-getting opener. So you two spent hours searching for the perfect joke to introduce the faith of Noah."

A sly grin crossed David's lips. "Do you know what state is mentioned in the Bible?"

"No, what state?" Leona played along, craving the light the precious memory brought to the darkness shrouding her soul.

"Arkansas."

"Arkansas?"

"Because Noah looked out of the ark and saw." Glimpses of the slick-faced twelve-year-old boy flickered across David's lined face.

They laughed until tears ran down Leona's cheeks. She put her arm around her son's shoulders. When had they become so broad? If only she could pull him into her lap, kiss away the hurt, and cover his wounded heart with a Batman Band-Aid. If only she could make everything better. But she couldn't. She wondered if even God could mend her boy's brokenness.

Leona dabbed her eyes, ordering that last wicked thought from her mind. Of course God could fix this. Hadn't he always been faithful in the past? But what if this time . . . Leona shook free of the unsettling despair rising within her. She returned her hand to her lap. "After choosing the Scriptures, you insisted on a practice run-through."

"Good thing. That's when we found out I couldn't see over the pulpit."

"So Daddy helped you make the stool." The baptistry heater

kicked on in the silent moment of Leona's sweet remembrance of that long-ago day. "You made him sneak it into place before the service started so no one would suspect. When it came time for you to give the sermon, you marched up there and stepped up like you owned that pulpit."

"And I got my first laugh." David had inherited his father's ability to poke fun at his shortcomings, a gift Leona had been denied. She marveled at the way the endearing quality drew people to her men like moths to light. J.D. would be so proud.

"I guess we failed to take into account that people might notice a ten-inch growth spurt right before their eyes," Leona chuckled. "But, from that day forward, not a single young man has given his first sermon in this pulpit without standing on your stool."

"Every boy wants to be like his father when he's twelve." David's eyes locked with Leona's. He took her hand. "But I'm not twelve years old anymore, Momma. I'm going to finish my term at Oxford. When I come home I'm—"

"Oh, David, you're coming home? I'm so—"

"To practice law." David's interruption halted Leona's excitement. "I'm going to tell Grandmother that I want the firm."

Leona felt as if she had just been yanked headfirst into the muddy pit of a nasty tug-of-war game. "Daddy never expected you to grow into his pulpit," she sputtered.

"Momma, it broke his heart when I walked away from his offer. I'm the reason Dad had a heart attack."

Leona's mind raced back in time to the image of a six- year-old boy with a tea towel tied around his neck insisting that the cape transformed him into Tea-Towel Man, defender of the defenseless. That same hardened determination now radiated from David's black eyes.

"You did not kill your father. Do you hear me?" She shook her son by his shoulders. "He wanted you to find your own way to serve the Lord, whether law, history, or preaching. God has placed a call upon your heart to help people. How you do that is between you and God."

The sanctuary heaters had long since cycled down. Cold crept toward the vaulted ceiling and brushed the nape of Leona's neck. A shiver raced down her spine.

What was it about David that compelled her to preach at him? Had she not learned anything from his extended absence? Why couldn't she just leave it at what a good man and son he was? Why did she have to back the truck and dump a load of guilt?

Guilt was Satan's secret weapon. She should know; the evil one kept the loaded cannon pointed at her head at all times. While nothing would make her happier than to see David use his talents in the pulpit, seeing him receive his eternal reward mattered more. The removal of this burden he carried would require some serious prayer.

She patted her son's leg and pointed at the stool. "Why don't you take that with you?"

"I think I'll put it back where it belongs." David took the center steps two at a time. He slid the little step into the dark recess of his father's pulpit. Straightening, he paused, placing his hands on the sides of the podium.

Holding her breath, Leona slipped the Lord a quick plea for assistance. What would it hurt? Surely God could send a little help in her direction. If David experienced some sort of divine stirring while he stood in his father's place, the blame would be on God's shoulders, not hers. Novel idea or Spirit's leading?

David's eyes slowly scanned the sanctuary, as if checking each empty pew for the face that belonged there. "Dad loved this place. . . . I'll pray that the next guy can fill it up."

The words *next guy* thudded heavy against the podium. "Prayer is always a good thing." She dared not say more for fear her voice would crack.

"Yes, it is." David came down from the stage and offered his hand. "Let's go home, Momma."

Had a tiny sprout of green breached the man's resistant hull? Or was she imposing her will upon the Lord? Leona searched her son's eyes. Where desolation had been, peace now resided. She took David's hand. "Good idea, Son."

The Holy Spirit had touched David Harper . . . Leona was sure of it. She couldn't wait to tell J.D.

Then it hit her. She'd never talk to J.D. again.

Chapter Eight

Maddie stuffed a lumpy pillow into a clean case. With an added punch, she attempted to fluff the foam before tossing it onto the open fold-away couch crowding her father's small parsonage study. Because Momma was a firm believer in hospitality, Maddie had made beds for unexpected company her whole life—from furloughed missionaries and university presidents to traveling evangelists and vagrants. The parsonage had always teemed with visitors and Momma expected her daughter to help things run smoothly.

For the most part, Maddie had enjoyed the kaleidoscope of people. But tonight she wanted to hole up with what was left of her family and keep the needy world at bay.

"Tater, get off Melvin's bed." She nudged the dog from his claim in the center of the clean sheets. The disturbed squatter jumped down. Tater came and sat at her feet, his adoring brown eyes awaiting her next command.

"That dog's a pain in the—"

"Grandmother, you don't have to watch me. I know how to

make a bed. In fact, you might be surprised at all I can do."

Her grandmother's thin brows rose slightly, but she made no effort to move from the doorway, her arms crossed over her suspiciously perky chest. "I didn't expect you to go to so much trouble for my hired help. My chauffeur can get a motel room."

"Momma says the Double D is full." Maddie avoided looking at her grandmother's breasts. The motel was not the only thing bursting at the seams.

"Well, my driver can sleep sitting up, so I'm certain he can make his own bed."

"Not in this house. Momma would have my hide."

"Here's a clean towel and washcloth for Melvin." Momma edged past Grandmother and laid them on the bed. "I just heard the weather. The roads won't be clear before morning; besides, tomorrow's Thanksgiving. . . . Oh no." Defeat dulled Momma's brave-fronted face. She sank onto the corner of the thin mattress as if someone had just let the air out of her tires.

Maddie dropped a blanket on Melvin's bed. "What is it, Momma?"

"Thanksgiving." Her mind racing, Maddie searched for the hidden meaning behind Momma's one-word explanation. "Thanksgiving?"

"I forgot to thaw a turkey." Momma hands came up to support her drooping head.

"For Pete's sake, Leona." Grandmother leaned against the door, examining her manicured nails. "You've got enough leftovers crammed into your fridge to have three Thanksgiving meals. Why do you need to roast a turkey?"

Momma lifted her head, her bewildered expression melting into a torrent of tears. "Because I always roast a turkey." Her head returned to its dejected position, sobs growing in volume.

This was not good. Maddie had not seen her mother melt down since David shouted out in church, "Daddy, please don't let Momma beat me again."

"Settle down, Leona." Grandmother crossed the room and put a hand on her daughter's shoulder. Her voice held a trace of unfamiliar softness. "Why don't you and the children pile into my limo, and we'll have Thanksgiving in the city? We haven't done it in years. We can go to the club, have an elegant meal, maybe even catch a movie afterward."

Tater growled.

Maddie squatted and smoothed the spiky hairs along the ridge of her dog's neck. Although the offer may have sounded good up front, she guessed she wasn't the only one who remembered the last time they spent the holidays with Roberta Worthington.

Tater ended up sequestered in the old woman's laundry room while the discount-store Harpers ate with haute couture stuffier than the dressing in the giant bird crisping under the country club heat lamp.

When they returned home, Momma promised her little family they'd never have to go clubbing again. In turn, Maddie swore the same on a stack of Bibles to Tater, and she never went back on her word.

But while going to the country club was out of the question, somehow holing up didn't feel normal either. As much as Maddie hated to admit it, having the house filled with people they knew and some they didn't—that was home.

"What about our tradition?" Maddie clasped her mother's knee, hoping Momma would pick up on her silent pleading to put an end to Grandmother's evil plan. "Does everything have to change?" She waited, hoping for eye contact despite the blur her own tears had caused.

Momma sniffed and slowly raised her head. The hint of an understanding smile tugged at the corner of her mouth. She used her thumbs to brush tears from Maddie's cheeks. "I don't know how to stop the changes that are coming, but for now we don't have to."

Her mother lifted her chin to Grandmother. "The kids help me wrestle the bird into a roasting bag the night before. Early Thanksgiving morning, J.D. pops the heavy thing in the oven so that I wake to the smell of roasting turkey." Momma blinked away the moisture rimming her lower lids, excitement mounting in her voice. "About noon folks without family start showing up. We set up card tables everywhere. The women talk while the men watch football."

Feeling the need to get into the game and run interference for Momma, Maddie joined in with all the enthusiasm she could muster. "And we eat until we think we're going to pop. Late in the afternoon, Daddy announces it's time for the parade."

"All of us file down to the corner of Church and Main." Momma's eyes glistened.

"For Mt. Hope's Thanksgiving extravaganza." Grandmother's sarcastic tone burst the hot air balloon Maddie and Momma's reminiscing had filled. "Don't look at me like that. You're forgetting that you've dragged me to that blasted parade for years."

Maddie hoped her cutting stare would slash the unfeeling woman wide open.

Momma placed a restraining hand on Maddie's leg then sent her a conspiratorial wink. "Face it, Mother. You know you love seeing which half of the trailer house Spinner Mobile will pull behind their semi this year."

"Don't be ridiculous."

Seizing the opportunity to help her mother lighten the tension, Maddie added, "And don't forget the Story sisters riding double on their lawn and garden tractor."

"Nobody can pop a wheelie like Nola Gay." Momma burst into laughter, clutched her side, and fell back on the opened couch.

Tater and Maddie jumped onto the bed and joined in the raucous howling, the fold-out's springs squeaking agreement.

"You two laugh while you can, but whether you want them to or not, things are going to change." Irritation radiated from Grandmother's lacquered face.

Reality ripped across Maddie's chest and silenced her laughter.

Momma sat up slowly. The laughter had vanished from her face, too. Her sobered mouth was a thin, straight line. "I'm sure they will. But they're not *fixin' to* change today." Rising, she swiped the tears gliding down her cheeks and squared her shoulders for business. She turned to Maddie. "Young lady, get both card tables from the garage. We'll send David to the church for more chairs in the morning. I'm going to dig that smaller turkey out of the freezer. If we soak it in cold water overnight, we can get up early and pop the bird in the oven in time for a late lunch."

Admiration swelled Maddie's heart. Her momma did walk on water, and tonight's impressive effort was not just some cheap sandbar trick.

Grinning ear to ear, she jumped up and kissed her mother's cheek. "I'll tell Nola Gay to start the phone tree. She'll round up a crowd if she has to clear the streets with her lawn tractor." As she and Tater Tot pranced past Grandmother, Maddie fought the childish urge to stick out her tongue.

The family car may have careened over a bridge, but it should come as no surprise to anyone, including Roberta Worthington, that Momma was holding her own against the current.

* * * * *

Leona removed the heavy pillow from her face and forced open her heavy eyelids. What time was it and why did she smell turkey? The fuzzy red numbers on her clock said 11:30.

"Oh no. I've slept through Thanksgiving." She threw back the covers and crammed her arms into a faded terry robe. She hurried to the stairs as her mother tromped up. "Mother, why didn't you wake me?"

"Your kitchen is not big enough for me and that *Brewer* woman." Her mother stormed past.

"What's going on?" Leona followed her mother down the hall. "Mother?"

Her mother stepped inside the guest room. "Call me when lunch is ready." She slammed the door in Leona's face.

Leona stared at the closed door. The solid wood plank

symbolized the barrier that had been between them for years. She could pound away, even try kicking it in, but the secret to what made her mother tick would never be revealed. The years had taught Leona one thing: her mother was a time bomb with a very short fuse. *Lord, just don't let her blow up here. Not today.*

Laughter filtered through the house and ascended the stairs to combine with the delicious smells escaping from the kitchen. Leona couldn't say how long she stood there listening for J.D.'s hearty roar among the gathered before it hit her she'd never hear his laughter again. Reminders of holidays past sucked the oxygen from the upstairs hall. All future family memories were now her lone responsibility. Long, leisurely breakfasts, tables filled with goodies, a house full of company, folding chairs borrowed from the church, eggnog and hymns around the piano, carving the turkey.

A round of giggles drifted from the kitchen.

Resolve snapped Leona's backbone into place. She swiped the tears from her eyes. Allowing the distance between her and her mother to alienate her from her own kids was not an option. Today she would be thankful. The Harpers had been given another opportunity to build relationships. How many folks would kill for a second chance like the one the Lord had graciously given her? David and Maddie were going to have a good Thanksgiving if she had to string her mother up by her ears on the backyard clothesline.

Leona pinched her cheeks to add color, belted her robe, and descended the stairs.

Roxie looked up from dicing stalks of celery. "I guess Bertie woke you when she lit out for the hills." She wielded the blade with the skill of a sushi chef. "Look at you. All gussied up and nowhere to go."

Leona ran a hand across the bump in her hair and pushed some wild strands behind her ears. "Not all of us wake up looking like we stepped out of a Chico's ad."

Maddie turned from sautéing onions at the stove. A pleased smile lit her face. "Aunt Roxie came early to help me get started."

"I see that." Leona grinned at the sight of her kitchen-shy daughter slaving over a gas flame. Maybe Maddie had absorbed some of her intensive hospitality training after all.

Roxie picked up the cutting board and scraped the pile of celery into the sizzling onions. "Baby, I'll watch the skillet. You pour your momma some coffee. Let's see if we can't fortify her with a little holiday cheer."

The onion-scented cloud rising from the pan made Leona's mouth water. "Is that for your famous dressing?"

"Girlfriend, don't think you can weasel Aunt Thelma's secret stuffing recipe out of me. You know I had to wait years for her to die to inherit it." Roxie tossed snatches of running conversation over her shoulder as she moved the enticing vegetables around in the skillet. "After you get some caffeine in you, why don't you hit the shower, clean up a bit before everyone gets here?"

Leona felt a sudden wave of warmth wash over the cold place J.D.'s unexpected departure had left in her heart. Everything did not have to change. They could go on. If the people she loved most could make this day happen, maybe it was a sign that God had not forsaken them.

"Roxanne Brewer, if your hair wasn't the color of hellfire, I'd think you were an angel." Leona devoured the smile of understanding lighting Roxie's face.

"Here, Momma." Leona took the cup Maddie offered proudly and kissed her daughter's cheek. "Thanks, sweetheart. The Lord does provide." She started for the door, but the phone rang, stopping her in her tracks. Few people had land lines any more but J.D. had insisted their congregants had a way to contact him day or night. Leona reached to answer it.

"I'll get it, Momma." Maddie bustled around her, lifted the cordless phone off the cradle, and punched the Talk button. "Harper residence . . . Justin, why didn't you call my cell? . . . You're where?" Maddie's face held the same fearful look Leona had seen the time J.D. discovered his little girl hiding inside his pulpit after her disappearance had delayed church for an hour. She scooted past her mother mumbling something terse into the mouthpiece.

"Who is Justin?" Leona could tell by the sheepish look on her best friend's face that she'd asked the right person. "Roxie, what do you know that I don't?"

"Maybe you better have two cups of coffee this morning." Roxie flashed her foreign-parts-are-comparable-to-American smile.

Never a good sign.

Something rotten was stinking up the room, and if she were a betting woman, Leona would bet dollars to donuts the suspicious odor wasn't coming from Aunt Thelma's secret fried-onion concoction.

Chapter Nine

David hesitated before he knocked on the guest room door. The moment his grandmother stomped upstairs, everyone downstairs had breathed a sigh of relief.

Why couldn't Momma just let Grandmother stew out of view? He knew why. Because his mother worried too much about what people thought. How would it look if the entire Harper family wasn't gathered around the Thanksgiving table, holding hands, and singing *Kumbaya?*

So when his mother pulled him aside and insisted he haul his grandmother to the table, he wasn't really surprised. He'd started to argue that Grandmother might be harder to manage after having been cooped up, but the tears swimming behind his mother's good front told him she was teetering on the edge of an emotional river. No way, was he going to let anyone push her in...especially not his grandmother.

He made a fist and lightly rapped his knuckles on the door. "Lunch is ready."

The chipped fluted-crystal knob turned slowly. Painted-over

ancient hinges squeaked as a crack appeared between the door and the frame. Through the slit, David could see his grandmother's eyes darting back and forth. "Is that Hayseed fellow down there?"

"Who?"

"Bay weed."

David's brow furrowed. "You mean Cotton?"

"Ragweed. Feed 'n Seed. Whatever his name is."

He knew good and well his Grandmother knew Cotton's name. She was just being contrary. Indignation pressed David through the door. The room reeked of Grandmother's trademark eau de money. He closed the door behind him. "What's the matter with you?"

"I find it extremely difficult to be civil to that man." Grandmother extracted a lace-edged hanky from the cuff of her silk blouse. Pinching the corner of the delicate linen between her thumb and forefinger, she snapped it open.

"Cotton's the nicest guy I know. What's he ever done to you?"

She raised the cloth and dabbed at her nose as if the mere mention of the janitor's name had fouled the air of her excessively perfumed habitat. "It's his eyes."

"What's wrong with his eyes?"

"The steely things drill right through me. They're full of

accusations."

David felt the muscles tighten in his jaw. "What kind of accusations?" he managed to grind out.

"That I caused J.D.'s heart attack."

"That's it." Now that Dad wasn't here to protect his pastor-parishioner privileged information, David intended to put an end to his grandmother's ridiculous aversion once and for all. "Fifteen years ago, the local bank was bought out. The new holding company cleaned house, leaving their sixty-year-old bank president, Cotton, without a job."

Surprise registered in his grandmother's eyes. "That corncob was a *bank* president?"

"He was." David waited, allowing the full force of his disclosure to sink in. For some reason, watching his grandmother chew on the incredulous details of the inside story gave him a great deal of pleasure. "Cotton was too young to retire and too old to be hired by anyone else. About that same time, his wife was diagnosed with terminal cancer. The man needed help, and my father gave it to him. Cotton wasn't just the church janitor. He was Dad's friend."

David started for the door. He stopped and turned. Going in for the kill, he closed his case. "That incredible man downstairs would have given my father his *own* heart if God would have allowed him a say."

Grandmother grabbed his arm, halting his huffy exit. "I can understand being good to your employees. I'm good to Marvin."

David removed her hand, unwilling to be sequestered by such a harsh judge. "Your chauffeur's name is Melvin."

Shrugging off his reprimand, his grandmother perched primly on the edge of the double bed. "David, I know you think I didn't care for your father, but that is not the case. I just feel the man never lived up to his potential."

The hairs on the back of David's neck stood on end. "What do you mean Dad didn't live up to his potential?" Was this the woman he wanted breathing down his neck every day for the rest of his life? "J.D. Harper was the smartest man I've ever known."

"Brilliant, but naïve." Running her hand over the faded chenille spread, she cleared her throat. "When your mother came home from college with this promising young business major, your grandfather and I were thrilled. We could tell things were serious, so your grandfather went out on a limb and offered the boy a place at the firm. But after law school, J.D. had some sort of religious experience. Said God had called him into ministry, of all things. We tried to tell him he'd be begging for scraps to feed his family the rest of his life."

Absently picking fuzz from the bedspread, she seemed lost in her thoughts. Her hand tugged at a stubborn bump. David waited, despite the voice in his head telling him to run. He didn't want to hear what she had to say, but an invisible hand held him in place, unable to move, unable to miss a word of the story he'd always wondered about. Why hadn't his father used his law degree?

As if the time had finally arrived for the disclosure of her well-prepped testimony, his grandmother lifted her chin and looked at him. Taking a deep breath, she continued, "But your father wouldn't listen. Instead, the fool convinced Leona they could live on faith. So she left her budding journalism career. He left a six-figure salary contract unsigned. Before we could do a thing about it, they married. Next thing we knew, they set off for parts unknown, determined to save the world. We didn't speak to them again until we received your birth announcement in the mail a couple of years later."

Rallying to his father's defense, David straightened to his full height. "Their life didn't turn out so bad."

"Look at this place." She waved her arm at the collection of garage-sale finds furnishing the tiny room. "Your mother was not raised to be a wet nurse to a menagerie of ne'er-do-wells." She stood and took David's hands in hers. "My dear boy, neither were you. I've seen to that." Her hand moved up to the watch she'd given him for his birthday. "Do not make your mother's mistakes. Live up to your potential. End this ridiculous toying with trying to find yourself. It's time you claim what is rightfully yours, young man."

David searched the fire licking the darkened pupils of his grandmother's eyes. An errant thought jarred him. He felt like Moses standing before a burning bush. And look where his willingness to give in to someone else's demands got him: dying on a mountain outside a Promised Land he could never enter.

David pried himself free from his grandmother's ironclad grip, efusing to let anyone compel him to assume a role he was unprepared to handle. "It's time for . . . lunch. Get yourself together and come downstairs." He turned and strode from the room.

Why hadn't he admitted he was ready to take his place at Worthington & Price? He'd caught glimpses of the empty void behind his grandmother's mesmerizing glow before and not backed away from the risks. Why now?

David stomped down the stairs. He ducked into his father's home study and shut the door. He slumped into the worn office chair and ran his hand along the top of the tiny metal desk. If he believed his Grandmother, his father had wasted his life. David roiled at the injustice. J.D. Harper was an impressive man. He could have had an incredible career, gone places, met important people, made a fortune . . . all of the things David wanted for his own life. Why didn't his father want the same things?

Drumming his fingers on the desk's cold surface, David let his mind skip across the church parking lot, returning to the swinging doors of the sanctuary. He saw himself slipping inside the quiet, eerie cavern. Adjusting to the dimness, he noticed a mist hovered above the baptistry, shrouding the stained glass cross and the jeweled path.

Suddenly his father strode through the fog, a smile spread across his rested face. David burst into an all-out run down the aisle, but the robust man ascended the stage and took the podium just as David arrived at the family's front pew. His father pointed and David felt compelled to obediently take a seat. Leaning forward, David watched with a silent helplessness as his father, a fireball of energy, a man on a mission, opened his Bible. A cold wind howled through the auditorium.

David strained to hear his father's sermon, but the words whipped out of his hearing. Without warning, J.D. Harper had vanished.

Hot tears stung David's eyes and brought him back to an empty parsonage study. He shuddered, trying to disperse the lingering traces of confusion. If Grandmother was right, how could she explain why his father had been so happy? How could she explain the glowing beacon that drew the lost and searching to his father like lost ships to a lighthouse?

David's thoughts and questions, sticky and balled together, bounced against the inside of his skull. He closed his eyes. Squeezing the bridge of his nose to ease the pain, he pressed harder, hoping to force some answers. But none came. He released his hold and opened his eyes. The darkened computer screen came into view. He ran a trembling hand over the keys his father had used to peck out his sermons.

A sudden jolt traveled through David's fingers, searing a path as it blazed up his arm and shot out his shoulders. When the sensation passed, a stinging numbness remained. Rubbing his arms, David attempted to restore a feeling of normalcy.

If he didn't know better, he could have sworn Momma had summoned her angel thugs to gag him, tie his bound body to the railroad tracks that ran through the middle of town, and restrain her son's floundering soul until he cried uncle.

It would serve Momma right if I let the train plow right over me.

* * * * *

Maddie managed to avoid her mother in the deluge of company that had come despite the last minute invitation. The need to be the hostess-with-the-mostest had done Momma a world of good. Although the members of Mt. Hope had always gotten on Maddie's last nerve, she had to admit watching the troops rally around Momma chipped at her walled heart.

Trying to remain inconspicuous, Maddie cleared the large dining table of scattered plates and wadded orange and brown Pilgrim napkins.

The Story sisters had Momma's undivided attention, regaling her with tales of cucumber blight. Hands full, Maddie retreated to the kitchen. She set her load on the counter. She put the stopper in the sink and squirted soap into the stream of warm water. Plunging her hands into the steamy suds, she gazed at the church building across the parking lot.

Living next door to the church had advantages and disadvantages. On the plus side, the preacher's family could leave one minute before the services started and still not be late. On the negative side, whenever anyone needed a key to get into the building on Monday mornings, they always felt free to drop in on the pastor, even if it was his only day off. No rest for the weary. No wonder Daddy had a heart attack.

But these minor inconveniences were nothing compared to the curse of the Story sisters. For the past eighteen years those shriveled twins had made it their practice to arrive thirty minutes early for church services, stop in at the parsonage, and park themselves on the Harpers' plaid couch until time for the morning worship to start.

Maddie remembered the first time they showed up

unannounced.

David had let them in, inadvertently trapping Momma in the downstairs bathroom wearing nothing but a silky slip. Once Momma managed to get Daddy's attention, she proceeded to inform him in a terse whisper that he was to remove the sisters by hook or by crook. Daddy went to the living room and invited Nola Gay and Etta May to join him at the church to hand out bulletins, saying the job required early birds with a keen eye for the lost and downtrodden. But the trick only worked once, leaving Momma no choice but to be fully dressed and ready to pass the old biddies' inspection by sunup every Sunday morning.

A fork splashed into the water, bringing Maddie back to the task at hand.

She resumed the scrubbing of dried turkey gravy from Momma's grocery-store china, but she kept an eye on Church Street. Checking the clock on the microwave, she figured she had about an hour before Justin's arrival ignited the fireworks. Maybe if she saw his car drive up she could sneak him in the back door, and she wouldn't have to face Momma until after everyone went home.

She jammed a handful of forks into the draining rack. Why did her boyfriend have to pick today to prove he could be caring and concerned? He'd avoided commitment this long. What was another year or two? Why couldn't he let things calm down a bit before—

"Need some help?"

Maddie dropped a fork and suds splashed across the front of her petal-pink sweater. "Parker, you scared me to death." She whipped the tea towel off the hook and dabbed at the splatters.

"Sorry." Parker deposited a stack of dirty dishes on the counter. "Let me dry."

"Excuse me?"

He pointed to the clean mound Maddie had on the counter. "The rack's full."

"Oh." She returned the towel to the hook. "Thanks, but I've got it." She submerged her hands in the soapy sink, anxiously searching for something to wash.

Why was she acting like an idiot? Of course Parker Kemp meant the dish rack. The guy wouldn't know how to come on to a girl if his corn crop depended upon it. She located a plate, rinsed it, and held it over the drying rack looking for an extra slot.

Without a word, Parker took the plate from her hand. He opened the drawer stuffed with dishtowels on his first try, acting as if he lived in this house and knew right where everything belonged. He toweled the plate to a sheen, put it in the cupboard, and removed another from the rack.

A slow burn worked its way up Maddie's puckered fingers. She thought about the non-confrontational approach Momma had used to put a stop to church members taking every opportunity to look inside the private nooks and crannies of their home.

The memory of her mother's ingenuity in rigging the medicine cabinet in the downstairs bathroom brought on a slight smile. The parsonage living room had been crammed full of primped and perfumed church ladies attending a Sunday afternoon bridal shower. Suddenly, the crashing sound of marbles hitting the porcelain put a pleased smirk on Momma's sealed lips and sent a red-faced Maxine Davis fleeing the scene without so much as a thanks-for-the-nice-time.

An evil chuckle escaped Maddie's throat as she lifted the stack of dirty dishes Parker had brought in. What made these people think their tithes entitled them to sit in the living room every Sunday morning or inspect the parsonage property whenever they had the urge? She immersed the plates in the water, dispatching any earlier fuzzy feelings with the tiny bubbles.

Maddie swiped away the suds on her cheek. She cut a sideways glare at her grinning drying partner. She opened her mouth to set him straight, but decided against it. Blaming some innocent guy she'd known most of her life would change nothing.

Silverware clanking against glass combined with an occasional cheer from the football watchers in the living room. Maddie was grateful Parker seemed content to allow the dead air to remain between them. Momma would have been proud at the restraint Maddie mustered in holding her tongue, but disappointed in her ability to show her appreciation for Parker's obvious support.

Maddie took a deep breath. "Had enough football for one day?" She cringed at the sugary-sweet tone of Momma's voice coming from her very own vocal cords. Sounding like her mother was the last thing she needed . . . or wanted.

"Not a big sports guy. Besides, it's a proven fact that if you stand after eating your food will fall to your feet."

Looking down at the man's size-thirteen loafers, Maddie laughed. "Why would you encourage that?"

"So I have room for another piece of pie." Parker grinned and patted his trim waistline.

"I'm not sure how you came by your medical information, but it could be suspect."

"You think?"

"I would stake the farm on it." She'd never noticed the unusual flecks of gold in Parker's twinkling eyes. They'd always been hidden behind windshield-thick glasses. Contacts or laser surgery had improved access to those deep wells of kindness and in the process improved his looks dramatically. Maddie gave herself a mental shake. Where had that thought come from?

Tater Tot's stranger-alert bark at the front door filtered back to the kitchen. A few seconds later, Nola Gay stuck her head around the swinging door.

"Maddie, your mother sent me to tell you there's some fellow with a snowboard waiting for you in the living room."

A sinking feeling rippled through Maddie. "Already?" She took a corner of Parker's towel and dried her hands. "I didn't hear his truck pull up."

"The boy says he's a half-pint champion."

"It's halfpipe, Miss Nola Gay," Maddie corrected. "He's an Olympic snowboard hopeful for the upcoming winter games."

"A snow what?" Nola Gay left the door swinging and tromped across the kitchen. She poked her face between Maddie and Parker. "I don't think I've ever met a real live Olympic hopeful before." Excitement bubbled in her scratchy voice. "Bet you run into those ski slope heathens all the time in Denver, right Maddie? What would bring a snowboarder to Mt. Hope? It's flat as a fritter here."

"Looking for love in all the wrong places?" Parker sang as

he winked at Maddie.

Admiration peeked around Nola Gay's cataracts. "Parker leads our singing on Sunday. Doesn't he have a nice voice?"

"I always thought so, Miss Nola Gay." Maddie smoothed her hair into place. Should she mention to the old girl that a simple surgery could take care of her cloudy vision? She caught a glimpse of Miss Nola's pride in Parker. Who was Maddie Harper to dispense unsolicited medical advice, let alone burst such an adoring bubble? "Maybe Mt. Hope's song leader should go to Nashville. I think our Parker would be a CMA hopeful."

Parker snapped the damp towel at Maddie. "I think I better stick to singing on Sundays or in a hot shower." He gave a quick nod toward the door. "You go on. Nola Gay and I will finish up."

The old lady jabbed Parker with a sturdy finger. "Speak for yourself. I want to get the heathen's autograph. Once they sign all those TV commercial deals, you can kiss your chances of getting near them goodbye."

"Justin's not famous, Miss Nola." Maddie shot Parker a look she hoped he interpreted as a plea for help. "And he's not a heathen."

Nola Gay plowed on. "Well, he might be someday."

"Famous? Or a heathen?" Parker proved quick on the uptake.

"Parker Kemp, you tease." Nola Gay's dentures clicked in

her broadening smile.

He handed the star-struck woman a fresh tea towel and turned her toward the sink. "Come on, now, Miss Nola. You're not fixin' to leave me with all this, are you? How about I wash and you dry?"

"Thanks." Maddie elevated herself on her tiptoes and pecked Parker's smooth Aqua Velva cheek. "I owe you one."

"I always collect." Parker swirled the towel in front of Maddie like a matador cape. "¡Ándale! ¡Ándale!"

Spanish? Where had Parker picked up Spanish? Maybe from some of the farmhands he met on the job.

Maddie flashed her perplexing dish-washing partner a weak smile. "No point putting off the inevitable." She lowered her head and charged past the waving tea towel.

Once in the safety of the quiet hall, she leaned against the wall, taking a moment to catch her breath and regain control over her racing heart. Apparently contacts weren't the only change Parker Kemp had made these past few years. But why in the world had she done a stupid thing like kiss him?

Panic. Pure and simple. History repeating itself.

The same thing had happened when they were in grade school, only Parker was the one who kissed her.

He'd insisted she ride double on the back of his new bike. But when he turned a corner too quickly, Maddie's ankle got caught in the spokes of the back wheel, crashing them instantly. Sprawled out on the ground, with blood spurting out from under the twisted bicycle wheel wrapped around her leg, she must have looked like she was dead. Next thing she knew, he kissed her right on the mouth. When he realized what he'd done, he jumped up and ran screaming for help.

Maddie rubbed her right foot across the quarter-sized scar on her left ankle, feeling as if she was once again snagged in bicycle spokes and unable to move.

Aunt Roxie stuck her head around the corner. "Maddie, you better come peel your mother off the ceiling."

From the tension in Roxie's voice, Maddie knew a tightrope had been strung across the parsonage living room. And her name was written all over it. If she was going to walk the wire between Momma and Justin, such a feat would require all the spotters she could rustle up. She could count on Cotton to be on one side of the safety net. And from the look of support on Aunt Roxie's face, she would be on the other. But it wouldn't hurt to have Parker on standby, which he would probably be happy to do now that she had kissed him. Surely Parker wouldn't think it meant anything.

"Madison, you have company." Irritation colored Momma's polite summons shouted from the living room.

Aunt Roxie waved her forward. "Get going, baby."

Maddie fluffed her hair and straightened her sweater, but she could not make her feet move. Given a choice, she'd rather brave the stuffed shirts at Grandmother's club than face the Grand Dame of Inquisitions and the born-again jurors willing to try and convict the pastor's daughter on the spot.

Chapter Ten

Bracing for rough winds, Maddie took a deep breath. She stepped into the living room. The thick air was reminiscent of the deadly spring night Maddie had tried for years to forget.

They'd been the last to leave church that evening. The air was heavy and still. As they crossed the parking lot, the wind came. They barely made it inside the parsonage. While her family sat huddled in the hall closet, she remembered feeling glad to be home. Safely tucked between people who loved her.

Then a tornado dropped from the midnight sky and scattered pieces of Mt. Hope across the map. Except for the lone tree standing on Main Street, each branch tightly wrapped with the shredded tin roof of the Cadillac dealership, the carnage took years to clean up. Every Christmas the Storys strung lights on the resilient evergreen, and Howard Davis threatened to sue the city for emotional duress.

If her father's death had taught her anything it was that feeling safe anywhere was a childhood illusion.

Tater Tot's anxious pacing cut a figure eight between

Momma's rigid legs and the snowboard case Justin was never without. Momma held the alleged boyfriend's hand, but her clenched nice-to-meet-you smile cut her low-toned small talk into jagged little barbs.

The poor guy fancied himself a rebel, able to deal with anything Mother Nature hurled at him. He had no idea he was standing in the eye of a tightly-wrapped storm and any minute the force would snatch his shoulder-length hair right off his head.

Roxie nudged Maddie forward with an encouraging shove. "Go ahead, baby. It's gonna be fine."

"Wanna bet?" Maddie pressed her hands against her aching middle. Maybe her appendix would burst, or her spleen would rupture, or her heart would stop and drop her on the spot, sparing her the suffering from Momma's double-barrel stare aimed right between her eyes.

Momma took Justin by the elbow and brought him forward. She presented the unkempt caller to Maddie as if he were the prime minister of a Communist country. "Madison, seems a young man has come all the way from Denver to offer his condolences." Her continued use of Maddie's proper name was not a good sign.

Maddie averted her eyes from her mother's obvious hurt. Leona Harper's anger was usually short-lived, but Maddie had seen her mother tend intentional slights to an over-ripened state.

Not telling Momma about her boyfriend qualified as one of those offenses.

If she had any guts at all, she'd run to the unsuspecting guy with the rugged stubble, smoldering gray eyes, and tight-fitting jeans and push him out of harm's way. But like the coward she'd always been when it came to Momma, Maddie stood immobile.

The eyes of the Thanksgiving crowd narrowed in silent judgment.

"There's my girl!" Justin flashed his I-intend-to-win grin. "Aren't you going to say howdy, Babe? Isn't that how the locals say hello in these parts?" He swaggered across the room, opened his arms, and sucked Maddie up by the roots.

Her mind whirled as he spun her around. A skilled surgeon would have been hard-pressed to snip her free of this mess. "Justin, put me down."

"Sure thing, Babe." He set her feet on the floor and planted a big kiss on her lips right there in front of Mt. Hope's incurably chaste crowd. The Story sisters riding topless in the Thanksgiving parade could not have attracted a greater number of appalled rubberneckers.

Maddie shimmied out of Justin's embrace. She palmed the

wrinkles from her rumpled top. Her eyes skated around the room, jumping from judge to judge. From the hostile looks, her boyfriend had not scored gold today. She prayed for a tornado to drop, snatch up the house, and whisk her away to Oz . . . or any place out of earshot of the tongue-lashing her mother was sure to give her when the crowd thinned. Damage control was her only option. She summoned her most charming smile. "Everybody . . . this is . . . Justin . . . my friend."

Tater growled.

"So he told us." Momma's response was extra sugary sweet, a sure sign she'd taken the injury in the heart. "Hush, Tater." She snagged the growling dog's collar, without taking her eyes off Maddie. "That's not how we treat *friends* in this house, especially *new* ones."

Maddie cringed. She hadn't meant to wound her mother, but that's exactly what her secrecy had done. All she could do now was try to staunch the hemorrhage. "Momma, I was—"

Roxie cleared her throat. "Leona, given the chance, I bet this boy would show us one of those Youboob videos of the tricks he can do on that tiny board in his fancy case."

"It's YouTube," Etta May corrected proudly.

"Whatever you call 'em, a little entertainment is just what this party needs." Roxie slapped Justin on the back. "But I'm forgetting my manners. You look hungry, son."

"Starved."

"I hear those athletic-types are always hungry," Etta May whispered to Bette Bob. "It's the steroids."

A lazy smile slid across Justin's lips, making him look more like a poster boy for Abercrombie underwear than a fit companion for a pastor's daughter. "It's not easy keeping this machine well oiled." He winked at Etta May and her mouth dropped open.

"We've got leftovers out the wazoo." Roxie stepped between Momma and Justin's snowboard case. "Maddie, you see what you can scare up for his fine specimen to eat." She nodded her head toward the kitchen. "Cotton and I will keep your momma company while you're getting him settled."

In her daring moment of brilliance, Aunt Roxie had never been more loved. "That's a great idea." Maddie snatched Justin's case.

"I'm sure that's exactly what your momma was thinking. Isn't that right, Leona?" Roxie wrapped an arm around Maddie's mother.

Momma's lips hardened into a thin, quivering line. "Absolutely." Outflanked, but not outmaneuvered, Momma released Tater Tot. The dog made for the hem of Justin's frayed jeans while Momma adjusted the kink in her bent-out-of-shape neck. "It's not Thanksgiving until you've swallowed a generous portion of secret stuffing."

"Good doggie." Justin's leg gyrated back and forth, his eyes beaming an SOS in Maddie's direction.

Maddie's eyes darted to Momma. Momma's disappointment had deepened into disapproval. Anger flared in Maddie's veins. Momma had made a judgment about Justin just by looking at him. She knew nothing of his effortless moves over the snow, stalwart determination, or gold-studded ambition.

Maddie tightened her grip on the snowboard case. "Tater." The cocker released his hold on the tattered pant leg and dropped to his belly, the corner of his upper lip lifted in a disapproving snarl. "Stay, Tater." Maddie led Justin from the room, miffed that she felt like the driver of a getaway car with flashing blue lights gaining in her mirrors.

"Don't know who has a worse bite, your dog or your mom," Justin whispered. Once in the hall, he pinned Maddie to the wall and smiled. "I've missed you." Dragging his stubbly chin along the curve of her neck, he rubbed his body up against hers and kissed her hard.

Maddie pulled free and hissed, "Have you lost your mind? Not here." She ducked under his arm. "You don't have a clue how close you came to being crucified in there, do you?" She noted his puzzled face. "Never mind. It'd take too long to explain. Come on. Let's get you something to eat."

He grabbed Maddie's hand and twirled her into his arms. "So this is Mayberry?"

"Knock it off, Justin." Maddie freed herself from his clutches.

Anyone would be uncomfortable in this delicate situation, she told herself. Fencing her rabid mother for any length of time would require barbed wire. The displeased woman could come charging after them at any minute, and there would be big trouble if she discovered them kissing. Maddie deleted the terrifying images from her mind. She took Justin's hand and escaped through the swinging door to the kitchen. Nola Gay dropped her tea towel. Parker looked up from the sink.

"Justin, this is—"

"Don't tell me. Aunt Bee and Andy." A cutting chuckle rumbled in Justin's throat. He sauntered past the stunned Nola Gay, flipped a kitchen chair around, straddled it, and draped his arms across the wobbly ladder-back. He poked his index finger into a bowl of leftover potatoes sitting on the table. He lifted his loaded appendage and sucked it clean. "Needs gravy."

Parker was the first to break the lull in the conversation. He stuck out a sudsy hand. "Barney Fife at your service."

Justin smirked, ignoring Parker's outstretched regards. "Keep a bullet in your pocket too?"

"At all times." Parker patted his rejected hand over his heart, taking the ribbing with the flawless stride of an expert in the art.

"Where are my manners? May I present the lovely Nola Gay Story."

Justin shrugged. "You people and your manners. It's the bomb."

Has my boyfriend always been this irritating or is my equilibrium out of whack with the trials of the past few days? Maddie removed a clean plate from the dry stack on the counter and snatched a fork for good measure.

Miss Story stepped forward. Justin made no move to rise in the presence of a woman. Maddie cringed, but before she could prompt her boyfriend into proper Southern etiquette, the old woman lowered her nose.

Nola Gay peered over the top edge of her wire-rimmed glasses. "Michael Phelps was a real gold medalist. And a gentleman."

"Justin, Miss Story would like your autograph." Maddie returned the plate to the stack, fork still in her hand. She jerked open her mother's junk drawer and frantically dug through the old coupons, rubber bands, and dried-up ink pens. "I know there's paper in here somewhere." When her hand struck an object that felt like a notepad, she tugged. "Here, I found something."

Nola Gay draped the dripping tea towel over the metal hook by the sink. "Keep your paper . . . and your rude half-pint skier,

Maddie Harper. I've changed my mind." She stomped out of the room.

"I guess I better help the Story sisters or they'll never get that tractor started for the parade." Parker gave Justin a quick nod. "Good to meet you. Any friend of Maddie's is a friend of mine." He focused his dark eyes on Maddie. "Y'all coming to the parade?"

Maddie felt a contemptible surge of color blush her cheeks. "Of course. We wouldn't miss it." She closed the drawer with her hip and leaned against the counter for support, tapping the fork against her crossed upper arm.

"We'll see you there." Parker exited through the swinging door.

Listening to the squeaky hinges, Maddie had the distinct feeling she'd been issued a time-out, even though Parker had been nothing short of . . . gallant. Why should she care what some guy from high school thought of her or her boyfriend?

She glanced at an oblivious Justin sitting at the table shoveling serving-spoon-sized mounds of stuffing into his mouth, straight from the bowl.

Acknowledging her stare, he stopped mid-bite. "What?"

"Ever thought of using a fork?"

Justin dumped the spoonful of dressing back into the container, waved the big utensil in front of his sideways smirk, and slowly dragged his tongue over the smooth, shiny surface. "That better?"

Maddie's insides melted. She sighed. If she was going to have to spend time in her room, she might as well make the most of her boy toy. She put the wrinkled paper back in the drawer, handed Justin the fork, and sank into a chair beside him.

Running her hand along the top of his leg, Maddie watched her boyfriend stab a piece of turkey off the large ceramic platter. "So, you missed me?"

"Sure." Justin crammed a hunk of dark meat into his mouth. He swallowed. "Got anything to drink?"

Maddie went to the drying rack and retrieved a clean glass. She listened to Justin chatter on about the band's latest gig while she took the milk jug from the fridge and filled the tumbler, but her mind drifted back to the look on Parker's face when she walked into the kitchen.

For a split second she'd seen . . . Well, she wasn't sure what it was. Discomfort maybe? But how had she made Parker Kemp uncomfortable? The guy had always been way too sensitive.

Justin put down his fork. "Milk?"

"You're in training."

"And a parsonage." He accepted her offering.

"You'll have to sleep on the sofa."

"What?"

"You heard me."

He winked at her. "Sure. Anything you say, babe." He tilted his head back and drained the glass. "My truck's got a heater. Maybe we can slip out and frost the windows."

Sensitivity had never been one of Justin's struggles. As Maddie watched his Adam's apple bob up and down, she couldn't shake the nagging feeling Miss Story might have diagnosed something she'd overlooked in her initial examination of their relationship. Since he'd come in, Justin hadn't asked her a single thing about her father's funeral, or how she'd managed these past few days sandwiched between her mother and grandmother. Had he always been so self-absorbed?

Maybe Justin was like the bent jigsaw puzzle piece she found years ago under the couch cushions while searching for Coke machine change. She tried to cram the piece into the new scene her mother had spread out on a card table in her sewing room, but she never could make it fit. Momma told her to throw the rogue piece away. But for some unknown reason, Maddie tucked the unyielding shape in with the old book reports and science projects she refused to part with.

Too bad men weren't like mathematical equations: plug in

the right variables, juggle things around, and presto . . . balance. Foolproof solutions with finite answers were solid comfort. Maddie eyed the stranger sitting in her father's chair. Justin was definitely an unknown quantity. She sighed. Maybe her prognosis about their future had been a tad optimistic.

* * * * *

A lightning-sharp twinge burned through Leona's nose, cutting through the gathering storm of her emotions. Hearing I told you so was the last thing she needed. She held up a stiffened hand. "Mother, do not say a word."

Her mother circumvented her exit. "This is what comes from giving Madison so much freedom."

If Leona did not escape immediately, the cloudburst brewing behind her lashes would beat the thunderous comments sure to roll off the tongues of her self-righteous guests. "I mean it, Mother. Don't mess with me." She executed a quick sidestep maneuver and broke for the stairs, but the staccato click of designer high heels trailed her breakneck retreat. Leona took the steps two at a time, anxious to reach higher ground.

"You let Madison wear whatever she wanted. You sent her off to those foolish church camps. You—"

Leona's foot froze midair. She wheeled and faced her mother. "Don't lecture me on how to raise a daughter. Maddie is a great girl. She's going to be a doctor, for heaven's sake.

And with absolutely no help from you." Planting both feet on the landing, Leona ignored the crowd forming at the base of the stairs. Her tongue, possessed by a mind of its own, slashed the roiling darkness like heat lightning. "Since when do you care about Maddie? You've never so much as sent the girl a birthday card."

Years of bottled-up emotions discharged like buckshot. Her mind gathered another load of unsettled scores and crammed them into the firing chamber. Leona raised her chin and took aim. "How do you think you made David feel, knowing you doted on him while you ignored his sister?"

David's face, cold and silent, fell into Leona's sights. Nausea swept over her. No matter what she thought of her mother, David didn't deserve to be the rope in this tug-of-war. She blinked, unable to see a thing through the tears threatening to run her off the road like a driving rain.

Her mother marched up the stairs, unfazed. "Well, I must say, it is gratifying to see that you've raised a daughter just like you."

"Like me? What is that supposed to mean?"

Mother charged up even with Leona and squared off face-to-face. "Now maybe you'll know how it feels when someone you've loved more than life itself throws everything in your lap and runs off with a no-account loser."

The acrid words slammed into Leona with the force of an eighteen-wheeler. But she'd had enough of her mother flattening her like some varmint on a stretch of deserted highway. "Is that what you really think, Mother?"

"You bet it is." Her mother's steel trap snapped shut.

Leona swiped away tears, but she could not escape Mother's vise-like glare. She would have to gnaw her leg off to break free. Her mind backtracked through the haze of thirty years of animosity. Leona remembered being young and impetuous, but she could not recall a deliberate plan to hurt her mother. Suddenly, comprehension cleared Leona's muddied thoughts, and the staggering weight of the fallout caved her shoulders.

"Mother, do you think I married J.D. to get even with you?"

"What other explanation is there? You up and married him without so much as a 'I wish you were here.'"

"We eloped because you and Father made it very clear that if J.D. chose ministry over the firm, he could not have me. Mother, I was never yours to give away. I belonged to God."

"Is that why God stood in my place before that justice of the peace? Not even a district judge." Mother brandished a pointed finger in Leona's face. "Who is this God you love more than your family? Where was God when you took your first step, lost your first tooth, or nearly died of pneumonia? This ludicrous *idea* you worship wasn't there to hold your hand on your first day of school or dry your tears when Sarah Michaels found a new best friend. Who was there? Your mother, that's who!" She raised a balled fist as if she were shaking it in the face of God, demanding a rematch on Leona's life.

Mother loves me. In her warped, possessive way, she loves me.

The startling realization smoothed the hairs standing along the ridge in Leona's neck. Right or wrong, her mother felt she had been dealt a dirty deal and somebody was going to pay.

Leona considered the blame forming a hard shell around her own heart. Why had God allowed J.D. to die and leave her in such a painful lurch? For the first time in three decades, she and her mother had something in common.

Leona twisted the thin gold band on her left hand, pondering the injustice she had swallowed in the past few days. Maybe nothing could wash the bitter taste from her mouth, but one thing she knew for certain: she refused to chew on it for the next thirty years.

The knot in Leona's tense insides loosened. She reached for her mother. "I know you—"

The agitated woman backpedaled from her touch. "If you knew how much I loved you, how could you throw it in my face and run off with that . . . preacher?"

"Because I loved him." Leona searched her mother's eyes, looking for evidence that the understanding she hoped to communicate had sunk in.

"You didn't have a clue about love. If you had, you would never have walked out our door. It killed me that you didn't have a big wedding and a reception at the club."

Leona stiffened. Why did her mother have to make everything about what people thought? Could the woman never see past herself? "If you understood love, Mother, you would have flung the door open and welcomed my happiness. But instead you slammed it shut." Leona caught a glimpse of David's accusing face.

Reality pricked her rod-straight backbone and deflated her spine. By insisting her own children live by her choices, Leona had become the very person she swore she never would. She had become her mother...a woman constantly worried about what other people thought. Fresh tears spilled down Leona's cheeks. While obsessing over the speck in her mother's eye, she had missed the log in her own. God, forgive me.

Her mother poked Leona's shoulder with a glossy nail. "You want me to fling the door open and walk out of your life? Is that what you're saying?"

"No, that's not what I meant."

Mother released her hold on the banister, both hands flailing the air as she plowed on with her tirade. "I can walk out that piece of plywood you call a front door and never look back." She pivoted her stylish heel on the landing, missing the first step.

Roberta Worthington tumbled head over heels down the stairs. She landed at David's feet with a loud crack and a sickening thud. One designer pump headed north, while the other shoe pointed south.

Staring at Roberta Worthington's still body, Leona was unable to move from the landing.

What kind of horrible person kills her mother . . . twice?

* * * * *

David lunged forward, but as usual, his feeble attempt was too late. He couldn't believe he'd witnessed such mayhem. Momma yelling. Grandmother backing down. Usually it was the other way around. His father's death had upset the delicate balance of the Harper world, maybe even the universe. Nothing was right. Nothing would ever be right again.

He knelt beside his unconscious grandmother, afraid to touch her. Conflicting emotions nearly doubled him over. "Somebody get Maddie!"

Parker pushed through the crowded hall. "What happened?"

Nola Gay grabbed Parker's shirtsleeve and shouted, "Mrs. Worthington is dead!"

Placing both hands on the old woman's shoulders, Parker spoke to her in a measured tone. "Calm down right this minute. Go to the kitchen and get Maddie." He drew his cell phone from the holster on his belt, snapping orders at the dumbfounded onlookers. "Maxine, I'll try calling Charlie. But he's probably got the ambulance in line for the parade. If I can't get him, I'll need you and Howard to run down to Main Street and see if you can find him."

Maxine shook her head and wrung her hands. "Melvin drove Howard to the Zip Trip for more ice."

"You call Howard's cell. Tell him to get Melvin and that limo back here. We might need it to transport Mrs. Worthington if we can't find Charlie." Parker removed Etta May from the fray. He placed her against the wall. "You gotta let the poor woman have some air."

"What can I do, Parker?" Etta May's lips quivered.

Parker's face softened. His arms enfolded the sweater- clad woman and she disappeared in his comforting hug. "Pray, Miss Etta May. Pray."

David envied the conviction he heard in Parker's voice. The guy spoke as if seeking God's help was the only thing to do. A wave of shame washed over him. Praying had fallen off of his to-do list since he decided to match God's lack of communication about his future with a silence of his own. From his place on the floor, David sat immobile, watching helplessly as everyone else sprang into action.

Momma silently clutched the banister, her face a pale shade of green. "Is she breathing?"

"Cotton." Parker motioned to the janitor. "If you can step over Mrs. Worthington without bumping her, I think Mrs. Harper could use a shoulder to lean on."

The custodian gave a quick nod. "I'll do it, Parker." He picked his way around the crumpled woman and bounded up the stairs to the landing. "Leona, I think you better hang on to me. You don't look so good."

"Watch her, Cotton." Roxie peeked through the painted balusters. "She's fixin' to pass out."

"Where's Maddie?" David could not take his eyes off his grandmother's face. He'd never seen her so peaceful. He could not resist the temptation to touch her wrinkle-free skin.

In a flash, his sister pushed past Parker and knelt beside him and their grandmother. "What happened?"

"I killed her." Momma wilted into Cotton's arms. How he managed to keep her from tumbling down the stairs before he got both of them seated on the top step, David couldn't say.

Maddie pressed two fingers against the vein in the old woman's neck. "Did anyone call an ambulance?"

"I'm trying to get Charlie." Parker towered over them. "And

I've sent Maxine to find Melvin and the limo."

David lifted his grandmother's hand, tracing the blue veining with his thumb.

"Don't move anything." Maddie gently removed their grandmother's hand from David's caress. "I need to check her injuries."

"Tell us what to do, baby." Roxie hovered over David's shoulder, blocking the light and casting a shadow over Grandmother.

"Pray." Momma lifted her head off Cotton's shoulder. "Pray the Lord spares my mother long enough for me to ask her forgiveness."

The sadness in his mother's eyes broke David's heart. "Momma, it wasn't your fault." He wanted to scoop his mother into his arms and make everything better, just like she used to do for him. But cartoon Band-Aids were no match for the destructive tilt of the earth's axis his father's death had caused or the inequities he had allowed his grandmother to heap in his favor. "She missed the step. It's my fault. I should have caught her."

"It was an accident." Maddie sandwiched David's face between her hands. "Do you hear me?"

Surely his bossy little sister knew his reluctant agreement was the result of her jerking his head up and down, but she appeared satisfied.

Maddie released her hold, returning her attention to her patient. Using the pad of her thumb, she raised Grandmother's eyelid. "She's alive. Maybe has a concussion." Her long, slender fingers quickly assessed the damage to the catawampus limb. "At her age, I'm almost certain she's broken a hip." Maddie nudged David. "I need more room. Bring me the cushions from the couch. I have to stabilize her leg."

"Why doesn't she open her eyes?"

"Brother, move it," Maddie ordered.

David's head understood his sister's command, but his legs were uncooperative to the urgency. This tragedy was his fault. He could have intervened. Put an end to the bickering. Dad always did. Time and time again, David had witnessed his father stand as a buffer between Momma and Grandmother's thrashing tongue. I'm not half the man he was.

"We need to get her to a hospital as soon as possible." Maddie appeared calm, focusing on her examination with the skill of a seasoned physician, unaware David had failed to move as she ordered.

From the lines creasing her brow, David had the sickening feeling the family physician wasn't telling him everything.

"What's all the ruckus?" Justin stood in the doorway, holding a plate of pumpkin pie.

Etta May's bowed head popped up from her clasped hands. "Leona may have killed her mother."

"And you without the decency to put down your dessert," Nola Gay snapped.

"Back off, lady." Justin crammed another bite into his mouth. Eyes taunting the old girl, he dragged his tongue over the pie filling stuck to backside of his fork.

"Nobody's dead." Maddie's confident admonition did not cure David's inability to stand.

"Young man." Aunt Roxie tugged at David's sweatshirt. "We need that ambulance. You see if you can't find Charlie. I'll get the cushions."

Parker pocketed his phone. "Let me help him." He slid his arms under David's armpits and lifted him to his feet.

Forced vertical, David tried to balance himself on his straw legs. "Maddie?"

"Get . . . that . . . ambulance." His sister enunciated slowly like she used to do when she tired of his teasing and threatened retaliatory action. "Have . . . I . . . made . . . myself . . . clear?"

David wobbled above his sister, grateful Parker's arm of solid support had not been withdrawn. He glanced up the stairs. Guilt had whitewashed his mother's face from pale green to a sickly yellow. "Momma, everything's going to be fine. God will not give us more than we can bear." Repeating his father's favorite words failed to rally the same reassurance David had believed as a kid.

What kind of a God expects a family to rely upon rhetoric any jury would find flimsy?

Chapter Eleven

The blaring siren sputtered as Charlie Copeland's vintage ambulance swerved around the corner of Church and Main. Lights flashing, the emergency vehicle sped past the held-up Thanksgiving parade. Steadying the gurney, Maddie ran through the emergency protocol she'd followed in spite of David's irritating interference, not to mention trying to mentally block out the squabbles between Nola Gay and Justin.

She'd checked her patient's vitals: heart rate, blood pressure, and breathing. Concerned about a possible head injury, she checked her grandmother's pupil dilation. Brain function appeared normal, but a CT would give a definitive evaluation.

After assessing the injury to the hip, she'd stabilized the leg to minimize internal damage to nerves and tissue. Finally, she'd covered the patient with a blanket to prevent shock. Maddie heaved a slow, pleased sigh. All things considered, she'd managed an A-plus performance. Why didn't she feel better about it?

Watching her grandmother's comfortable respirations normalize her coloring, Maddie chafed at the ebb of her self-satisfaction. Any moment Roberta Worthington could sit up and spout off something catty about her care. After all, stabilizing a leg and calling an ambulance hadn't magically healed their broken relationship.

I did my duty. Provided the best medical care I knew how. Truth was, the unconscious woman lying on the stretcher didn't concern Maddie nearly as much as the blank stare coming from the woman standing on the opposite side.

"Keep that ice on her hip." Maddie regretted the snappy edge the adrenaline rush had given her voice. She added a softened explanation. "It will reduce the swelling."

Momma adjusted the plastic freezer bag Aunt Roxie had frantically thrown together after Howard and Melvin returned from their convenience store run. "I'm doing the best I can." Momma's flat-line tone matched her expressionless features.

Emergencies had always been Momma's strong suit. Nothing thrilled the pastor's wife like a chance to bark orders and assume command. So her mother's insistence she ride along in the ambulance hadn't come as a surprise, but Maddie had never seen the color drain from her mother's face. She didn't need two patients on her hands.

Maddie reined the panic rising in her throat. Think. Ask

questions. Observe. "How are you doing, Momma?"

"Fine."

Short answers. Profuse perspiration. Unhealthy pallor. It didn't take a brain surgeon to interpret the evidence. Maddie never thought she'd live to see it, but the trauma of the last few days had finally teetered the Tower. Instead of satisfaction, a deep loss rolled over her.

Desperate to stanch the emotional flow draining her mother, Maddie searched for a topic of distraction. "Do you remember the first time I tried using your old Singer sewing machine?"

Her mother's brow furrowed into a puzzled crease. "I told you not to." She changed hands on the dripping bag, wiping away the excess moisture on her slacks.

"You made everything I wore. I watched you whip garments together. The whole time, I was thinking, how hard could it be?"

Momma kept her eyes on the ice pack. "You did a good job laying the pattern and cutting out the pieces."

Encouraged by her mother's attempt to follow her train of thought, Maddie hurried on. "But when I tried to stitch the first seam, my finger was in the way of the needle. The evil thing plunged straight through my nail bed. I'll never forget the popping sound of being impaled." Maddie made her eyes wide for added effect. "It was so cool when they pulled it out and there was this little geyser of blood."

Momma glanced up, beads of sweat glistening on her forehead. "I thought I was going to pass out." She swiped the back of her free hand across her brow and focused her attention on the assigned task, swaying with each dangerous turn of the ambulance.

For Momma not to gag at the mention of blood meant only one thing: her emotional shock had escalated.

Panic snapped at the taut sinews holding Maddie's professional resolve in place. She pawed through Charlie's first aid kit, wishing the volunteer paramedic stocked his antique station wagon with something more useful than gauze and cotton balls. *Keep her talking.* "You were as calm as a neurosurgeon. You calmly lifted the presser foot, unscrewed the needle from the arm, and drove me to the ER."

"I'm glad you don't remember me driving like a crazy woman or melting into a heap on the waiting room floor."

Maddie was relieved Momma seemed to be tracking well enough to make a joke.

"Do you think I hate you, Madison?" Momma's words were barely audible over the crackling wail of the siren.

Not sure how to respond, Maddie stared at her mother. "What?"

"I didn't live up to my mother's expectations, and she hates me for it." Tears splashed the blanket tucked around

Grandmother. "Did I expect too much from you?"

Maddie's gaze darted around the vehicle, seeking alternate escape routes. Maybe Charlie would drive the ambulance off a bridge before she was forced to answer these loaded questions. If Momma was busy thrashing around in a river, she wouldn't have time to delve below the surface of their strained mother-daughter relationship.

Some things were better left unsaid, and their feelings were one of those things. Maddie noticed the vacant glaze of her mother's eyes and halted her search. Shock had Momma by the throat.

"Momma, I want you to take some deep breaths through your nose."

"I didn't mean . . ." Her airy voice cracked. "To expect too much from you."

"Breathe, Momma."

"People can see me through the walls of the parsonage. I had to be perfect. Did you feel like they could see you too?"

Diving into a river to save Momma was one thing. Being her confidant was out of the question. They were mother and daughter, not BFF's, nor would they ever be. Momma's spiritual compass pointed toward heaven while Maddie's spun around in search of a true north.

Bumping around in the back of that rescue vehicle, Maddie

caught a glimpse of her future in the tired face of her mother. Suffering a lifetime of paralyzing guilt because she failed to reach an unattainable standard did not interest her in the least.

Trying to shore up the sagging mother-daughter borders, Maddie steered the conversation toward something generic. "Is that why you never threw away a single stashed pickle in the back of the pantry?"

Her mother gave a labored, confused nod. "I hate pickles. But Ray Story is our trash man. He would have hauled the evidence straight to his sisters." She reached across Grandmother's slow-rising chest. "Did you hear my question? Did you feel like you had to be perfect?"

Shock or no shock, taking a bone from Tater would be easier than shaking Momma once she sank her teeth into a train of thought.

When Maddie didn't answer, Momma continued, "Why didn't you tell me about Justin?"

The blunt question shamed Maddie. If her life was so great, why didn't she want to share it with her parents? Why had she felt the need to keep her boyfriend a secret? He wasn't a forbidden tattoo or piercing to be hidden until Momma and Daddy caught up with the times. He was the person who made her happy, and that should make her parents happy, right?

"I'm sorry—"

Tears spilled down her mother's cheeks. "Did you think I would stop loving you?"

Maddie knew shock victims talked irrationally, but this conversation had careened toward disaster. She had to take the wheel, change the subject, or run the risk of dealing with her mother in uncharted waters. "Breathe, Momma. In through the nose, out through the mouth." Maddie used the calming physician's voice med students practice in front of their bathroom mirrors before rounds. "Let's not try to solve the world's problems today. Once we get Grandmother—"

"I didn't tell my mother about J.D." Momma's pupils appeared fixed on a point in the distant past. "I fell in love with a man who could never meet Roberta Worthington's expectations. I failed my mother. I knew she'd hate me for it. And when she found out, she did."

Momma had kept things from her mother? Impossible. Imagining her mother struggling to break free of her own cocoon bordered on heresy. Momma's fear of capsizing would never allow her to rock the boat of convention.

"Grandmother doesn't hate you." Maddie patted Momma's hand. Her mother's skin felt cool and clammy. "She is a bitter old woman who has made it her life's ambition to make everyone else miserable."

"I'm the cause of that bitterness."

"Don't be ridiculous." Maddie tightened her grip. "Momma, look at me. Your theory is flawed."

Confusion furrowed Momma's brow. "What?"

"If I disappoint you, can I expect you to hate me?" Maddie shook her mother's arm. "Is your love conditional?"

"No." A pained expression contorted Momma's face as if the question was preposterous. "There's nothing you can do to make me stop loving you."

"I know that." Maddie wondered whether Momma's blanket statement included moving in with a member of the opposite sex, but now was not the time to lob that grenade.

Maddie could feel the rise and fall of her grandmother's chest under her outstretched arm. Roberta Worthington defined happiness by how she was treated, not how she treated others. When people failed to meet her expectations, disappointment consumed her like a flesh-eating bacterial infection. Momma wasn't like that, was she?

But what if true unconditional love was a myth? Or merely something mothers claimed until their children defied them? Maddie searched her mother's red-rimmed eyes for reassurance, for proof her hypothesis was invalid.

Momma let go of the ice pack and clasped Maddie's hand. "If you want an Olympic snowboarder, Justin is what I want for you. Is he what you need, sweetheart?"

"Need?"

What she needed was for this surreal conversation to end and this rough ride to be over. It would only be a matter of time before the woman's uncanny way of seeing straight into the heart of the real question would expose the awful truth. If she wasn't sure what she needed, how could she ever know what she wanted?

Maddie pulled free of her mother's grasp, unwilling to be jerked around by strings the woman refused to cut or condemned by a standard she could never live up to. "Take deep breaths, Momma."

When would Momma admit her daughter was no longer a child in need of extra eyes to bring the future into focus? Maddie squeezed her eyes tight, wishing she could erase the sight of what was in store for her. Right before Charlie closed the ambulance door Justin had pulled her aside and told her he was going back to Denver.

What kind of man tosses his snowboard in his truck and leaves without a backward glance? Maddie adjusted the blanket covering her grandmother. What kind of fool pretends it doesn't hurt?

* * * * *

Leona craved fluids. She, along with nearly all of Mt. Hope's congregation, had been sitting in the hospital waiting room for hours. She popped the plastic lid from the Styrofoam cup and gulped the lukewarm coffee Roxie had brought up from the hospital cafeteria.

"Go easy on the caffeine." Roxie pried the cup from Leona's trembling hands. "You're just now getting some color back in your face."

The last swallow slid down Leona's parched throat, her mind muddier than the liquid she had just consumed. Her brain felt too big for her skull. Pressing her fingers to her temples, Leona attempted to thwart the escape of all of her common sense. "Roxie, tell me again what the doctor said."

"Bertie has a slight concussion and a broken hip. She'll be out of recovery and in her own room in about an hour."

"Maddie nailed the diagnosis." Leona lowered her hands and smiled weakly. "She's going to be a great doctor, isn't she?"

"The best." Roxie pursed her lips on the tip of her straw and slurped up the last of her Diet Dr. Pepper.

Leona surveyed the cramped room.

Over in the corner, Cotton and Melvin had David occupied. Against the wall, Parker was treed by the Storys. Out in the hall, Howard and Maxine were in deep conversation with two other board members, Hank and Harold. *Board members?*

Leona leaned forward in her chair to see if she could hear their whispers, but a sudden wave of dizziness made deciphering their conversation impossible. From Maxine's animated gestures, it couldn't be good. Leona fell back into her chair and closed her eyes.

Bette Bob McDonald bustled into the room, toting proof of her firm belief in the combined powers of chocolate and prayer. "I've got homemade fudge, chocolate chip cookies, and warm brownies. Prayer warriors need their strength."

"Let me help you with that, Bette Bob." David flew across the waiting room like he was saving a baby from a burning building.

Curiosity niggled Leona from her stupor.

"Why, thank you, David." The corners of Bette Bob's lips lifted in a pleased grin. "I brought Amy some lunch too. Do you mind holding it while I slide this tray onto that end table?" A paper sack dangled from her hand.

"Happy to take the heavy tray off your hands," David offered.

"No, I believe you taking care of Amy will help me more." Mt. Hope's dessert diva dropped a brown paper bag into his grasp.

David stared at the lunch sack. "Amy had to work on Thanksgiving?"

"Someone's got to work the holidays, right?" Bette Bob wiped her freed hand across the front of her pink wind suit, leaving a brown swath of chocolate. "Or there wouldn't have been anyone here to take care of your grandmother?"

David nodded agreement.

"Mrs. Harper?" A vision in pale blue scrubs appeared in the doorway.

Leona had been so busy watching David she hadn't even seen Amy come in. But when she glanced at her son, his spellbound stare proved he had not missed the entrance of the beautiful, young nurse.

Well, this was a complication she had not considered. If David was interested in Amy, how could she have Parker married to her by Easter? But then how could her son choose a wife when he couldn't even pick a vocation?

"Mrs. Harper?" Amy's gentle touch startled Leona.

"I'm sorry, what did you say?"

"You can come on back if you'd like to see Mrs. Worthington for a few minutes before we move her out of recovery."

"I'll go with you, Momma." David was at Leona's side before she could organize her thoughts into a coherent answer.

"Follow me." With military precision, the pretty nurse executed a pivot turn.

"Amy, I brought you Thanksgiving dinner." Bette Bob called out after them. "If you get a break, come get some of these brownies you love."

Amy turned. "Thanks, Aunt Bette Bob."

David held out the sack. "Here."

"Thanks." Poker-faced, Amy took the crumpled bag.

She led them down a long, tiled hall. Trailing behind, Leona felt her chest tighten with each squeak of Amy's rubber-soled shoes. They rounded a corner, and Amy palmed a large silver button on the wall. Slowly the automated double doors swung open.

"Bed two." Amy pointed. "Behind that curtain."

David touched the nurse's arm. "I appreciate you taking such good care of my—."

"It's my job." Clutching her sack lunch, the tight-lipped young woman spun on her cushioned heel.

Well, she had spunk. Leona had to give her that. And she'd need every ounce of it if God had paired her with the conflicted pastor's son. *Says, the conflicted pastor's wife who's getting ahead of herself again.*

Leona put her hand on the curtain, but hesitated before entering. She couldn't remember everything she and Maddie had said in the ambulance, but she had the distinct feeling her attempt to patch things up had been botched. What were the odds she could convince her mother to bury the hatchet? *Lord, help me.*

Cautiously, Leona peered around the nylon curtain. Maddie, wearing a white paper smock, stood beside her grandmother's wired body. The matching shower cap reconfigured her mass of golden curls into a look reminiscent of a lunchroom lady. She studied a chart just like the real doctors on TV medical shows. Pride surged through Leona and crashed head-on into her guilt. *I do not deserve such an incredible daughter.*

"I'll get that." David reached above her and gave the lightweight curtain a tug, sending it whizzing around the metal track attached to the ceiling.

"Hey, Momma." Maddie closed the chart she held and slipped it into the holder at the foot of the bed. She came over and kissed Leona's cheek. "You're looking better."

"I did feel a bit green."

"Definitely not your color," Maddie teased. She turned and gave David the once-over. "I can see you've regained your legs, Brother."

"You keep Grandmother alive. I'll keep Momma out of jail."

"Fair enough." Maddie's chuckle reminded Leona of the soothing trickle of water washing over the smooth stones of the feng shui fountain Roxie had in her entryway.

The IV pump beeped beside her mother's bed as a jarring reminder that all was not well. Leona studied the machine. A suspended bag of fluid glistened in the fluorescent light. Her eyes traversed the clear tubing taped to top of her mother's hand. Feeling woozy, she could have sworn the constant drip was forcing liquid blame directly into her own veins. A guilty scum formed in the back of her throat and choked her breath.

"How is she?" she sputtered.

Maddie brightened. "I think the old girl's got a few good miles left on her."

Leona stepped forward and stood at the foot of the bed. Steadying both hands, she clasped the strap of the purse slung over her shoulder. "What can you tell us?"

"Small hospitals are great. You're never going to believe all they let me do today. Katie Beth is going to be pea-green with envy." Maddie chattered a mile a minute. "At first some charge nurse tried to run me out of the emergency room, but Amy told them I was almost a doctor so they let me stay." She stopped abruptly and cocked her head. "David, do you know Amy? She says she's met you. Asked me if you were always so rude."

David's eyes narrowed. "What did you say?"

"Only since puberty." Maddie flashed a sly grin. "Amy said, 'If he hasn't outgrown it by now, it's doubtful he ever will.' I like her."

"Me too." Leona said.

"Good for you." David scooted a chair toward his mother. "Want to sit, Momma?"

"No, I'm fine." Fake it until you make it, Leona thought. "So what did they operate on exactly?"

"Grandmother has an intertrochanteric hip fracture, which is better than a femoral neck fracture. These fractures do not have the issues with damage to blood flow to the bone."

"Neck? You thought Grandmother had a broken neck?"

"Femoral neck, Momma."

Leona felt lost in the medical mumbo jumbo swirling in the soup that had once been her brain. "Maddie, how about you run that by me again . . . slowly . . . in layman's terms."

"Basically, we were able to repair the break in Grandmother's femur with a metal plate and screws instead of doing a more extensive hip replacement procedure."

"We?" Leona said.

"We!" Light radiated from Maddie's eyes. "When they wheeled Grandmother into surgery, Dr. Patel remembered me from that time I jumped off the sanctuary stage and broke my leg. He said he'd heard J.D. Harper's daredevil daughter was studying medicine so why didn't I scrub in and get a firsthand look at an orthopedic surgery?" She stopped to take a quick breath. "Momma, I got to watch the surgeon set the pins and everything. Absolutely incredible. Much better than working with cadavers or shadowing doctors on rounds."

Medicine was a queasy world, in Leona's opinion. Her sensitive stomach was prone to protestation when she nicked her legs shaving. Past picking up a prescription, she didn't care to know a thing about doctoring. But from the glow on her daughter's face, it was obvious broken bodies didn't faze Maddie. Healing was what her girl had been called to do, no question about it.

Maddie's concentration strayed to the flashing red numbers on the monitor. She retrieved the chart. Leona watched her daughter carefully record important information, speaking as she wrote. "According to the MRI she didn't have any cerebral contusions or lacerations, only a mild concussion."

The foreign words scrambled Leona's brain. No wonder they had so much trouble communicating. When had the simple child she raised beamed up to a different planet? Acquired that alien glow?

Leona refused to allow the regret stinging her eyes a chance to make a tearful entrance. If the complex workings of the human anatomy mattered to her daughter, she'd just have to find some way to share in those pursuits. Discover the key to unlocking her daughter's heart. Wriggle past the chest of drawers stuffed with resentment Maddie used to block the door of their relationship.

She touched her daughter's arm. "Explain concussion to me."

Maddie ceased her scribbles and closed the chart. "She'll have a monster headache when she wakes up."

"Will she remember . . . ?"

"That she was a horse's rear end?" Maddie's probing eyes appeared as if she, too, searched for common ground. "I doubt it."

Leona released a relieved breath. "If your grandmother's misfortune furthers your education, I guess it's the least she can do for you."

The sound of Maddie's unrestrained laughter soothed the raw places the day had scraped across Leona's heart. Oh, how she missed J.D.

"So what happens next?" David drummed his fingers on the railing of his grandmother's hospital bed.

Chart tucked under her arm, Maddie checked the IV monitor. "I'm sure she'll be here a few days. Once she's stable we'll move her to that new rehab facility next door. Sooner we get her up and walking, the better. Grandmother is in excellent health. She should be up and around in no time."

A sudden urge to touch her mother's leg came over Leona, but she couldn't pry her hands from her purse strap. "Do I need to stay with her?"

"I'll stay tonight. You can come in the morning." Maddie guided Leona away from the bed. "Momma, you did great on the ride over here. I couldn't have done it without you. David, would you take my assistant home?"

David scanned the room. "Is there a back door?"

Maddie raised a quizzical brow. "Back door?"

"So I can avoid the nurse who thinks I have mad cow disease."

Maddie laughed. "Maybe she has some sort of miracle cure."

"I doubt it." He kissed his sister's cheek. "Taking Momma home is the least I can do, especially since I wasn't much help to Parker."

"Parker?" Maddie asked.

"The guy has nerves of steel. He had his cell phone out and Charlie tracked down before I could even get up off the floor." Admiration twinkled in David's eyes.

"Parker?" Skepticism sounded in Maddie's voice.

"The guy was cool as a Story cucumber. He kept Etta May and Nola Gay out of your way. Even offered Justin a ride to the hospital with us."

"I knew Parker had emergency training in stem rot, but never guessed he knew broken hips as well." Maddie's green eyes sparkled. "I'll be sure and commend our local extension agent on his blue-ribbon emergency showing." She didn't say a word about where Justin was.

"You do that." David took Leona's elbow. "Come on, Momma."

"Give me a minute, David." Leona stepped around the foot

of the bed and came to the head.

She focused on her mother's serene face. The woman would be ticked if she knew hospital lighting had erased her frown lines better than her last Botox injection.

Leona leaned over the bed rail and placed her lips against the downy skin near her mother's temple. The familiar scent of Olay and the pulsating sensation of life awarded her a peaceful reassurance. "I love you, Mother." Leona tucked the blanket around her mother. "Take good care of her, Dr. Harper."

Maddie grinned. "Will do, Momma."

Leona slipped her hand through David's arm. Surely God wouldn't give her this second chance and snatch it away before she could make things right.

Chapter Twelve

Lukewarm water pounded Leona's aching muscles. Much as she wished she could shut out the world and hide in her bathroom forever, she had things to do and bills to pay. The past few days of dealing with her mother had been a painful peek into how difficult life was going to be without her J.D. Everything was up to her now.

With a resigned sigh, Leona twisted the corroded bath knobs. Water pooled over the slow drain J.D. had promised to fix. Her husband had always done the handyman chores.

In some ways, her mother was right. She and J.D. had divided the duties of managing a family. Which had left her feeling ill-equipped in the areas he'd always covered. Managing the finances was one of those areas. She didn't even know how much a plumber charged? And she wasn't about to ask Howard Davis if the church would pay to unclog a drain. The last thing she needed was for the board to start worrying about how much it was going to cost to keep her in the parsonage.

Leona tugged on the shower curtain. Her skin prickled in the chilly morning air. She dragged each dripping foot over the edge of the claw-foot tub then wrapped a towel around her shivering body.

Two long steps and she landed on the mat in front of the sink. Resting against the vanity, she cleared the mirror with her forearm. She peered at the sunken face reflected in the blurry swipe.

The trouble with her mother had only worsened once the anesthesia wore off.

She woke up confused and meaner than a bear emerging from hibernation. More than once these last couple of days, Leona had considered asking that cute nurse David kept avoiding if it was possible to increase the dosage on her mother's morphine drip. Managing her mother without J.D. as a sounding board was hard.

Leona dug through the drawer and found a comb. She yanked at her tangled curls. Her children were floundering. Her mother was raving. Fear nipped at her ankles. If God didn't step in soon, she'd fail to keep her family together. What would people say if their pastor's family fell apart? Tears spilled over the purple circles rimming her eyes. She tossed the comb in the drawer and slogged toward the bedroom.

She opened her closet and stared at the four dresses hanging from the rusty rod. One of her husband's pet sayings had been, "Sunday comes around every week, four times a month." Rotating her limited church attire worked out fine, except for those pesky five-Sunday months. The dropped-waist floral print was up for this week, but that one had been J.D.'s favorite.

The flood of tears refused further restraint. They burned her cheeks. The dread she had held at bay now weighted her shoulders. How could she attend church without her husband?

In the space of a heartbeat she had been removed from the Pastor's Perch and relegated to Widow's Row.

Images of being crammed into the backseat of a car full of blue hairs on their way to the cafeteria flashed in her mind. She shuddered at the thought of having nothing better to talk about than her last doctor's appointment.

Over the years, she'd mastered the art of redirecting the conversation away from the health issues of those needy women.

Bessie Wilcox had been the worst.

Show Bessie the slightest interest, and she would rattle off the long list of foods that kinked her antiquated bowels or worse, give every detail of the operations she'd undergone to unclog them. Her complaints kept her in and out of the emergency room on a regular basis.

Leona remembered telling J.D., "Bessie's hospital trips are merely ploys to garner attention. If we don't run up there every time our resident hypochondriac calls, she'll give up her diabolical schemes." So the next time the gray-haired fossil was admitted, they didn't go.

That night Bessie died . . . alone. Shame pierced Leona's conscience. What excuse could she offer for the way she'd brushed off the lonely, avoiding them as if dead spouses were contagious?

Leona crossed her arms over her damp towel and briskly buffed the gooseflesh from her arms. In the deathly quiet of her bedroom, she understood the longings of the companionless . . . the need, the desperation to have the sound of their voice make contact with a human ear.

Would those happily coupled now divert their gaze or pretend they didn't see her? Was she destined to be the token fifth-wheel people invited to lunch out of pity?

Could God be punishing the smug way she flaunted her noisy life of devoted husband and children? She didn't really believe the Lord to be spiteful, but remembering the biblical story of how God took out the braggart who built bigger barns struck a guilty nerve in Leona's chest.

She thumbed through her dresses. Maybe she should stay home from church today. It's not every week a woman buries her husband and nearly kills her mother. If the happily married had the nerve to fault her, they should watch their backs.

Unexpected tragedy could head-butt them into her sad boat.

Leona turned to her shoe rack. Someone had put the shipping box with the red shoes on the shelf where her brown flats always sat. She'd forgotten all about sending them back. She yanked the box out to search for the receipt. New shoe smell rose from the wrapping paper. She fingered the red bows. "You want to wear red shoes, wear 'em, darlin'," echoed in her memory.

She crammed the supple suedes back into the box and took down the pair of fuzzy slippers David had given her years ago. She stuffed her bare feet inside the matted comfort wishing she had a tenth of her husband's courage.

Hands trembling, she pushed back the louvered door on J.D.'s side of the closet. Except for the navy pinstripe he wore to his funeral, his three remaining suits hung in the order of their rotation. Today would have been the herringbone tweed.

Leona ran her hand across the rugged Shetland wool. It had given her a great deal of pleasure to surprise J.D. with this expensive coat. The dear man had been struck mute when he learned she'd bought the jacket with pennies saved by clipping coupons.

Seeing the gratitude on his face had been worth every single thing she'd done without. Come to think of it, what had she done without? Leona brought the woolen sleeve to her nose and inhaled. She couldn't remember.

"Momma?"

Leona jumped, dropping the jacket sleeve. "Maddie, you startled me." She hurriedly closed the door on J.D.'s side.

Maddie crossed to the closet and removed Leona's floral print. "Wear this. Daddy loved it."

Who was this insightful young woman standing before her? More tears stung Leona's eyes, but she hurriedly blinked them away. Maybe she hadn't totally screwed up this child's life, but it was hard to tell for certain. Maddie had been so busy at the hospital the last few days they'd not had a minute to talk. Leona was anxious to get their relationship repairs underway.

"Good idea." She took the offered hanger.

"Daddy would expect us in church."

"That's never bothered you before." Where had that come from? Leona clamped her lips, hating the jagged barb she'd just hurled at her daughter. This was no way to make the amends she longed for. She remembered a magazine article Roxie had given her. The world-renowned grief expert claimed anger would not be far behind the shock and denial. Whatever the source of this raging desire to lash out, Leona didn't want her child taking the hit.

"I'm sorry, Maddie." From her daughter's blank expression, Leona could tell her apology hadn't erased the judgment she'd heaped upon her daughter. Why had she subjected her child to the curse of caring what others thought? "I'm not your God, sweetheart."

"I'm going to get the Storys their coffee." With supersonic speed, Maddie had maneuvered her emotions behind the invisible force field she kept between them. Short of firing a laser, Leona didn't hold out much hope of cracking the shield. "I'll be back in five minutes, and I'll expect you to be dressed and ready." Maddie stormed toward the door.

Feeling the need to do something, Leona blurted out, "Is Justin going with us?" *What is wrong with me?*

Maddie stopped in her tracks. She stiffened and turned slowly. "He left. Remember?"

Lord, please don't let the look I see in her eyes be contempt. Disagreement she could deal with, but disdain would put her in an early grave. She summoned strength from a reservoir she didn't know she had and made another pass at peace, determined to smooth over this rift in their relationship.

"I do. I just wanted your boyfriend to feel welcome here and was wondering if—"

"If Justin went to church?"

"No…yes."

"Justin's not big on organized religion."

"But he's big on you, right?" Leona continued. "Today is

going to be rough. Sitting on the Harper pew without your father . . . I just thought you could use the support."

"Momma, I'm not like you. I don't need a man to tell me I'm valuable." With that, she was gone.

Leona opened J.D.'s closet door. His row of suits hung lifeless from the rod. She slid the herringbone tweed from the hanger. Threading her arms through the sleeves, the cool silky lining glided over her skin. Leona shoved up the sleeves and slowly buttoned both leather-covered buttons below the anguish in her chest.

Closing her eyes, she waited for the wool to trap her body heat and tame the needle-sharp prickles running up and down her spine.

Examining herself in the full-length mirror, Leona noticed J.D.'s jacket covered her from neck to knees. Realization froze the reflection staring back at her. She'd hidden behind her husband for years.

Leona Harper was no longer a preacher's wife, who had to worry about what other people thought. If she owned a halter top and a red feather boa, she could sashay up the sanctuary aisle and not give a flip about who whispered what.

But would I want to?

The magnitude of the question boggled Leona's mind as she grappled with the buttons. Hot tears wet her cheeks. She'd been Mrs. Harper or someone's momma for so many years she couldn't imagine being anything else. Without the labels she'd worn longer than her husband kept a suit, who would she be?

Leona unbuttoned the coat and returned it to the empty hanger. She wrestled the next dress in her rotation over her head, kicked off the slippers, reached past the red heels and dug out the brown flats. Accepting her daughter's right to find her own path didn't even scratch the surface of the letting go she had left to do.

* * * * *

David eyed the cluster of biddies pecking their way through the foyer crowd to get at the Harpers.

Momma's insistence that they attend church the first Sunday after burying his father rubbed him as raw as the starched collar of his pinpoint oxford shirt. If another person declared his father blessed to be in a better place, he planned to say something Momma would classify as un-Christlike. And he did not plan to feel guilty about how embarrassing such a blunt retort would be.

He clutched the stubborn woman's floral-print-clad elbow. "Where do you want to sit, Momma?"

"My usual place." Momma's voice cracked.

He clenched his jaw and whispered in her ear, "You sure?"

"I'm positive." His mother's eyes were girded with

determination. "You get Cotton and Maddie and meet me up front. I want to stop by the Storys' pew and say hello."

"But the sisters just left the house."

"It won't hurt to greet them again."

David shrugged, chalking up Momma's irrationality to residual shock. Who knew how long it would take for things to level out . . . if they ever would?

"Mrs. Harper?" The female voice came from behind.

David cringed, recognizing the voice. Fighting the urge to bolt for the door, he didn't join Momma in an about-face.

"Amy, is something wrong?"

David couldn't leave his mother to face bad news alone. He turned. "Good morning, Amy." The credit for his cheery greeting belonged to his momma because his own sinful nature found nothing good about the morning and would have preferred to avoid this woman.

"David." Amy's sterile hospital look had been scrubbed away to reveal a soft blush that matched the angora sweater clinging to perfect curves. Sunlight showcased the blonde curls framing her face and hanging loosely about her shoulders. Except for the unflinching gaze, laced with the red streaks of someone who had worked the night shift, the nurse appeared . . . angelic.

What am I thinking?

Biting his tongue, David reined his aroused curiosity. This was no angel.

"How are you, David?" Her disconcerting eyes were locked on his.

"Fine."

One perfect brow rose slightly. "I doubt that."

Why couldn't she cut him a little slack? After all, he'd just buried his father when they met. He hadn't meant to be rude, well he had, but not to her. He didn't even know her—which probably made it easier to dump his anger. She didn't deserve his barbs. What she deserved was an apology.

"Look, Amy, I'm—"

Amy cut him off and spoke directly to Momma. "Mrs. Harper, I checked on your mother this morning. I knew this would be a rough day for you, so I ran by the hospital before church."

Relief erased Momma's grimace. "That was so thoughtful."

David planted his feet, assuming his most formidable lawyer stance. He towered over those blonde curls that smelled of spring, an amazingly irritating feat in late-November. "How was the wicked witch of the west wing?"

"Mean as ever, but making progress."

David hadn't meant to, but he laughed. "Your bedside manner is so reassuring."

"You're the one who called your grandmother a witch." Amy

spun on the heels of classy pumps and disappeared into the pressing crowd.

He had always thought of his training in reading women like his mother, grandmother, and sister had prepared him to read all women. Obviously, his training had its limitations.

"She's incredible, don't you think, David?" Momma's eyes suddenly seemed less burdened.

"A real Florence Nightingale." David placed his hand on the small of his mother's back, unwilling to concede defeat. "Let's get this over with, Momma."

* * * * *

Sandwiched between Momma and Cotton on the Pastor's Perch, Maddie resisted the urge to shift closer to her old friend. The childish move might make it easier for her to breathe but today wasn't about her struggle to break free of her mother's expectations.

A beautiful baritone voice drew Maddie's attention to the stage. Parker held the songbook in one hand and directed the congregation with the other. Praise emanated from someplace deeper than his powerful diaphragm, as if he'd been mysteriously transported past the brick walls of the sanctuary and into another realm.

Examining the words on the hymnal page, Maddie searched for clues to Parker's power source. As a child, she would wedge in between her parents to get a closer look at their curious luminosity, convinced the radiance came from candles they refused to hide under bushels. For years, Maddie waited for the power to remove her bushel so light would shine from her candle.

And then it happened. While helping a missionary doctor in the jungles of Guatemala, she stayed with a native family struggling to keep food on the table. Despite her host family's abject poverty, their tiny home was filled with an abundance of love. On her last night, they prepared every morsel of food they had and served a surprise meal in Maddie's honor. After the feast, the Guatemalans circled her and sang "The Lord Bless You and Keep You" in broken English.

For the first time in her life, Maddie had felt the spark, the euphoric heat generated by selfless love. She came home aglow with the determination that nothing was impossible with God. But a few months after her return to the States, she learned the Guatemalan mother had died of tuberculosis. The reality bushel fell and snuffed her idealistic light.

What kind of a God allows mothers to be ripped from their children? Fathers to die in the pulpit? Maddie dropped the hymnal into the wooden rack with a defiant thump. *If Parker leads "It Is Well with My Soul," I'm out of here.*

Maybe her experience with the light had been a fluke. A

fleeting feeling rather than a scientific fact. Not only did people die, but they hurt each other, and more often than not, they inflicted their damage in the name of the Lord. A catty remark here, a slighted invitation there. Those were facts a preacher's kid could chart. She'd watched her parents endure every form of criticism and snub known to man. How could God allow two devoted servants to suffer such indignities and call himself loving?

Maddie cut her eyes at Momma giving the chorus an added forte it did not deserve. The radiance shining in her eyes was not a facade. It was real.

Parker finished the song. He came down the center steps and took a seat on the front pew. He glanced over his shoulder, flashing a smile in Maddie's direction. A strange flutter in her stomach made her wonder if she was coming down with something.

She didn't have time to be sick. By the time she got back to school she'd be so far behind she'd never catch up. Maddie wrote it off as a hunger pain. A blinding glare jarred her from her self-examination. She had failed to notice that Howard Davis had taken the stage. The painful beacon originated from the light bouncing off the elder's bald head.

Cotton draped his arm across the back of the pew and around Maddie's shoulder. "A united front," he whispered. "For your momma."

Maddie nodded.

Howard opened his Bible and cleared his throat. "Brothers and sisters, hear the Word of the Lord." The elder reached inside his suit coat and retrieved his glasses. Eyes magnified, it appeared he had headlights. He eyeballed the congregation over the edge of his Bible.

"'Moses my servant is dead . . . As I was with Moses, so I will be with you; *I* will never leave you nor forsake you.'"

Jolted by the audacity of Howard's words, Maddie quickly surveyed her mother. Had Momma caught the billiard ball's implication that he intended to be the take-charge savior of this tragic situation? That he was the man to fill Daddy's shoes? If so, what was going to happen to the Harpers? So much for his promise to care for the widowed and orphaned.

Momma's grip crushed the circulation in Maddie's hand. A seething darkness roiled behind the sunken sockets where the Tower's beacon of faith had been moments before. At last, the stalwart bushel had fallen.

Let the holy wars begin.

Chapter Thirteen

Once again, the bathroom mirror gave Leona a true reflection of her new reality. She stared at her haggard reflection. The dark bags under her eyes now resembled the overstuffed suitcases missionary families lugged back to the field after an extended American furlough. Gripping the chipped tile counter, she inhaled and exhaled slowly. Ever since her grocery store meltdown, she'd struggled to force air around the fear double-parked on her chest.

On Sunday, she'd managed to hold in her anger at Howard's bold move.

On Monday, David and Maddie had returned to their respective schools.

On Tuesday, Leona went in search of an over-the-counter sleep aid. In retrospect, her decision to cut through the produce department at Royce's Sack-n-Pay on her way to the pharmacy had been a terrible mistake.

She had been so tired she'd believed she saw cabbages hovering above the bagged lettuce and broccoli crowns. They swooshed overhead like luminous Christmas pageant angels singing something about ain't no mountain high enough.

Bulldozing through the winged heads, Leona had smashed into the stock boy. But when the young man implied she was the one with a bulb loose, she'd deserted the rusty buggy and fled the market before anyone else had seen her.

She remembered fumbling with the car keys and screeching out of the parking lot, but the escape route was a blur. Next thing Leona knew, she was wrapped in Roxie's plush Turkish bathrobe, clutching a cup of strong coffee, and sobbing uncontrollably.

"Your shock is wearing off, girlfriend. Good chance your new reality is gonna hurt like nobody's business."

"That's not what hurts." Leona blubbered. "J.D. hasn't been gone two weeks and Howard and Maxine have …"

"You don't know for sure what Howard and Maxine have done." Roxie refilled the oversized mug and added two lumps of sugar, but Leona didn't remember drinking a drop.

Taking a long look at the stranger in the mirror, Leona sighed.

She would never eat slaw again. Nor could she imagine being able to show her face in Royce's any time soon.

She had not left the house since Roxie took her home and wouldn't be going out now, except for Howard's Wednesday night visit. He and Maxine had stopped by the parsonage after she missed prayer meeting to offer a few suggestions on how she might deal with her grief in a more productive manner.

Word travels fast in a town with only one grocery store.

Rummaging through the vanity clutter, Leona found the tube of dark-circle concealer. She pumped the wand and dragged pale liquid under each swollen eye, effectively creating two lavender half-moons. The cosmetic that could hide the telltale signs of sleepless nights and backstabbing elders had yet to be invented. She jammed the useless stick into the creamy hole and screwed the lid tight. Daubing on buff-colored lipstick, Leona choked back the disappointing way she'd yelled at that poor produce guy. That scrawny little fellow did not deserve what he got, but then neither did she.

What is happening to me? This is no way for a pastor's wife to behave.

She capped the silver cylinder and returned it to its proper place in the drawer.

The only thing J.D. Harper despised more than her need to please was a prideful, painted woman. Leona took a tissue and blotted the natural-tone lips that were already missing the brush of J.D.'s mustache.

She yanked open the vanity drawer. Who was she kidding? She was no longer a pastor's wife. For the first time in her life, the only person she had to please was herself. She fished around in the back until her fingers came across an ancient tube of fire engine red lipstick. She popped the cap and dragged the dried-out color across taut lips.

That'll teach you to drop dead and leave me to my own devices, J.D. Harper.

Forcing air into her constricted chest, Leona felt a heady rush of oxygen. She tossed the lipstick on the counter.

"Ready or not, world, here I come." She crossed the small master bedroom, stopping to grab the navy sweater flung across the king-size bed. "Tater, get off there." Leona nudged the dog from the bed that now seemed way too large for the room.

Tater jumped to the floor and stretched at Leona's feet, gratefully diverting her gaze from J.D.'s untouched pillow. If she dwelt on the overwhelming uncertainty his death had introduced into her world, her mascara would run.

Can't have raccoon eyes on the first day of the rest of my life.

Stuffing heavy arms inside worn sleeves, Leona focused on the framed cross-stitch hanging over the headboard. She repeated the verse, the sounds barely brushing past her lips. "This is the day the Lord has made; let us rejoice and be glad in it." Hoping the inspired words would bolster her spirits, she waited for a miraculous infusion of strength to catch up with her new resolve.

But as she looked around the lifeless room, she knew . . . nothing had changed.

She hiked the strap of her navy handbag over her shoulder and trudged toward the sound of Roxie flipping channels on the TV. Tater Tot's nails faithfully clicked on the wooden floor behind her.

Stepping into the den, Leona forced a smile. "How do I look, Roxie?"

Her best friend pressed the mute button on the TV remote. "A real looker."

What else could Roxie say? After all, what were best friends for if they couldn't join in your denial? "I guess I better get going." Leona adjusted the strap on her shoulder. "How responsible would I appear if I was late to my first job interview in thirty years?"

Roxie's brows furrowed over stormy eyes, causing Tater to seek cover behind Leona's legs. "Okay, that's it, girlfriend. I can't lie to you."

"You'd unleash your true opinion while I'm in my darkest hour of need?"

"Especially now." Roxie came and put her arm around Leona. "I'd be doing you a great disservice if I didn't say you look just like a member of the local newspaper cartel."

"The Downys?" Years ago, the overall-wearing family had staked their claim on the busiest intersections. From there, they made their living selling Sunday papers to passing motorists. Bristling, Leona pulled away. "I'd be more qualified to sell newspapers than write them that's for certain."

"You'll need overalls." Roxie's melodious laughter filled the room with a warm normalcy, wrapping Leona like a wooly couch throw. She'd never forget the first time she heard that contagious cackle. She and Roxie had gotten stuck scraping dried pancake batter off the griddles at the PTA fund-raiser, but Roxie's unassailable sparkle had turned a sour situation into a sweet friendship. A skill Leona wished she possessed then . . . and now.

Still chuckling, Roxie said, "Remember the lost look on Papa Downy's face when Howard Davis told him he could no longer sell his little stack of newspapers in front of the Cadillac dealership?"

"I remember."

"Well, that's you."

"Toothless?"

Roxie swatted at her playfully. "You know what I mean."

"For your information, I'm doing the best I can."

"I know." Roxie took Leona's hand and led her to the couch.

"But ragtag plain Janes don't get the job. You're gonna have to break down and buy an outfit manufactured in this century. Something to go with those red shoes I saw in your closet."

"You were the one who put them on my shelf?"

"And took the receipt so you couldn't send them back."

"Roxie!"

"It wouldn't hurt to spend a couple of hours at the Fake Bake. Tan some color into those pale cheeks."

While the entire community of Mt. Hope regularly overlooked Roxie's affinity for dramatic overstatement, she did not have that luxury.

Leona's blood pressure rose like a teakettle over a high flame, pushing her up from her seat. "What's wrong with what I have on?"

"For starters?"

"Well, that's as good a place as any."

"No one has worn Peter Pan collars in fifteen years."

"I'm afraid to spend any money before Saul gets J.D.'s affairs in order."

"You wait around for your lawyer to settle with the insurance company, and you'll be out on the street with nothing but your resoled shoes."

Leona dragged the top of her worn brown slip-on across the back of her leg. "Roxie, I don't think the board will ask me to leave the parsonage until I'm ready."

"Where will they put the new pastor?"

Good question, but a better question would be, where would they put their old pastor's wife? Visions of crawling back to her mother's guest apartment over her three-car garage hammered Leona between the eyes. She pinched the bridge of her nose. "The search process will take months. I don't think the board is in any hurry."

"So Howard insisting you find work was merely a suggestion?" Roxie framed the word suggestion in air quotes. "Something to keep your mind off your troubles?"

"He's right. I'm going to need a job. We barely have a dime in savings."

"Just because I'm a dyed-in-the wool Episcopalian, don't think I don't understand the depths to which a desperate Baptist can sink. I'd bet my store that Howard is not about to let you sit in the parsonage and collect dust." Roxie stood and shook her finger. "Any man that would put an end to the livelihood of the disadvantaged Downy cartel is gonna want you out so the new preacher can move in. What's to become of you, Leona?"

"Fortunately, Howard doesn't have the only vote. Harold and Hank are good Christian men. They'll see that I'm treated right."

"Wake up, Leona." Roxie slapped her well-toned thighs.

"Those two puppets wouldn't know an opening prayer from a closing one. Howard pulls their strings, and they vote exactly how he wants. It's time you grew a backbone and told that grumpy old so-and-so he can take his key to this dilapidated old parsonage and shove it where—"

"Roxie, please. Antagonizing the board chairman is hardly the best route to take at this moment." Leona's knees gave out, dropping her to the couch. "I need time to figure out what in the world I'm going to do with my life. I've been a preacher's wife for thirty years and now . . . what am I? The only skills I can list on a résumé are Sunday school teacher and potluck planner. I doubt there's a big market for calculating the gallons of tea Ivan and Modyne might drink in a month down at the Messenger."

Roxie plopped beside Leona. "Girlfriend, I refuse to allow you to sell yourself short. You are proof that it takes two men a week to get done what one good woman can do in an afternoon. Once you're not pouring every ounce of your energy into that church, things over there will start to fall apart. But I don't think you can count on Howard to suddenly figure out what a wonder you are and how lucky he's been to have you for the last eighteen years."

"Let's hope Ivan sees my potential. I want to have some kind of a job before the kids come home for Christmas and Mother gets out of rehab." Leona patted Roxie's hand. "I know you're just looking out for my best interests, but I don't have it in me to fight over this house right now."

"I'll do your fighting until—"

Leona shook her head. "It's not your battle . . . it's mine."

Tears glistened in Roxie's eyes. "You're going to end up banging on Bertie's door."

Leona clenched her jaw, heaving her pocketbook strap over her shoulder. "I'll live on the street before I move in with Mother." She rose and marched toward the front door. "Tater, stay. Momma's got to get a job."

A familiar voice stopped Leona's I-mean-business exit in mid-stride. She scanned the room, convinced she'd heard J.D.'s distinctive baritone proclaiming today was the day Leona Harper began to trust herself. Easy for him to say. He was strolling heaven's golden streets while she was making a fool of herself dodging levitating cabbages on aisle three.

Leona checked the television. Muted.

She glanced at Roxie's satisfied smirk. Not a word.

And finally Tater, his tongue lolling from the corner of his upturned face.

If she thought the dog spoke, maybe she was losing her mind. But talking canines were no more far-fetched than this sudden inexplicable conviction that she could actually land a real, paying job.

Chapter Fourteen

Thirty minutes later, Leona stood in the middle of Roxie's posh master bedroom clutching a file folder containing two copies of a still-smoking, freshly printed résumé and a glowing letter of reference from Roxanne Brewer, owner of Brewer's Auto Parts. "I don't think it would look professional if you tagged along to my interview."

"Take a chill pill, Leona." Roxie stepped out of her walk-in closet, loaded with several clothing options. "I'm just saying it won't hurt Ivan Tucker to remember Brewer's Auto is one of the Messenger's best advertisers. And that's not even counting the expensive Christmas center spread we take out every year." She held a jacket under Leona's chin, wrinkled her nose, and tossed it on the bed. "I don't have a problem reminding the editor he owes me a few favors." She dumped the pile and returned to the closet. The sound of hangers whizzing along the rod got mixed up with her mumbling.

"Roxie, if anyone owes you . . . it's me." Leona laid the folder on the dupioni silk duvet, a testament to her business-roughened friend's softer side.

Roxie came out armed with one more choice, a stunning Liz Claiborne suit, complete with crisp white cotton blouse, and black Anne Klein pumps. Not bad for a parts lady. "Black is slimming."

Leona squirmed her way into the worsted-wool skirt and tugged on the zipper. The expensive fabric felt foreign, like she was a sausage stuffed into someone else's skin. Leona wiggled her toes around the wad of toilet paper Roxie had crammed into the toes of her half-size-too-large shiny shoes. "I hope I don't break my neck trying to walk in your slingbacks."

"So hate me. I couldn't bear sending you into the world dressed like a charity case." Roxie tucked a stray strand of Leona's hair behind her ear, a pleased smile lighting her face. She turned Leona's body to face the bank of full-length mirrors lining the wall opposite the massive poster bed. "Now you look like the ace reporter you are."

Leona had to admit the transformation was astounding. "Reporter-wannabe."

"Same thing." Roxie led her to the tailored-suede chaise. "We've got a minute. Let's go over this résumé one more time."

"I don't—"

"You want to end up selling car parts with me?" Roxie opened the file. "I didn't think so. Besides, I'm not willing to risk the undoing of our delicious friendship with too much togetherness." She perched her reading glasses on the end of her nose. "So, tell me, Mrs. Harper, tell me about your responsibilities down at the church?" Her dead-on imitation of Ivan's nasal drawl brought a shared snicker.

Taking a moment, Leona considered her sparse options. She could list the Ladies Day Committee she headed every spring. Pulling off the spiritual extravaganza sucked up a lot of time, plus it forced her to work with Maxine Davis, so she should get extra credit for that one.

Leona chewed on her lower lip. She probably had a couple of gold stars in her crown for eighteen years in the toddler nursery. Sunday school teachers were hard to come by. But did her points count if she secretly hoped to move or die to get shed of all those runny noses? Oh, she almost forgot. The annual Silver Servers Sweetheart Banquet was her baby. Folks had been known to say they were fifty-five a few years early in order to get an invite.

Leona ran a mental tally and sagged. Even if she counted the little entertainment skit she wrote for the banquet, none of what had occupied her life for the past thirty years amounted to a hill of beans on a job application, or in life for that matter. Heaving a sigh, she settled on, "I completely remodeled the parsonage for the next pastor."

Fire rimmed Roxie's blue pupils. "Wrong answer, girlfriend."

Leona snatched the folder and slammed it shut. "How would you translate mother of two, preacher's wife, and general church flunky into marketable job experience?"

"Calm down. I've got it all figured out." Roxie removed her readers.

"You do, do you?" Leona did not like the plotting look swimming around in Roxie's fishbowl eyes. She fell for it once, the time Roxie convinced her eggplant was the new shade of brunette, but she had no intention of being suckered into such a monumental catastrophe again.

"I do."

Turn tail and run flashed in Leona's mind, but the confidence on her friend's face, coupled with her own unquenchable curious nature, compelled her to ask, "And?"

Roxie waited, her dramatic pause reeling Leona in the way a spider retrieves a stuck fly. "You're going to tell Ivan you've been the Director of Creative Arts."

"The what?"

Ignoring the question, Roxie thumped the manila file with the earpiece of her glasses. "I've tweaked your résumé."

Indignation snapped Leona's shoulders stiff. "I can't mislead Ivan."

"No, you can't."

The spring on Leona's pressure gauge went slack. "Good. I'm glad we agree upon something."

"But—" an impish grin curled the corners of Roxie's lips— "there's no law against me polishing up the rough edges." She charged full-steam ahead, undeterred by Leona's rolled-eyes. "Here's how I see it. Creating something out of nothing is a talent, and no one does it better than you. I've seen you throw a full-scale seniors' banquet armed with nothing more than a can of tuna, a hot glue gun, and a ream of construction paper. If that's not creative, I don't know what is."

"But Ivan's one of our deacons, for Pete's sake. He knows what I do and have done at the church—"

Roxie held up her hand. "I've seen children entertained for hours climbing through your bedsheet tunnels, and there's not an old codger in town who'd miss your senior citizens' night." She snapped her fingers. "Wake up, Leona. You *are* the Director of Creative Arts, whether you want to believe it or not."

How in the world did her exasperating friend manage a successful business with such a deplorable lack of logic? Frustration collided headlong with Leona's ailing self- esteem. The ugly concoction raced through her veins and raised her voice to a shriek. "Are you thinking Ivan needs someone to fold his weekly publication into paper party hats?"

Roxie's face hardened. She waved her arms like a worked-up televangelist trying to raise pledges. "Hell's bells, Leona, you didn't just throw church parties. You sold relationships. Every time people gathered around your banquet tables they came away with a better understanding of each other." Roxie paused and took a breath. Still panting, she lowered her chin and arched a plucked brow. "Anybody can hawk a few newspapers, but not everyone can sell goodwill. And there's not a business in this dying town that couldn't stand to sell a lot more goodwill. People will line up to buy what you're selling."

Her friend's pep talk sizzled in the air. Leona studied Roxie's confident face. What had she ever done to deserve such undying loyalty and love? Not a single thing she could think of. It reminded her of J.D.'s sermons on grace and the unmerited favor God bestows on folks, even when they could never earn it. Grace was a gift, free to all who were willing to reach out and take what he offered.

But therein lay her problem. To receive the gift, the recipient had to grab hold.

Leona blinked back tears. She didn't have the energy to lift a finger, let alone latch on to a rope and dally over dangerous rivers of deception or jump through the flaming hoops Roxie had lined up between her and the newspaper editor. This was a job for Super Christian, not a freshly widowed pastor's wife.

Lord, I can't do this.

Suddenly a firm pressure conformed to the curvature of Leona's spine. Glancing over her shoulder, Leona saw no one . . . but for some reason, she was not surprised. The calming touch belonged to the hand of God. She was certain. Not since a premonition alerted her to Deacon Hornbuckle's affair with his secretary had she been this sure of a holy presence.

A warming started at the tips of her toes. It surged fast as a caffeine rush through every weary particle in her body, intensifying the beat of her heart. Pumping strength into her limbs. Renewing her spirit.

Leona squeezed Roxie's hand. "Just when I think I cannot take another step through this dark valley the Lord sends somebody to me." She rose from the bed and kissed her best friend's cheek.

She picked up her borrowed Dooney & Bourke handbag, along with the file folder touting her adapted credentials. Roxie gave an approving nod. While Leona regretted that time did not afford her the opportunity of marinating in the Divine's presence, she rejoiced, secure in the knowledge that she no longer faced this battle alone. Never had. Leona laced her fingers through a proffered invisible hand.

Shoulders squared, she wobbled through the open door wearing shoes she could never fill, walking faithfully toward a job she was far from qualified to do.

* * * * *

Leona wheeled the minivan into an empty parking slot along Mt. Hope's busy Main Street. She threw the gearshift into park. The rusted hunk of metal idled in gyrating gratitude. She hoped wasting a little gas would allow the sputtering heater a chance to thaw her cold feet before her appointment with the newspaper editor. How could a red- hot faith cool in the time it took to back out of a driveway? She swallowed, the disappointment of her short-lived confidence refusing to go down easy.

Through the cracked windshield, she could make out the gold-leafed letters **Mt. Hope Messenger** stenciled across a large plate glass window. She had been in the newspaper office a hundred times over the years, and her stomach had never rebelled before. But dropping off church news articles was an entirely different ballgame than interviewing for a reporter position.

She checked the center console for the bottle of antacids J.D. downed for the indigestion that turned out to be heart trouble. Pouring the last of the chalky tablets into her hand, Leona prayed her arteries were clogged, and that maybe she'd drop over before facing Ivan.

Next door to the paper, a grimy haze coated the diner window, distorting the cup-and-saucer-shaped neon sign into a saggy-looking eye. The Koffee Kup had been there so long that the regulars, retired men escaping honey-do chores at home, did not need a clear view of the flickering advertisement.

Locals called the restaurant the Dirty Spoon, but never to the face of Ruthie Crouch, the plump proprietor. Legend had it that during the Korean War, Ruthie's flat-footed husband ran off with a soldier's widow, leaving Ruthie with a bun in the oven and keys to the greasy cafe. To her credit, the crusty woman had made a successful go of both.

Leona reached across the stained passenger seat and opened the glove box. She extracted a bulging envelope of newspaper clippings. Every article submitted to the paper about Mt. Hope's church picnics, fund-raisers, and Christmas pageants had been saved, each piece secretly affirming that her efforts had been worth the time and trouble. On top of the little stack rested her most cherished work: her husband's obituary.

In the past week and a half, she had nearly worn the inky-black words off the page running her finger over the newsprint during the sleepless hours of the night. Leona held up the scissored strip to the afternoon light streaming in through her van window.

James David Harper, loving husband and father, left this world with honor and dignity.

Did the concise wording make it appear that she had callously dumped J.D.'s full life into a trash compactor, snapped a switch, and allowed a machine to spit out a justified-two-inch-wide-shortened-condensed man? J.D. Harper's accomplishments could have filled a book. Anyone would be a fool to attempt to sum up such a fine man.

What made me think I could do it?

A tear splashed on the thin paper, dousing the words *left this world* to illegibility. Leona folded the newspaper write-up carefully and laid it on the pile. She dug a tissue out of her borrowed bag, flipped open the visor mirror, and dabbed at the streaks of mascara running down her cheeks.

What a mess.

She checked her watch. If she hurried, she could run into the Koffee Kup, duck into the bathroom for face repairs, and maybe even down a few swallows of Ruthie's stout coffee before her interview. A little caffeine might loosen her toes and steady her nerves. Leona returned the clippings to the envelope, stuffed them into the file folder, and tossed the bundle onto the passenger seat. She killed the engine, grabbed her keys and purse. When she stepped outside, the wind cut through Roxie's worsted-wool jacket and rattled her fragile bones.

A bell above the diner door jingled as Leona bustled inside.

The smell of the lunch special, fried chicken livers and mashed potatoes, mingled with the lingering odor of fried eggs and bacon from the breakfast special. Doubting Roxie's extra spritz of perfume would hold up to the stale assault of the hash house, she was tempted to prop the door.

Ruthie Crouch dragged a sponge over the deserted lunch counter. "You need somethin', Leona?"

"A mirror. Oh, and a cup of coffee, please." Leona smoothed her windblown hair into place.

"You know where the washroom is." The veteran server tossed the sponge over her shoulder. It landed with a splash in the tiny sink behind her. She pulled a pad out of her apron pocket and scribbled Leona's order. "After you get cleaned up, I'll get that coffee out to you."

"I'm in a bit of hurry, Ruthie. I've got an appointment."

"I guess that explains why you're gussied up in that Brewer woman's clothes." She stuck the pencil behind her ear. "Trying to get yourself a job?"

Leona bristled in her borrowed suit. "Yes."

"About time."

Amazing how all those hours spent doing the jobs at church that no one else wants do not count as real work. Fighting the urge to point out that Crouch rhymed with grouch, Leona stormed toward the bathroom. As she passed the last booth, a glint bounced off the dome of a familiar bald head and halted her hasty retreat.

"Howard?" Leona backed up, cocked her head to the side, and perused the sticky table littered with half-full coffee cups and a stack of papers. "Harold? Hank? What are you guys doing here in the middle of the afternoon?"

Color emptied from the faces of the three board members stuffed in the back booth like too many socks in an underwear drawer.

"Leona." Howard crammed papers into a folder and snapped it closed. "What a surprise." He pushed the file toward the flushed-faced fellows wedged on the opposite side of the table. "Don't you look nice this afternoon? Good to see you somewhere besides your mother's rehab room." Howard slithered over the cracked vinyl, coiling his rangy frame on the edge of the seat. "Care to join us?"

"Thank you, but I'm really in a bit of a hurry. I've got an interview with Ivan in just a few minutes."

"At the newspaper?" Harold's voice croaked with more of a hopeful air than an inquisitive one.

"Yes."

"So we've heard."

Word travels fast. Discovering the elders knew of her job interview shouldn't have fazed Leona. But the pointed reminder that the pastor's wife's business was considered public domain, and therefore fair game for the rumor mill, grated her nerves.

Leona gritted her teeth. "When Ivan brought over some extra copies of J.D.'s obituary, he suggested I come by and talk to him. He says Modyne's husband is insisting she retire by early spring so they can hit the road in their new RV. Henry's afraid they won't get to spend a dime of their children's inheritance if they don't put the pedal to the metal."

The men smiled politely at her smoke screen of humor. Making light of people's inquiries had proven to be her only line of defense in preserving her sanity after years of continual prying into her private life.

Howard shimmied free of the booth and took Leona's hand. "Good girl. Glad to see you taking the bull by the horns. Getting on with your life."

His used-car-salesman tone nettled Leona. The last time Howard Davis good-girled her, she ended up teaching the hormonal junior high girls for ten years.

Leona cut her eyes at Harold and Hank. Something was not right about the way they were squirming. Either those two guys were in serious need of a little more elbow room or they were in cahoots with Howard. She counted their lack of direct eye contact good reason to suspect the latter.

Alarm bells reverberated in her mind. Trying to think over

the clanging racket, Leona stalled for time. "It's not been easy, but by God's grace I'm making it."

"Amen." Harold gulped down the remains of his cup of cold coffee.

"And amen." Hank nodded.

Silencing his sidekicks with a look, Howard swiveled Leona toward him, her back to the table. "Grace is the only way any of us are going to get through this terrible tragedy."

Proceeding with well-honed caution, Leona sweetened the saccharine edge curdling her tongue. "I've been meaning to call you, Howard. I think you did a fine job Sunday filling in for J.D."

"Well, your husband left some mighty big shoes to fill. But I'm glad you brought up the subject of the pastor's job, Leona."

"You are?" Leona's eyes darted around the empty diner looking for clues that would shed some light on this awkward meeting. Her sights landed on Ruthie's craned head. When the startled woman ducked her pudgy face and attempted to busy herself pouring coffee, the alarm bells morphed into the peal of emergency sirens.

Howard cleared his throat, shifting from one expensive-slack-clad leg to the other. "The pulpit is a heavy burden. Proclaiming the Word of God takes a lot out of a man."

Leona stiffened. "Church work can kill you if you're not careful."

"My point exactly." Patting her hand, Howard gave a concurring nod, as if his sudden conversion to her side should soothe the bitter welt death's sting had left upon her tongue. "I don't know how long I can carry the burden of preparing sermons, what with a trailer of next year's Caddies fixing to hit my lot just any day."

Leona capped her anger, unwilling to be the first to play her hand in this game of church politics. Yet unwilling to let it drop. "Watching J.D. prepare week after week, nobody understands that heavy responsibility more than I."

"A good Christian woman like you would be the first to say Mt. Hope cannot allow J.D.'s vacated pulpit to remain at the mercy of whoever is available that week. Folks come to church expecting a first-rate worship experience. You and I both know how much the success of that experience hinges on the pastor's sermon."

The room became a merry-go-round. Leona reached for a vintage channel-back diner chair. Strangely, her mother's words from long ago zipped through her mind. "Hang on to the center pole, Leona, or the thing will sling you on your butt." Every time her thoughts whizzed past Harold and Hank, their faces grew redder and redder with their treachery.

Realization launched Leona into action. She whipped herself around, the chair toppling with a clatter on the black-

and-white tiles. She snatched the folder off the table. "These are résumés, aren't they?"

"Now, Leona, don't get yourself all worked up." Howard took a step toward her.

Reeling and dizzy, Leona waved the file in his face. Papers flew everywhere. "J.D. has not even had time to color-code his suits in the closet of his hilltop mansion, and you're already boxing up his office for the next guy?" She slapped the empty file down on a smear of dried mayonnaise, knocking over two coffee cups. "Is that why you suggested I needed to find a job less than two weeks after my husband's death?" Leona grabbed a quick breath. "Are you telling me it's time to put on my walking shoes?" She gasped at the red flush to his face. "That's it, isn't it, Howard? You're kicking me out of my home and putting me out on the street with nothing."

"Why would you think that?"

"Why? I'll tell you why. So you can hire yourself some thirty-year-old whippersnapper, his Barbie-doll wife, and their two-point-five children."

"Now, calm down, Leona. We don't know who we're looking for at this point. We just started getting inquiries."

"You expect me to believe résumés just miraculously showed up in the mail? Howard, if you're going to claim that, you're going to have to finally admit the power of the Holy

Spirit." Leona watched a cornered look flash across Howard's face. "I didn't think so. So you tell me, how did the word get around that Mt. Hope's pulpit was empty?"

Harold avoided eye contact and ripped a handful of napkins from the tabletop dispenser. "Well, we might have taken out a few advertisements in some church publications." He mopped coffee off the stained pages.

"Was this shenanigan executed before or after my husband lost his life working for you bozos?"

"Now, Leona. You know we've been satisfied with J.D. all these years." Howard attempted to lead her away from the crime scene, but Leona planted Roxie's heels on the checkerboard tiles, locked her knees, and refused to budge.

"Don't give me that. Every church is looking for someone who is thirty and photogenic. You've been thinking for some time that J.D. and I are old and shriveled up."

"Leona, you're far from shriveled—"

"Don't try to placate me, you bald-headed buffoon. You just wait until J.D. hears about this—"

"Leona." Howard put a hand on her shoulder, sorrow softening his firm touch. "J.D. is not going to hear about it."

The truth smacked with the force of a cast-iron skillet.

Without J.D. the church was without a preacher. Without a preacher, Leona Harper was not a preacher's wife. Without her husband, who in the world was she? A woman who'd just been handed her walking papers, that's who.

Leona pivoted in her borrowed shoes. Heels clacking, she charged toward the door. She marched past the diner proprietor leaning against the counter. "What are you looking at, Ruthie Crouch? Haven't you seen a homeless person before?"

Hitting the door with gusto, Leona shouldered it open and stomped over the threshold. Her heel caught in the cracked weather stripping. When she tried to jerk it out, the shoe broke free, but the stiletto remained wedged deep in the aged rubber.

"Hell's bells." Leona heard the door's faint jingle behind her as she limped back to the van.

If Roxie wanted the rest of her expensive shoe, she could march her bright ideas down to the Dirty Spoon and pry it loose.

Leona pawed through her borrowed purse searching for her keys while the wind whipped her hair in a million different directions. She unlocked the door, climbed in, and sank into the driver's seat. Placing her hands at ten and two on the steering wheel, she let her head drop at twelve.

Lord, what in the world am I going to do now?

* * * * *

An insistent tap, tap, tap on the van window roused Leona's pounding head from the wheel.

"You coming in?" Deacon Tucker held up the broken heel like it was the championship trophy of the senior citizens' church bowling league.

Leona rolled down her window. "Where did you get that, Ivan?" She snatched the heel from the newspaper editor and hurled it to the floorboard.

"Ruthie brought it over. Said my next headline was slumped over the wheel of a rattletrap vehicle parked in front of her establishment. Claims your loitering is ruining her business. She's threatening to have you towed."

"What a sweetheart." Leona let her aching head fall back against the seat.

"Nothing a little salt and light couldn't cure." Ivan opened the door. "Come on. Let's get you in where it's warm."

As she stared at his proffered hand, shame washed over her. She couldn't believe how quickly she'd released the hand of God and charged out on her own. Did she think the answer to her dilemma was awaiting her arrival on the other side of that hash-house door? No. Nothing in life had ever come that easy. But did her lapse mean she had to be homeless?

What am I going to do?

Visions of Ivan's wife ran through Leona's mind.

Once Hathleen Tucker got wind of the embarrassing public tirade, Leona could never face Ladies Bible Class again. Hath was the class secretary, and as such, felt duty bound to report every congregant blunder to the women's group. Not a single hospitalization, separation, or humiliation got past the church bloodhound.

Leona was sure the news of her run-in with the chairman of the board would hit the flock's communication airwaves faster than news of the pastor's vacated pulpit had made the brotherhood's job listings. But it really didn't matter whether word got around by Howard or Hathleen; truth was her days in the parsonage were numbered.

She allowed her gaze to come level with the editor's patient stare. "I don't know if I'm up to an interview today, Ivan."

"Why don't you come in? Have a cup of hot coffee. We'll decide if we should reschedule."

Ivan's years of saving ink had condensed his speech to short, concise sentences. But the kindness in his twinkling eyes matched his unabridged heart and generous checkbook. Even the all-knowing Hathleen was unaware of Deacon Tucker's secret funding of the missionary family's emergency return to the States last fall.

But Leona knew . . . one of the few perks of being on the inside loop. Secret sins often knotted the guts of a church, but once in a while the quiet, unassuming Ivans of the world selflessly loosened Satan's grip and restored Leona's faith in mankind. In that respect, she would miss the loop.

Leona heaved a weary sigh. If she went home she'd appear ungrateful. And if she'd learned anything after thirty years in ministry, it was that only a fool refused to accept help on those rare occasions when it was offered.

"Let me get my résumé." Leona reached for the folder lying on the passenger seat. Dipping past the mirror, she caught a glimpse of her mascara-smudged cheeks and wind-styled hair. *This is not going to be pretty.*

Chapter Fifteen

Leona buried her face under J.D.'s pillow, praying the Lord would let her drown in the fading trace of bay lime aftershave. Inhale. Exhale. Inhale. Exhale. Still breathing. She pulled the pillow tighter. She didn't know which was worse: that the lumpy foam failed to suffocate her or that she could still hear the muffled sound of snapping roller shades as her best friend flitted around the room rehashing yesterday's sordid mess.

Roxie lifted a corner of the worn pillowcase and peered at Leona. "You're not the first to tongue-lash a temple money changer, and I doubt you'll be the last."

"I called Howard a bald buffoon."

"Fiddle-faddle. I've called him worse. One time that skinflint returned a thousand-dollar parts order. Said our merchandise wasn't up to Cadillac standards. So I told him he could—"

Leona cast the barrier from her face and held up her hand to stop the certain flood of profanities. "I can't bear to think of you plummeting toward the eternal inferno because of my deplorable lack of self-control."

"That's better."

The gleam of success lighting Roxie's eyes irked Leona. Where did a person get the guts to plow through life heedless of what anyone thought?

Leona retrieved the pillow and crammed it behind her head. "Okay, I came up for air. Are you happy now?"

"Will be once you're out of that bed and back on your feet."

Eyeing the woman whose persistence could drive a nail without a hammer, Leona shook her head. "Ivan must have thought the Lord had called him to tame the shrew by the time he got me out of the van and into the newspaper office. Modyne looked at me like I was something the cat dragged in. But that probably didn't scare them half as bad as listening to the ugly tale of what transpired in the diner."

Roxie shrugged. "They're reporters, Leona." She wrestled with the stubborn louvered closet door until she'd wrangled it open. "They're trained to deal with gore." Roxie took Leona's robe from the hook. "Come on."

Humiliation weighted Leona's shoulders. "I won't be able to show my mug in Ruthie's establishment again."

"Who'd want to?"

"She'll paper those greasy walls with my wanted poster."

"Probably."

"I'll have to take my lunch to work for the rest of my life."

Leona covered her face.

Roxie pried Leona's stiffened fingers from her tear-swollen eyes, her grip on Leona's wrists firm and sure. "Your hard-earned money will spend in the Dirty Spoon good as the next person's. Ruthie may be hard-nosed, but she won't turn down an honest nickel." She snatched the robe and tossed it at Leona. "Besides, I've seen your wily charms win over many a tough old bird. Ruthie better *crouch* behind the counter because she wouldn't know what hit her if you unleash your magic." Roxie flashed a Cheshire cat grin at her successful manipulation of the restaurant proprietor's name. "Now, get out of that bed."

"I'm afraid Ruthie found my charm harder to swallow than her sour cream pound cake."

"Let it go, Leona. She asked for it. And Howard deserved every bit, and then some, of what you gave him. The board chairman is delusional if he thinks folks will just stand aside and allow you to be kicked out of your home." Roxie plopped on J.D.'s side of the bed and crossed her arms. "Now, if you're not going to get up, I'm going to sit right here until you tell me everything Ivan said." When Roxie Brewer got that steely look in her eye, her target might as well roll over and cry uncle.

A cornered moan escaped Leona's lips. Snatches of Ivan's conversation zipped through her mind. The bewildering impact of their meaning seemed far too private to share. Didn't admitting she enjoyed Ivan's complimentary remarks about her work border on vanity? J.D. considered the need for flattery a sign of spiritual immaturity.

Leona adjusted her pillow, stalling for time. Ivan's confidence in her abilities had been misplaced. That had to be the only plausible explanation for what happened.

Squirming under Roxie's determined gaze, Leona knew the sooner she shared every last detail, the sooner she could seek God's forgiveness for her shallow need to have her ego stroked. Odds were Roxie already had a pretty good idea what happened at the Messenger. Since the moment they met, keeping secrets from one another had been deemed a lost cause.

But laying her feelings bare had never been Leona's strong suit. People who let it all hang out risked being judged. And the verdict could only go one of two ways: acceptance or rejection. The possibility of rejection was more frightening than getting into an overloaded vehicle crossing a raging river. She'd been raised a Worthington and Worthingtons believed in confidentiality. Becoming emotionally involved or exposing those emotions was certain to weaken your position. This was a staple as important as their country-club-brunch diet.

Who was she kidding? What position? Her widowed status,

the fact that her kids were scared to death she would become a noose around their necks, or perhaps that she had absolutely no equity, savings, or any sort of financial security in her future. The only position she could claim at this moment was one teetering very close to the edge of a cliff.

Leona took a deep breath. She started with Modyne pouring hot coffee down her raw throat.

"Ivan said J.D.'s write-up was the finest obit he'd ever printed. He thinks people will line up to have similar tributes written about their loved ones." Leona paused, waiting for a flicker of judgment in Roxie's attentive stare, but true to the record of their eighteen-year friendship, there was none. "As you know, the only thing growing in Mt. Hope is the cemetery. Ivan needs help with the brisk rise in the obituary business."

"When Cadillac sales increase, coffin sales aren't far behind," Roxie interjected, her authoritative voice tinged with a wisp of sadness. "Puts a hurt on the replacement parts business."

Leona hated it when people got so wrapped up in their own fears and problems they couldn't see the concerns of others, and now she'd done the very thing she despised. That was the trouble with the sea of self-pity—before a person knew what happened they could be adrift on the raft of egocentricity. "I'm sorry. I didn't even consider Brewer's Auto."

Roxie flashed a brave smile and waved away Leona's guilt. "Don't you worry a minute about Tom and me. You think we intend to peddle parts forever? No way. Someday we'll sell the business and retire in Florida. I'll be so tan you won't even recognize me."

Unwilling to imagine another person missing from her life, Leona changed the subject. "Before Modyne retires, Ivan wants me trained to work with Wayne at the funeral home. Once I get my feet wet, Ivan says I might even move to reporting on the school board meetings and the city council."

Pride beamed from Roxie's eyes. "I can't wait to see Leona Harper's byline above that cesspool of political intrigue."

"Waders are required gear for church workers, so I'm set."

"But it wouldn't hurt to make sure those rubbers haven't sprung a leak."

Roxie and Leona giggled at the allusion to the unplanned conception of Roxie's fourth child. A pinprick of light breached the darkness of Leona's tunnel and a surge of energy, a tiny spark of hope, rode the sunbeams warming the room.

Leona blinked away the moisture forming in her eyes. "I have to confess."

"Of course you do."

"When I walked into the Messenger, the smell of newsprint tickled my nostrils and the sound of ink hitting recycled paper made my heart pound." She pushed herself up and leaned against the headboard. "I've never told anyone this, Roxie, but . . ."

Roxie scooted close, poised for the divulging of every last shred of the deep, dark truth.

"I've always wondered what it would have been like if I had continued my journalism career. Who knows what amazing news stories I might have uncovered. I could have been the next Woodward or Bernstein."

"You would have been a lot cuter than Dustin Hoffman, but Robert Redford would be hard to beat."

"They weren't the real Woodward and Bernstein."

"Don't burst my bubble, girlfriend."

Unrestrained laughter worked better than any painkillers, relieving the tension at the base of Leona's skull. The phone rang, interrupting her emotionally induced high.

Roxie glanced at the caller ID on the nightstand. "It's Maddie." She picked up the phone. "Hey, baby . . . Yes, your momma is feeling much better. She's getting some color in her cheeks . . . Why don't you ask her yourself?" She handed the receiver to Leona, patted her leg, and slid off the bed. "I'll let you tell your daughter the good news of your gainful employment. I'll expect you downstairs for coffee." She tiptoed across the bedroom and eased out the door.

Leona held her hand over the mouthpiece, allowing herself a moment to marvel. The door of opportunity had not been slammed shut, despite her ungraceful passage through it. She felt as if her feet had come in contact with solid ground, and she was only a few steps from the shore. Thank you, Lord.

If her new job wasn't an example of the unmerited favor J.D. preached, she didn't know what was. She certainly had not earned this second chance. Truth be known—and she was sure both God and Roxie already knew—imagining herself at a desk and working on a computer sent waves of panic rippling across her stomach.

What if I can't hold up under the weight of the gift, God?

* * * * *

Maddie snapped her cell phone off.

A strange mixture of relief and loss tumbled around inside her head. Momma would be self-supporting, which was good. Real good. Piling more debt atop of her outstanding med school loans had been a paralyzing thought. Now she could breathe easy. Right? Why wasn't she? Why did she feel her breath was trapped in her chest? Why did she have this nagging feeling that having Momma busy starting a new life was . . . bad?

I don't want Momma to have a new life.

Shame drooped Maddie's head over the kitchen sink. Had she almost said those appalling, selfish words out loud? Did she really think her mother didn't deserve a chance to pursue her own dreams? Did she seriously begrudge her mother trying to find a way to make a living?

How self-absorbed had she become to think Momma must focus all her attention on two grown kids consumed with establishing their own lives? For years, Momma had hovered over them like a helicopter. She couldn't imagine her life without the whir of those rotor blades and for the first time, she realized she would miss it.

A gnawing emptiness pressed Maddie toward the cabinets. Dried-out turkey pepperoni, stale crackers, one small can of tuna. She opened the fridge. The lone bulb spotlighted a stalk of shriveled celery, a gallon of expired milk, and a slice of apple browning on the barren shelves.

Maddie slammed the door. Putting her back to the laminated vinyl surface, she slumped against the front of the appliance and slid onto the floor. Pulling her knees to her chest, she wrapped both arms around her bent legs.

"So how was your mom?" Justin's question startled Maddie.

She looked at the man towering over her. "I didn't hear you come in."

"You've been your own world ever since you came back." He held his new snowboard, a Vapor-something, light as a bag of feathers. Not the board of his dreams, but the board he was hoping would help him nail a couple of decent sponsorships at Nationals. "I said, how's your mom?"

Maddie followed the enviable caress of Justin's hands on the board's sleek lines. He'd spent hours poring over websites and YouTube videos. He hadn't been willing to part with the little bit of cash he'd made working the ski lifts on the weekend until he'd tracked down the board of every winner. She remembered it was this intense focus and drive that had attracted her to him in the first place. Had she been a fool to think he would invest that same energy in a relationship? Disappointment echoed in the empty hole of Maddie's heart.

"She got a job."

Justin's brow crinkled skeptically. "Doing what?"

She searched the smoky-blue eyes destined to grace sports ads. "My mother is not inept."

"Not sure what that means, so I'm pretty sure I didn't say that."

"Are you asking about my family because you really care or because I threw a fit when you came back to Denver without me?"

Justin bristled. "Hey, I paid to fly you back."

"You didn't even bother to come to the hospital and check on me before you left." Maddie planted her hands against the cold linoleum floor and pressed her back against the fridge.

"Justin, why did you drive all the way to Mt. Hope?"

"How high are you going to make me jump?" He pulled over a kitchen chair and put his boot on the seat. "I've landed tricks easier than you."

Anger clenched Maddie's jaw. "I'm not one of your tricks."

His glance rolled down his perfect nose. "Katie Beth said she'd kill me if I didn't."

Tears stung Maddie's eyes, her pride struggling to freeze them in place. "You came because my roommate made you?"

"Look, Maddie, quit making a big deal out of this." Justin shoved the chair back to the table with his foot. "I gave up a chance to work some sweet halfpipes in Vermont over the holidays. For what? So I could twiddle my thumbs in the flatlands of Mayberry?"

Fury blazed through Maddie's veins. "My father had just died. My grandmother was in serious condition, and the whole time you were worried about flipping around in some stupid snow tunnel?" Her voice had raised an octave.

Justin heaved an exasperated sigh and placed his board on the table. He squatted in front of her. "Look, I'm sorry about your dad." His voice had taken on the dreamy quality that melted his groupies. "You didn't deserve that." The back of his hand caressed her cheek.

Why did she feel as if sandpaper had removed the

epidermal layer, exposing raw nerves? Maddie searched Justin's eyes, desperate for an inkling of reassurance that the man cared for her as much as he did for his snowboard.

"I can't bring the guy back." The force of Justin's matter-of-fact words stung.

Maddie jerked her face away. "I'm not asking you to bring my father back. I just wanted a little attention and maybe a little concern. Is that asking too much of you?"

"Yeah, it is." He stood and picked up his board. "I didn't sign on for that."

Recoiling as if the point of Justin's scuffed ski boot had kicked her right in the pit of her stomach, Maddie crossed her hands over her chest. "I don't recall asking you to sign anything." She swallowed hard to keep the tears from thawing and spilling over the dam.

Justin flipped the snowboard over his shoulder. "You're a mess."

"I'm a mess? And this coming from a guy who looks like a hobo with a knapsack tied to the end of a stick." Insulting Justin's cherished snowboard inflicted a jab Maddie hoped hurt him as much as he'd hurt her. She kept on punching. "You planning to hop the next train out of town? Are you walking out on me?"

"Hey, we're not married."

"Thank God."

"From the beginning, we agreed this was just for fun. You're leaving in the spring to be some high-powered doctor, and I'm headed for New Zealand for Olympic training. It wouldn't have worked. I'll get my stuff tomorrow." Justin grabbed his ski jacket. "Go home, Maddie. Take care of your mom. Forget Denver." He opened the door and looked back over his shiny new board. "Merry Christmas."

As the man Maddie thought she'd marry closed the door behind him, fear swept over her. She was alone. Completely and totally alone.

Before her father died, she'd never felt alone. Knowing her father was only a phone call away made it seem he occupied the wooden chair squished against the old roll-top desk.

Daddy.

The man never missed a single event in her life. Now he would miss watching her become a doctor, walking her down the aisle, and holding his grandkids. Loss welled up and burst forth in hot, bitter streams.

"Momma." The word rang in Maddie's ears.

Who had spoken? She brushed away the moisture blurring her vision, certain the voice was not Justin's. She listened intently. No one was in the apartment.

She closed her gritty eyes. The face of her mother appeared

on the backs of her lids. Her mother smiled and opened her arms. Maddie saw herself running, like a slow-motion movie, and falling into the welcome embrace, but when she opened her eyes she remained cross-legged on the floor. She squeezed her eyes tight, rubbing her temples, willing the comforting image to return. But there was only darkness.

"Go home." Again the voice spoke, this time firm and commanding.

Maddie's eyes flew open. A wintry gray light filled the window above the sink, but no one was there. Calm down. You've studied grief. Physical ailments or heightened senses are not unusual manifestations of gut-wrenching emotions. Maddie rubbed her eyes and looked around. She wasn't hearing things. Stress had caused her mind to play tricks on her.

God had allowed all of this to happen. She hadn't heard from him in years, so why would he be talking to her now? Besides, even if he sent her a special delivery letter, God didn't have a single thing to say to her that she wanted to hear.

Feeling empty as her cabinets, she fished her cell phone out of her jeans pocket. Scrolling to the number Parker had given her, Maddie dismissed the likelihood he would question her. But, if he did, he did. What choice did she have? She pushed Send.

"Hey, Maddie." Parker answered on the first ring. His voice didn't carry the slightest inkling of the put-out tone Justin's had when she asked him earlier about the possibility of going home with her for Christmas.

"Parker . . ."

"Maddie, what's wrong?" Uncertain of her ability to restrain any residual tears, Maddie hoped Parker would pretend her little fib was the truth. "Nothing."

"You sure?" He sounded unconvinced. "Is it your mother? I can be over there in two shakes of a lamb's tail."

"No, it's not Momma." How could she explain the strange urge prompting this conversation when she didn't understand it herself?

"Did something happen to Mrs. Worthington? I know they moved her to rehab, but I thought she was doing better. Causing quite the ruckus, but making progress."

"Parker . . ." Maddie cleared her throat. "I'm thinking about coming home early for Christmas."

"Great . . . I mean . . . I'm sure your mom would love—"

Maddie cut him off. "I want to surprise Momma."

"Surprise?"

"Can you keep a secret?"

"Have I ever told anyone you kissed me in second grade?"

"I didn't kiss you; you kissed me."

"That's not how I remember it."

"You thought you killed me and panicked."

"I seem to remember—"

"Look, Parker. Can you pick me up at the airport or not?"

"I'll be there." Parker's firm voice possessed the clarity of purpose Justin's never achieved despite the slew of voice lessons. "Name the day and time."

"Thanks. Probably Friday or Saturday. I'll be in touch."

Maddie closed her eyes and let her head fall against the fridge. The vibration of the motor hummed along her spine, sending a buzzing sensation into her extremities. She took the fact that her limbs had feeling as a sign Justin's scalpel-sharp words had not severed all of her nerve endings. But her vitals must have dipped to desperate depths, sapping the oxygen from her brain. What other possible explanation could account for the stupid decision to call Mt. Hope's resident extension agent and beg him to bring her home early?

Taking in a ragged breath, Maddie pushed herself up from the floor. She brushed off her hands. *If God thinks he can scare me back into the fold, he doesn't know Dr. Maddie Harper.*

Chapter Sixteen

Leona considered printing an alias on the blank name tag the receptionist shoved across the front desk of the nursing home slash rehabilitation center, but Penny's glare dared her to claim she was no relation to the raving woman in room 110. Uneasiness crept up Leona's neck and flushed her cheeks. She scribbled her name, ripped off the backing, and lightly pressed the sticky paper to the lapel of her new navy suit. If the blasted thing left one of those gummy rings, she'd see to it that her mother paid the dry-cleaning bill.

Summoning her most caring voice, Leona picked up the sign-in clipboard. "So, how is Mrs. Worthington today, Penny?"

The young woman's expression soured faster than expired milk. "You want the truth?"

Shaking her head, Leona lowered her eyes and busied herself, logging in on the line below the unsteady signatures of Nola Gay and Etta May Story.

"She's progressing nicely." Penny's pursed lips flattened into the same health-professional smile Leona had noticed on

Charlie's face as she followed him to the ambulance.

A wave of tears blurred her vision. Would she ever get a handle on the assortment of odds and ends that could trigger her grief when she least expected it? Desperate to halt the watery flow rimming her freshly applied mascara, Leona changed the subject. She would not be waylaid. Not today. "Are the Story sisters still in with Mother?"

Penny nodded. "They were here before the breakfast trays came out. Said something about shining light down a dark hole. You might want to get back there."

Or turn around and run out those automated doors.

"Thanks for the heads-up, Penny." Leona squared her shoulders. Placing one wobbly new pump in front of the other, she set out down the gleaming corridor of Mt. Hope's rehab center.

The clinical smells were not those of a luxury hotel, but she couldn't help that. Her mother needed rehabilitative care, help getting back on her feet. Surely the woman would understand limbering a stiff hip was not for amateurs. A rehab center was the obvious and only solution. And the only rehab offered in Mt. Hope meant her mother had to temporarily become a resident of the local nursing home.

Who was she kidding?

Leona cringed, remembering the time her mother took on

the physical education teacher who wouldn't allow her daughter a break on the cramping days of her monthly. Nothing that poor teacher said or did could convince Roberta Worthington that a little exercise would not kill her daughter. Leona wasn't sure what happened, but the next semester they had a new P.E. teacher. Proof positive that tangling with Roberta Worthington was not something people should ever line up to do.

Leona rounded the corner. Escalating voices shook the suite at the end of the hall. Clutching the metal safety rail, she paused. *Lord, have mercy.*

The last two weeks without J.D. had been tough, but she had never missed him more than she did at this very moment. She wished she could pawn her mother off on the eternally optimistic man. Her reasons weren't entirely selfish. The guy hated to miss a good fight, and from the snarling sounds emanating from room 110, the gloves were off. But since the good pastor was probably preaching to the choir, she had no choice but to handle this situation on her own. Get a backbone, as Roxie would say.

Leona tugged on the hem of her new jacket, straightening her spine along with her notched-collar polyester. The determined clack of her high heels filled the empty hallway. Picking up steam, she bustled through the swinging door of her mother's room as if she was happy to be there.

"Morning, Mother," she chirped.

From her hospital bed, Leona's mother snarled, "About time you showed up."

The reprimand stopped Leona in her tracks. Her eyes dropped to her shiny shoes, her guilt reflecting in the patent leather. She mentally scolded herself for reverting to the cowardice of her youth and tried to step forward. Something was wrong with her new shoes. They would not move. Lifting her eyes, she encountered the impatience on her mother's face. "I had a few errands before I could come."

"I see you forgot my coffee. What am I going to do? The sludge they serve in this place would choke a horse."

The fiery blast from the bedridden dragon melted Leona's resolve into puddles that oozed between her stationary toes.

"Don't mind her, honey." Etta May tugged at the thin blanket covering Roberta's legs. "I think she's chilly."

"If you ask me, I think she's had one too many dill pickles." Nola Gay settled into the recliner in the corner and shifted her purse to her lap. She cranked the footrest lever, and her thick ankles popped straight out in front of her. "Ah . . . that's better."

"What do you think you're doing?" Mother squawked. "You don't have the right to make yourself at home in my room." Leona's mother struggled to raise herself, but fell back with an exhausted huff. "Get these pickled broads out of here."

Breaking free of the force holding her feet to the floor, Leona inched forward, her shoe rolling across something on the floor. "They're just here to cheer you up." She looked down. Pink sponge rollers littered the floor. Smoldering emotions sparked into flame. "Mother, why did you rip these out?" She bent and stuffed curlers into her jacket pockets. "It took me an hour to roll your hair."

"They were uncomfortable. I've sent my driver to fetch my hairdresser." Her mother ran her fingers through the haywire strands crowning her head. "Look at this mop. It's been nearly two weeks since I've had my hair done."

Would this woman's ability to incite Leona's feelings of inadequacy and reduce her to a freckled-faced schoolgirl ever diminish? Leona had spent years working with packed sanctuaries of crabby old coots, and none of them peeved her as quickly and completely as did her own mother. "I did your hair last night, Mother."

"You missed one, dear." Nola Gay pointed, directing Leona's attention to a roller wedged under the door.

"Thanks." Leona jerked the roller free, and the door slammed shut.

Nola Gay fiddled with the recliner lever. "We told your mother that Earlene over at Snippers does a fine job with a wash and set."

"We even volunteered to bring Earlene over here." Etta May picked up an overlooked roller near the bed and handed it to Leona. "But your mother insisted that poor chauffeur fellow drive all the way back to the city."

"If I wanted blue hair, I would have asked for your hairdresser's name," Mother snapped.

Nola Gay pushed herself up on her elbows. "Bertie, I don't understand how anyone could be so attached to a skunk stripe down the middle of their pointed head. You need your roots done."

"Sister," Etta May interrupted, casting a reproving look her twin's way. "Do not grow weary in doing good, and at the proper time, you will reap a harvest."

Nola Gay considered her sister's chosen Scripture for a moment, "Well, you know how I adore a good harvest." She wiggled back into the recliner. "But her roots are horrible."

"Get these blue-haired Twinkies out of my room." Leona's mother pounded the bed with both fists. "Next thing you know they'll be wanting to anoint my head with oil just like those idiots you call elders. Look what that greasy stuff did to my hair."

"Mother, that's enough." Blame or no blame, Leona felt the strong urge to strangle the hostile woman. "These people just want to help. To let you know they care about you." She wrenched open the bottom dresser drawer and emptied her pockets.

"If they think they can grease me up good enough to slip through the bars of heaven, they're wasting their precious oil. How long do you think it would take your God to realize I didn't belong on his side of the pearly gates?"

Nola Gay gasped, her saddened eyes seeking out Leona. "Everyone has their cross to bear, and she is yours, dear."

No kidding. Humiliation buckled Leona's knees as her mother's blatant blasphemy yanked the bottom card from Leona's reared-in-a-godly-home image and toppled the whole fabricated construction like a house of cards. How could she ever look the Storys in the eye again now that they knew what kind of a family she really came from?

Etta May cleared her throat, and Leona braced for the rebuke she deserved.

But it didn't come. Instead, without missing a beat, the seasoned woman jumped into the lull in the conversation as if ignoring irreverence was the best way to save the pastor's wife from the deadly rot of her heredity. "Leona, a little birdie told us about your job. We're so excited for you." A proud smile spread across her stained dentures.

Roberta arched a tattooed brow. "What job?"

"Your daughter is going into the newspaper business." Etta May's face glowed. She put a hand on Roberta's pajama-clad shoulder and leaned in as if she was about to divulge her secret pickle recipe. "Leona is the new reporter down at the Messenger."

"You got a journalism job?" Her mother's surprised tone carried a sharp-edged note of hurt, poking a hole in Etta's excitement.

Leona hated the wounded and worried look creasing Etta's face. The Story twins were mostly thorns in her flesh, but everything they'd ever done had always been done in love…including sharing their pastor's wife's personal information. And she appreciated the support. But she couldn't help wishing that just once she could have been the one to tell her own news.

That's what she got for allowing pride to take over her better judgment. If she hadn't wanted to make sure the job would work out, she could have told her mother herself. But the thought of admitting failure knotted her stomach. Would she ever get past wanting to please her mother?

Willing herself to clear the tense air, Leona offered a cautious response. "Ivan has attended church with us for years. I think he hired me out of pity."

"If you wore that Peter Pan collar, I'm sure you're right." Her mother yanked the blanket across her chest and held it in place with her crossed arms.

"Is that all you're going to say about it, Mother?"

Her mother kept her eyes on the lint she picked from the thin cover. "It's about time you bought yourself a nice suit."

Nola Gay and Etta May exchanged uncomfortable glances, but no one said a word. In the strained silence, Leona could hear the second hand on the wall clock methodically click its way around the face of time.

Pinching blanket fibers between her thumb and forefinger, Mother ignored the eyes honed on her.

Etta May cleared her throat. "Don't you even want to know what Leona will be writing?"

Leona's mother sighed, looked up, and glared at Etta's hopeful face. "Oh, all right. What section?"

Success illuminated Etta's face. "Obits," she crowed, as if Leona had just won a Pulitzer.

"My daughter is going to write obituaries?" Mother tossed the accumulated fuzz ball on the floor and fluffed the back of her flattened hair with her chipped nails. "Now there's a position one should aspire to."

"She did a terrific job on Reverend Harper's write-up. Everyone said so." Etta May pulled a folded piece of paper from her purse. "Sister and I have jotted down a few things and would appreciate it if you could work up ours as soon as possible." She pressed the paper into Leona's hands.

Leona felt her jaw drop, words tumbling in all directions. "You want me to write your obituaries now?"

"Why certainly, dear." Etta May's yellowed dentures filled her smile.

Mother's hands slapped the covers. "But you're not dead, you old fool."

Nola Gay shook the unyielding recliner lever with two hands. "If we wait until we're dead, we won't be around to read them when they come out in the paper. Where's the fun in that?" She swiped at the perspiration forming on her brow.

"You know how we love to see our name in the paper." Etta May stepped across the room, put a foot on the stubborn lever, and dropped Nola Gay's Easy Spirits to the floor with a jarring thud. "We haven't had our name in the paper since our pickles took first at the county fair." She offered her sister a hand.

With a heave, Nola Gay popped out of the overstuffed chair. "Besides, if we take a look at your work, we can eliminate any embarrassing inaccuracies before the paper hits everyone's front porch."

Etta freed the back of her sister's dress caught in the waistband of her panty hose. "Once Modyne typed 1902 instead of 1912, and in a keystroke, Lucille Ellis departed this life ten years older than necessary. Lucille would have been mortified."

"Leona, I would think you, of all people, know how protective women are about their age." Nola Gay leaned in and whispered, "Claiming to be forty when they're really fifty."

Squirming in her fancy shoes, Leona wondered if the surprise fiftieth birthday party J.D. had thrown for her would haunt her the rest of her life.

Etta May grinned, waving away Leona's need to set out on another guilt trip. "Truth is we'd like to have a few copies framed for Ray's kids."

Nola Gay turned to the wild-haired woman whacking a TV remote controller across her flattened palm. "Bertie, you might want to think about having Leona go ahead and write up your obituary."

Mother dropped the remote. "What?"

"Well, if you're not willing to work to get yourself out of that bed, you might as well be dead."

A swath of red blazed up Roberta's neck and exited her ears in a mushroom cloud of steam.

Leona took a step back, warning bells clanging in her head. But before she could broadcast an eruption notice, the rumbling volcano grabbed a ribbon-wrapped Mason jar off the swivel bed stand and heaved it across the room. Spicy vinegar dripped down the pristine wall, trumping the smell of hospital disinfectant.

"That is what I think of your soggy pickles!"

"What a waste." Nola Gay shook her head.

"And she doesn't mean pickles." Etta May directed her pointed gaze at the breathless woman who had maneuvered two stiff legs over the edge of the bed.

"Bertie, if you're feeling well enough to chuck pickles, it won't be long before you're up and around." Nola Gay let her purse strap drop into the crook of her arm.

"Get out!"

Etta stepped over the spreading syrupy puddle. "We're praying for you, Bertie."

"You know what I think you can do with your blasted prayers," Roberta growled between clenched teeth.

Nola Gay nodded. "And that's never stopped us before."

"Thank God." Leona threw an arm around the neck of each sister and whispered, "Thank you. That's the first sign of life I've seen in her since the accident."

"Our work here is done." Nola Gay patted Leona's arm and backed from her embrace. She took Etta May's elbow. "Let's go, Sister."

Rendered speechless as the sisters shambled from Roberta's room, Leona turned and regarded her mother. Pity pricked as she watched the cursing woman struggle to reach the aluminum walker parked beside her bed. Leona started across the room, but some unseen force stopped her.

She took a moment. For the first time in her life, she examined her mother with the eye of one gifted at ministering to the hurting rather than that of a slighted daughter. Why had she never thought of doing this before? From this vantage point, she could see the demons of anger, disappointment, and emptiness consuming the aging woman the way cucumber rot destroys a healthy vine. *Lord, help me find the courage to get to the bottom of this darkness.*

Undulating peace covered Leona. She wouldn't help her mother reach the walker and she would not feel guilty about it. Like a butterfly wrestling to break free of its tightly woven cocoon, her mother had to do it for herself if she had any hope of finding her wings.

Her mother's condition was helpless, not hopeless. Roberta Worthington was a cucumber ripe for pickling, but the transformation would require a canning expert. Imagining God rinsing out a Mason jar brought a smile to Leona's lips, and a spark of hope to her heart.

* * * * *

David checked his messages before he punched in his mother's number. He hoped the time difference wouldn't catch her crying in a lonely bed. As he waited for the connection, he considered Momma's surprising reaction to his career announcement. No fit, no tears, no trying to talk him out of it. Grief must have muddied her thinking. David felt a twinge of guilt for using his legal training to strike in the midst of her vulnerability.

"Hello." Momma's greeting sounded terse, but not the least bit groggy.

Probably still not sleeping would be his guess, and Momma didn't function well without her beauty rest. David remembered the few times she tried to sponsor the youth group's all-nighters. She'd be the life of the party until the clock struck midnight; a werewolf could not have sprouted claws and fangs faster. Momma believed the best way to avoid youthful temptation was to forbid frolicking after midnight, much to David's embarrassment as a teenager.

"You rang, Momma?"

"I did."

"What's up? Grandmother giving you grief?" David yawned, unable to hide his own inability to catch some decent winks.

"Yes, but nothing I can't handle." The trademark confidence in her voice was probably for his benefit, but David greedily indulged in the comfort anyway.

He stepped away from the small window of his flat overlooking a quiet side street. Since his return to England, he hadn't been able to shake the feeling that someone had stuffed him into a tiny, damp box and closed the lid. Leaving the cramped, claustrophobic quarters tucked under a canopy of gray skies in exchange for the wide-open spaces of the heartland had a distinct appeal he had never felt before.

"David?" Momma's irritation snapped his attention into place. "This is costing money."

"I'm sorry, Momma. I was just thinking about how it doesn't surprise me that you're managing to deal with Grandmother."

"Well, in a manner of speaking."

"What do you mean?"

"She's being a little stubborn about her pain meds and therapy. The doctor says it's normal, but if she doesn't get those joints moving, the muscles in her legs may atrophy. I've threatened to wheel her into the country club and let all her tennis pals push her around, but she says she'll sue if I do. Can she sue her own daughter?"

"In a heartbeat," David laughed. "But can she win? That's the important question."

"Unbeknownst to the old girl, she may have slit her own throat by sending you to law school." Momma's evil chuckle was reminiscent of having satisfactorily corralled rowdy teens.

"So you called to see if I'd represent you against Grandmother?"

"No." Her hesitation alerted David that his cross-examination had struck gold.

He was right. Something was wrong. Momma never phoned overseas just to chat, and he doubted this call was an exception to her penny-pinching rules. His pulse quickened. The last time his mother's number showed up on caller ID, it had not been good news.

"What's the real problem?"

"I need legal counsel."

"What have you done?" David swiveled the desk chair and sat down. "Are we talking jail time?"

"No . . . well, maybe."

He put his feet up on the desk and made himself comfortable. Getting to the bottom of this convoluted mess was going to take a while. "What's going on, Momma?"

"As you know, I've got a job at the paper."

"I'm proud of you. You'll be great."

"Thanks for the vote of confidence."

David squelched the urge to nudge her to the point. Her fragile self-esteem did not need to catch wind of his impatience. "When do you start?"

"As soon as I scrub this pickle juice off my suit." Momma decked in business attire was an impossible image to conjure.

"What kind of juice?"

"Never mind. I'm in the rehab lobby, but on my way to the

office. Here's the thing. I don't get paid until the end of the month."

"Didn't Dad have some money?"

Why had he asked such a stupid question? What preacher ever had extra money? Miss one paycheck and of course, Momma would be strapped. The thought of making his own wife live like every dime could be the last was the very reason David had no interest in ministry. He waited, praying that somehow Momma's answer would surprise him.

"I don't know for sure. Saul says it could take months to get everything sorted out and settled." Momma's overdone chipperness did not mask the worry in her voice.

A half-unpacked bag sat on his cot-sized bed. David fought the urge to cram everything back into his bag, skip his finals, and catch the first plane home. "Estates can take a bit of effort, but Dad's should be simple to sort out."

"There's a mountain of paperwork to plow through. But I have to wait on the death certificates before I can start filing any of it."

"If I had any money, Momma—"

"David, I'm not asking for money. How could you give me money? You haven't even started your job." Her voice sounded apologetic.

If only Dad had died a year from now. Things would be

different. I'd be settled at the firm, making some serious money, and in a position to help. David railed against a God with such poor timing that a son would be denied the ability to care for his widowed mother. He added this new injustice to the mounting evidence list he intended to present in God's prosecution case.

"I would think the church could float you a few bucks until you get things straightened out."

Momma snorted. "That's the problem."

"The church?"

"No, Howard." Momma's tongue came down hard on the d in Howard. It reminded David of the times she used his full name, James David, to express her anger.

"What's old Chrome Dome up to now?"

"He's bringing in a guy to interview for your father's job."

David whipped his feet off the desk and jumped up. "Already?"

"Claims we'll lose members if the pulpit sits vacant too long."

"It's been two Sundays." David paced the length of his tiny place. He may not want his father's pulpit, but why did the thought of someone else having it fly all over him? "You're telling me that old goat is kicking you out of the parsonage less than a month after my father died?"

"That's what it basically comes down to."

The anger in Momma's voice brought David a warped sense

of satisfaction. Maybe now she would see that his decision to walk away from the pulpit and into a lucrative legal career had been the right one. Why would anyone want to live at the whims of an incompetent board who could toss a family from their home whenever the mood struck them?

While struggling to interpret the call of God, maybe he'd overlooked the obvious. He had legal expertise because God had given him the educational opportunities.

Perhaps the Lord had chosen him to be a defender of those who could not defend themselves. Dirty job, but someone has to make sure Christians treat each other like they should. If he was to be the enforcer, the sooner he accepted his place in the Kingdom, the happier he'd be.

"I'll be home by the end of the week, Momma."

Chapter Seventeen

Racing from the rehab center as fast as her fashionable pumps could navigate the slippery sidewalks, Leona sucked in pained gasps of the cold morning air. Her son was on his way home to help her make everything right and she intended to do the same with him. If she could see her mother in a new light, surely the Lord would assist her in building some sort of bridge over the chasm separating them. She yanked open the door of the van and climbed in.

Leona dropped her cell phone into the sticky, briefcase-sized handbag Roxie insisted she buy to accessorize the new outfit for her return to the working world.

She opened the glove box and dug out a couple of unused Dairy Queen napkins. She scrubbed at the vinegary syrup splattered across the front of her pinstripe suit. Good thing Mother's aim was off, or she'd be wearing pickle juice between her not-too-much-but-not-too-little earrings Roxie picked out.

She wadded the shredded napkin and tossed it onto the floorboard. Why hadn't she thought to stick in that bottle of Cotton Blossom body splash Roxie picked up at the strip mall?

But how could she have known? The average person does not expect to be pelted with canned goods while visiting their sick mother.

Some catastrophes just could not be prepared for . . . like a person's husband dropping dead, being forced into the working world without a minute's notice, threatened with eviction from her home, or the sudden realization that God had prepared both of her children for such a time as this.

God had not left her destitute.

Cranking the ignition key, Leona shot the Lord a quick prayer of thanks along with a request that today would not be the day the van chose to be temperamental. Appearing professional while smelling like a sweet pickle would be tricky enough without showing up late her first day on the job. The van coughed to life, and Leona let out her first deep breath since her narrow escape.

Accumulating snow flurries glossed the pavement. She eased from the rehab parking lot and turned right onto Main Street.

Driving past Mt. Hope's struggling downtown, Leona thought about how much David sounded like his father. She blinked back tears. Having her son in J.D.'s corner at next week's board meeting would be a comfort. Once David cleaned Howard's clock, maybe Maxine would back off the crusade to get the Harper boy in the pulpit. Leona suspected the preacher parade idea had been Maxine's ploy to force David home. Although there was nothing she wanted more than for David to preach, the decision was between him and God.

Guilt pricked Leona's conscience. She'd put more pressure on David than Maxine ever could. What kind of a mother pressures her son into taking the pulpit simply because she needs a roof over her head? Accepting the call of the Lord was not the same as acquiescing to extenuating circumstances. And there was no way she was going to let David get the two confused.

Leona's freshly manicured nails clicked rapidly against the steering wheel. This time, Howard and Maxine had gone too far and messed with the wrong momma.

Exactly what she intended to do about the situation, she wasn't sure. She needed something that would knock the legs right out from under Maxine's plan, make her sorry she had trifled with Leona Harper.

But what?

And just how evil could her plan dare be?

Leona maneuvered the van into the tight parking space in front of the Koffee Kup. Before she killed the ignition, the flashing blue neon warning signal registered with her preoccupied brain.

"What was I thinking? I can't park here." She slammed the gearshift into reverse. Relishing her sinful fascination with retaliation had nearly cost her another run-in with Ruthie.

Leona backed out, drove around the corner, and cut through the alley. A trash truck blocked the only open space behind the brick building. Bouncing her left knee, Leona backed out and circled the block. She glanced at her watch. In less than five minutes, she'd be late. This was an emergency. Stomach in a knot, she slid down until only her eyes peered over the wheel. Coasting into the only available spot, she prayed Ruthie was still too busy with the breakfast rush to notice.

Through her cracked windshield, Leona checked the diner window. Ruthie, her broad back to the street, flipped something greasy on the grill. *Thank you, Lord.* Leona fumbled with her keys, snatched her new handbag, and sprinted toward her employer's door.

Modyne glanced up and frowned.

Leona drew her purse tight against the pickle stain on her chest, hoping her less-than-graceful entrance had not ruined her only opportunity to make a good first impression. She flashed a rectifying smile. "Morning, Modyne."

"Heat ain't cheap, Leona." The news icon returned her attention to the computer screen.

"Sorry." Leona gave herself a mental kick in the seat of her new suit pants as she closed the door and her mouth.

Across the room, Ivan continued clicking computer buttons, shouting over his shoulder, "Be with you in a minute."

"No rush." Sooner or later she would have to open her mouth and catch a breath, but for now she'd settle for whatever air she could inhale through her nose. The scratchy combination of paper, ink, and the rancid smell of scorched microwave popcorn tingled her nostrils.

According to Ivan, the press only ran on Friday. Without the clanking ka-chunk, ka-chunk, ka-chunk of the ancient machine, the atmosphere in the cluttered office seemed peaceful.

Toes cramping in her new heels, Leona surveyed the dingy space, her perusing gaze lighting on an empty desk. A little dusting and she could see herself seated there, creatively moving words around on the page, her concentration not suffering in the least . . . especially once Modyne's constant pecking was retired.

Ivan pushed his chair away from his desk. Metal scraping against the scarred wood floor jarred Leona from her daydreams. "Care for some coffee?"

"Sure. That'd be great." Leona had practiced condensing her sentences in hopes of making a good first impression. First impressions were everything in setting the tone for a copacetic working relationship. If church work had taught her nothing else, it had taught her that digging out of the hole of perceptions-gone-awry was an impossible task.

Modyne continued to tap away on the computer keys. "Make mine black."

Leona had made coffee and smiled about it her entire married life. She couldn't believe such menial Christian service had given her a handy expertise in the marketplace. Maybe she should pinch herself.

"Happy to, Modyne." Leona removed her wool coat and draped it over a folding chair.

Following Ivan to the coffeemaker hidden behind stacks of papers, another thought occurred to her. Once she got settled, she could offer to tidy the place up a bit. Coffee and cleaning. Two things she knew well. She'd see that Editor Tucker got his money's worth if she had to get down on her hands and knees and mop every warped board in the press room.

Ivan wiped the insides of two stained mugs with a paper towel. "You can bring a cup from home if you want." He poured a thick black liquid into the mugs and filled a dusty Styrofoam cup nearly to the brim. "Here. Care to see your desk?"

"Of course." Leona opted to ignore the oily film rising to the top of the disposable cup.

Keeping her eyes on the back of Ivan's sparsely-sprigged head, she carried one mug and the paper cup to the front desk without sloshing a drop. She never imagined all those years of walking with a book on her head to perfect her posture would bestow yet another marketable skill.

"Here you go, Modyne." Leona added a dash of levity to her voice for good measure.

"Thanks."

"You're so welcome, Modyne. I'm here to help any way I can."

The ace reporter lowered her nose and peered over her half-glasses. A hint of a snarl formed under the shadowy mustache the older woman no longer waxed. Leona waited politely for a response to her offer, but was met with a stony silence. Apparently congenial dialogue was not Modyne's strong suit.

Leona brandished her Sunday smile.

Modyne's frosty demeanor might have deterred the less seasoned, but as a pastor's wife, she was way ahead of the competition when it came to dealing with the cantankerous. Church work had given her years of experience dealing with irascible personalities. Crock-Pots, J.D. called the Modyne-types. Always on simmer. But given time, these slow cookers would eventually crank out a fork-tender rump roast. On more than one occasion, the pastor's family had even been invited to share in a feast of reconciliation. All Modyne needed was a little time to warm up to the idea of another woman in the office and she'd be falling all over the new hire.

"We use Quark to build a page." Ivan leaned over the empty desk in the corner, pushed a button on the computer, and the dark monitor came to life. "You're familiar with the program, right?"

Visions of the assorted and confusing TV, VCR, and DVD remotes scattered across the parsonage coffee table danced before Leona's eyes. She took a deep breath, smiled, and plunged ahead hoping Ivan considered honesty the best policy. "I think I mentioned I can use Word, and I e-mail occasionally, but after that, I'm afraid I'm . . . technically challenged."

He managed an encouraging nod. "Well, I guess we'll start with Word."

Modyne's eyes cut above the rim of her glasses. "She'll have to learn the page designer sometime."

"Let's get her feet wet before we dunk her." Ivan pulled out the empty desk chair. "Why don't you try out this seat? Do I need to adjust it for you?"

Leona fought the urge to saw off an arm and lay the bloody stump before Ivan as a sacrifice. J.D. had told her of Ivan Tucker's many kindnesses, but being on the receiving end was more than she expected or deserved. She would prove to Modyne that Leona Harper was a good hire if she had to stay up nights reading every yellow Dummies manual in Royce's checkout line.

Offering her best it-will-work-out smile, Leona resisted the urge to peer at Modyne's screen to see if the old woman's typing speed was real or merely an intimidation tactic. "You'll see, Modyne. I'll catch on so fast, you'll be out on the open road before the first wildflower shows its color."

"Sure you will." Modyne's nails picked up their frantic pace as she glanced over her shoulder at Ivan. "Wayne Darling called. Councilman Pond died last night."

"Oh no. Poor Goldie." Leona felt the starch drain from her legs. "What will she do without her Owen?"

"Sit down, Leona. You don't look so good." Ivan eased her into the desk chair. "You sure you're up to dealing with obits?"

"No, I'm not sure." Leona's tears refused to be held back. Through blurry eyes she could make out the smug smile under Modyne's hairy lip. Leona swiped at her damp cheeks. "But I can't sit around. Idleness is the devil's playground. I need to keep my mind busy. If I can make things better for Mrs. Pond, that makes things better for me, right?"

Ivan pulled a hanky from his pocket. "Good girl."

Good girl? The malarkey she'd just spewed made her blood boil. How could helping someone else possibly make her own pain go away? She made a mental note to frame the foolish rhetoric that had just rolled off her tongue as a tangible reminder that clichés offered no comfort to the hurting. She would think twice before touting those hollow words to another in the throes of grief.

"You hired me to proof write-ups." Leona took Ivan's hanky and dabbed her eyes. "I think I can do that."

When she'd first learned that Ivan was not hiring her to actually write anything original, she'd done her best to swallow the disappointing news. After all, she couldn't expect the resumption of a career after a thirty-year hiatus to begin at the top of the heap. Given time, she could work her way up. But the jury was still out on whether or not she was up to the climb. Since J.D.'s death, even getting out of bed required monumental effort. How could she ever muster the stamina to start her life over?

Ivan tapped his long fingers. "I'm afraid your job's a little more involved than we originally discussed."

The troubled look on Ivan's face, coupled with Modyne's silent keyboard, gave Leona pause. "In what way?"

"Usually Wayne brings the write-ups to our office . . ." Ivan fiddled with the pencils in the coffee can on Leona's desk. "But he's shorthanded at the funeral home. I'm afraid I'll have to send you over there to pick up any piece he needs to submit."

"Can't he e-mail?" Leona regretted telling Ivan how to run

his business the second the words leapt off her tongue. Apparently, the transition from being in charge of nearly every church project to doing just her job would take some getting used to. "Sorry, Ivan."

The editor waved off her apology. "Wayne feels this sensitive material deserves a personal touch. Quirks of the service industry." Ivan's tolerance reminded Leona of how much she had to learn.

From the corner of her eye, Leona could see Modyne's gnarled fingers poised as if anxious to type a career obituary the minute the greenhorn dropped. Leona stiffened in her chair. This dog pack wasn't big enough for two females. One would have to be dominant . . . and Modyne wasn't going to give up her spot without a fight … no matter how big her new RV.

Leona squared her shoulders, praying the added height gave her added punch. "Just let me know when you need me to go."

"This morning." No one would ever accuse Modyne of a media blitz the way she doled out information segments in short, controlled blips. "Wayne's expecting you."

Leona swallowed any grandiose idea of being pack leader anytime soon. "Tell him I'm on my way." She donned her coat and headed into the darkening day.

Chapter Eighteen

Tiny snowflakes salted Leona's shoulders as she hurried out on her first official assignment. She got into her van and twisted the key in the ignition. Pumping the gas pedal, Leona held her breath. When the fickle engine convulsed to life, she exhaled and gave the Lord credit. At least car trouble wasn't plaguing her upside-down life.

Starting the wipers, she noticed a piece of paper flapping under the flimsy blade. She followed the arc of the note, but could not read the streaky words smearing the windshield. She turned off the wipers, jumped out of the van, and freed the soggy paper.

Customer parking only. Violators towed. Koffee Kup Management

"That brazen hussy." Leona wrenched open the van's rusty door and hurled Ruthie's threatening notice to the floorboard. The newspaper's next headline flashed before her eyes: "Pastor's Widow Drives Family Vehicle through Local Restaurant Window."

Leona revved her engine. She threw the gearshift into

reverse and floored it. With a fiendish chuckle she smiled at the significant portion of her bald-tire rubber now embellishing Ruthie's coveted space.

The van fishtailed around the slick corner of Main and Elm. Better calm down and get control before I have a wreck. Lifting her foot from the accelerator, praying for her enemies came to mind, but she quickly pushed the charitable thought from her head. In less than two weeks, Satan had summoned his whole army, formed an intimidating line of assault, and attacked her on every front. Family, finances, church. If she prayed anything, the petition would be one of King David's psalms begging God to give the adversaries an extra helping of what for.

As she came within sight of the bland brick of the funeral home, large wet flakes splat upon her cracked windshield. Leona cranked the steering wheel and pulled in under the funeral home's portico, parking alongside the hearse. From her idling vehicle, she stared at the gleaming black car that had transported J.D.'s abandoned body to Oak Lawn.

Shivers rippled down her spine. Her head knew her husband was not lying out in this miserable cold, but her heart wanted him in where it was warm. Wanted J.D. Harper home. Wanted the man she loved sitting in his old recliner with a book in his lap. Wanted her husband's strong, safe arms wrapped around her. Stinging tears trickled down her cheeks.

Leona removed Modyne's file from her large handbag. She reluctantly killed the engine and sat in the frigid quiet. She wiped her cheeks while waiting for the aching gush from the crevice in her heart to harden like the precipitation icing her windshield. *Lord, I can't do this. Help me.*

Next thing Leona knew, she stood before the mortician's receptionist, manila folder tucked under her arm, completely unsure how she'd walked through the office door.

Pine wafted from green Christmas pillars, but the pleasant scent did not mask the aura of death hovering in the room. Nor did the radio talk show host droning from the out-of-place boom box on Rosie's desk camouflage the lethal quiet. A wave of nausea crested in Leona's hollow gut.

Rosie Cass stuck a pencil into the indentation in her beehive hairdo and smiled. "I've been keeping up with the weather." She fiddled with a dial and lowered the radio volume. "Modyne called and said you were on your way. How are you, Mrs. Harper?"

How did the woman think she was? Less than a month ago she was in here picking out her husband's coffin. Was anyone ever fine after that?

"Hard to come back in here, isn't it?" Compassion sparkled in Rosie's eyes.

"Excuse me?"

"After my Morris died, I never wanted to set foot in a funeral home again. But when I couldn't pay the interment bill, Wayne offered me a job. That was twenty years ago, and I still can't go into the casket selection room."

The woman's quiet confession pricked Leona's conscience. She'd been to enough funerals in this one-funeral-home community to know Rosie Cass could stride up the aisle and seal a coffin as well as the funeral director.

But not once had she taken the time to notice the secret pain hidden behind those horn-rimmed glasses. Blinking back tears, Leona whispered, "Thanks, Rosie."

"You'll make it, doll." Rosie winked and wheeled her chair away from the immaculate desk. "Mrs. Pond is in with Wayne now. Why don't you sit here and warm up a bit while I make sure they're finished in the back." The spry woman bustled from the room, leaving Leona alone . . . again.

She glanced around the spotless waiting room. The candles burning in glass holders set on oak end tables flickered like silent tributes to all the sadness that had passed through these heavy doors. No doubt Rosie used the noise of the low-pitched radio announcer to drown out the haunting quiet the same way Leona flipped on the TV at night while she picked at one of the casseroles in her fridge.

On the surface, the living-room coziness of funeral homes

removed the chill of death. But if experience had taught her anything, it was that there weren't enough candles and soft music in the world to fill the empty hole death left in the lives of the bereaved. Dropping into the upholstered chair, Leona was grateful for the opportunity to stabilize her shaky legs.

"Leona." Face flushed, Wayne appeared in the doorway. "I'm so glad you could make it." He extended a hand of welcome, and Leona complied, tamping her desire to check for any traces of embalming fluid lingering on his mummified mitts. "We'll try to keep this brief, but Owen was a pretty important man in the community. We need his obit done up right." He offered a pasty smile and gestured for her to rise.

"I'll do the best I can." Leona clutched Modyne's file under her arm and dragged herself out of the chair. She prayed her legs would not fail her as she followed Wayne across the hall.

The funeral director whispered over his shoulder as if he might wake the dead. "Goldie insisted we wait for you after I told her you were the one who wrote J.D.'s obituary. Said she thought his write-up was exceptional and so she wants you to do Owen's." He offered the same satisfied-salesman smile he had the day Leona opted to upgrade J.D. from a pine box to something with inner-spring coils.

Leona shuddered, but Wayne did not seem to notice as he stepped aside like a true gentleman and allowed her to pass first into his office. The sight of Goldie Pond sitting in the exact same chair she had occupied so recently stopped Leona cold.

Curled up on the Liz Claiborne wool slacks of the councilman's wife was the whitest cat Leona had ever seen.

Wayne pressed his palm against the small of Leona's back, propelling her into the ornately decorated office. "Mrs. Pond, Mrs. Harper is here."

The woman dabbed her dry eyes with a linen hanky. "Thanks for coming, Leona."

Gathering her scattered wits, Leona shoved from her mind how she must have looked sitting in the same situation, minus the cat, of course. "Mrs. Pond, I am so sorry about Owen." She paused, racking her brain, careful to avoid any of the trite phrases people had thrown at her after J.D.'s death. Things like "He's in a better place." "At least the pastor didn't suffer." And Maxine's take: "Apparently the Lord needed J.D. more than you, Leona." Why in the world would the creator of the universe need a worn-out preacher? She settled on, "Nice cat."

The widow's French manicured nails combed the cat's luxurious coat. "This is Pinkie Pond, my husband's prize Persian."

When the plastic surgeon ironed out Goldie's wrinkles last year he must have pressed her emotions flat as well. *But who am I to judge?* Everyone handles grief in their own way . . .

another information perk of the experience learning curve.

Leona nodded and took the chair next to the icy widow and the pampered fur ball. She prayed her allergies would not kick in before their business was complete. Once her eyes swelled shut, she wouldn't be able to proof a word for hours. She cleared the mucus collecting in the back of her throat. "Pinkie is . . . beautiful."

"Owen thought so." Goldie fingered the rhinestone collar wrapping the feline's furry neck. "He left her everything."

"Oh. How nice," Leona stammered. "I mean, for the cat."

Goldie's green eyes locked with Leona's as she tucked a stray blonde hair into the nape of her French twist. "I want my Owen to have the obituary he deserves."

"Absolutely. I can certainly understand that. I'll do everything I can." Leona shifted, but could not squirm out from under the piercing emerald gaze.

"Good." Goldie's eyebrows lifted without making a single crease across her taut forehead. "I want Owen exposed for the cheapskate that he is . . . was. I read J.D.'s obituary and was quite impressed."

Leona gasped, "If you got the impression my husband was uncharitable, I'm certainly not the person for this job." Before she could storm out, Goldie clamped her hand on Leona's arm and pressed her back into the hot seat.

Wayne sought cover in the seat behind his desk. He flashed the Messenger's inexperienced obit writer a silent plea for help.

"Find someone else to do your dirty work, Goldie."

"Settle down, Leona. We wouldn't want *you* to have a heart attack. I only meant you depicted your husband's true colors. Everyone in town knew Reverend Harper to be an exemplary community servant and an outstanding family man. I feel I owe Owen the same due acknowledgment." Goldie's intense scrutiny was a sharp contrast to Pinkie's aloof indifference. Apparently coming into a large sum of cash really did calm the savage beast.

Leona weighed the odds of shaking the evil threesome, but from the looks of things she had stepped into a bigger mess than last year's Christmas pageant. The trap had been sprung, and when the spring was lifted she would be the unfortunate little church mouse with her chops on the cheese.

What an idiot. What made me think I could waltz back into the workplace and succeed at a real job?

Her gaze darted from frosty widow . . . to frantic mortician . . . to filthy rich feline. "Well, if you give me what you've written, I'll proof it and make sure there are no errors."

"I don't intend to write a thing." Goldie stroked Pinkie's long, shiny coat. "That's what you're paid to do."

Tension escaped Leona's rigid shoulders. "Technically, I'm

not. I'm just a proofreader. You see, today is my first day on the job." She plastered on her committee-negotiation smile and charged ahead. "Tell you what, Mrs. Pond, why don't you let me call Modyne? Get you some experienced help on this matter."

"I don't want Modyne. I saw what that old battle-axe did to Lucille Ellis. Owen would roll over in his grave if his final press release had such a horrendous mistake. Politicians live or die by publicity . . . but even negative publicity better keep the facts straight."

"I'm not really authorized to write obituaries. I'm supposed to pick up what you've written, proof it, and give the piece to Modyne." Suddenly Leona remembered the folder in her lap. "If you don't know where to start, I have forms you can fill out." She fumbled with the file, searching through the blurred headings for the right piece of paper.

Wayne threw himself across the desk, landing with a thud. "Leona, I'm sure you can see that this is a delicate situation, one that needs a seasoned hand." He drew his hands together as if praying to the Almighty.

Grown men begging had never impressed J.D., and now Leona could see why . . . it wasn't pretty.

"That's just it, Wayne. I'm green as a Story cucumber." Leona stood. "It's my first day at the Messenger."

"Leona." Wayne heaved himself up from the desk. "After all those years of sorting through church troubles you have more public relations skills in your little finger than most PR firms have in the whole building." His pleading face looked as if he were on the verge of dropping to one knee and giving her half of his sorry little mortician kingdom. Which, considering the brisk business the single man did, was an offer a lesser woman would have jumped at.

Goldie flipped the metal clasp on her beaded bag and removed two folded pieces of paper. She handed one to Leona. "Here is a list of my husband's political friends. It's short. Shouldn't take long to give them a call." She pressed a second paper into Leona's hand. "But after talking with them, if you can't fill a column, call his enemies. I'm sure you'll have more than you need by the time you've contacted each of them."

"Obits are purchased by the inch. An entire column will be very expensive." Leona gave herself a mental pat on the back for thinking of this clever point. If she hadn't just paid for J.D.'s obituary, she wouldn't have known this little funeral business secret. Amazing how God can use every piece of sorrow to his glory. In the future, she would be more willing to give experience the credit it was due. "Surely a destitute woman would find the newspaper write-up a perfect place to scrimp."

The golden flecks in Goldie's eyes twisted like the holiday-scented candle flames. "Pinkie can afford every line."

Leona released the folder. Forms fluttered about her feet. "But—"

"Wayne has Owen's biographical information." Goldie snapped her purse closed. "One more thing. Don't you dare write that my dead husband is resting in the arms of Jesus." She scooped up the feline heiress. "Now, if you'll excuse us, Pinkie doesn't do well in snow." A sly smile glossed her collagen-plumped lips. "I'm afraid the uppity little thing will catch her death, should she accidentally be left in the cold." Mrs. Pond floated to the door and paused before executing a perfect pivot turn. "Leona, be sure and mention Pinkie. Owen would have wanted it that way."

Leona's stunned lips refused to move. She watched Goldie exit the funeral director's office, a long, fluffy white tail swirling from under her arm.

"Here you go, Mrs. Harper." Wayne ripped off the top sheet of a legal-sized yellow tablet. "This is Owen's bio. If you need any more information, give Rosie a call." He raced around the desk. Stooping, he gathered the scattered papers and crammed them inside Modyne's disheveled file folder. He grabbed Leona's elbow and whisked her past Rosie. "Glad to see Ivan got himself some first-rate help." He hustled Leona out the door and into the blowing snow before she could utter a word of protest.

The heavy oak door slammed shut, leaving Leona out in the cold with a car battery as dead as her husband and without any hope of resurrecting her career in journalism.

Chapter Nineteen

Leona rubbed her hands together, waiting for Cotton's signal that he'd successfully connected the jumper cables.

Snatches of what sounded like J.D.'s voice howled around the raised hood of the van and whipped through her open driver's-side window. "What's the point of having a cell phone if you don't keep it charged, or worse, forget to take it with you?" the gusty wind accused.

Cranking the stubborn handle a couple of turns, Leona managed to raise the scratched glass several inches, but she failed to roll away the ache settling in her bones.

She didn't know what hurt more—missing her husband's loving chastisements or not knowing who to call when she had car trouble.

Thankfully, Wayne had been holed up in his office by the time she rallied enough courage to step back inside the funeral home and phone the church. Shirley, the church secretary, promised she'd pull Cotton from his custodial duties and send him in a flash, and in her efficient manner, she'd been true to her word.

Cotton poked his head around and gave a thumbs-up. "Try it now, Leona."

Holding the key, Leona prayed Cotton's mechanical magic had conquered the corroded battery posts. Modyne would be chomping at the bit if she didn't return to the office soon. After a few grinding seconds, the engine roared to life, and Leona let out the breath she had been holding. "You're a prince, Cotton," she shouted through the cracked window.

"Don't go peeling out of here." He removed his cables and slammed the hood. Wires in hand, he approached her window. "You take your time and be careful on these roads. They're not safe."

"Thank you, Cotton," she mouthed.

After a nod of his head, he threaded himself between the nose-to-nose truck and van.

Leona put her hand to the window lever. She concentrated on coaxing the window shut instead of running after her steadfast friend and burying her face in his sturdy shoulder. A deserted sense of loss seeped into the cold as she watched him toss the cables into his truck, get in, and back away. She forced the shifter into drive, pushed the play button on her CD player, and pointed her car in the direction of the office. She focused on the treacherous road while the Gaithers sang "He's Got the Whole World in His Hands."

Trolling Main Street at a crawl, Leona prayed for an empty parking space in front of the newspaper office. Suddenly, brake lights lit up a familiar two-toned Buick hogging two slots.

She hadn't expected her little crisis to bring Shirley downtown in this weather. She could have just called Modyne.

Traffic stacking up behind her, Leona drummed her nails on the steering wheel as she waited for Shirley to back out and free up the premium parking.

Once the four-door tank cleared, Leona wheeled into one of the vacated spaces, relieved she'd snagged a slot out of the jurisdiction of the Koffee Kup's management. She made a mental note to ask Ivan about parking and Modyne about Shirley's visit.

The canvas awning over the Messenger window drooped with accumulating snow. File folder in hand, Leona risked a daring dash across the perilous sidewalk.

"Seems you're a popular girl." Modyne leaned across her desk, thrusting a few pink notes in Leona's direction. "You left your cell. So my phone's been ringing nonstop. And your husband's secretary just left."

"What did she want?" Leona brushed the snow from her shoulders.

"This ain't church. Everything is not my business." She waved the notes. "And I'm not your secretary."

"Right." Leona ceased her pawing. "Guess I'll just give these folks a call." She snatched the phone slips. "During lunch. On my own time."

"You do that." Modyne's unflinching gaze dared Leona to break another rule. "You got that obit on Owen?"

Leona hesitated. "Not exactly."

Modyne's brow arched above the rim of her glasses. "Not exactly?"

"I have some biographical information, the time of the funeral, interment plans, and where to send donations."

A wry smirk eased out from under Modyne's hairy upper lip. "Sounds like an obit to me." The dog-eared ace spun around in her chair and attacked the keyboard with a vengeance.

"But I also have a list of friends Mrs. Pond wants me to call before I—" Leona shuffled her feet, praying the scraping of heels on wood would camouflage the knocking of her knees— "write the piece."

Modyne's fingers froze … mid-peck. Leona tried not to fidget while the news sank in. In the old days, reporters hated being one-upped on an exclusive. From the daggered glare Modyne shot over her shoulder, territorial boundaries hadn't changed all that much during Leona's working-world hiatus.

"Write?" Modyne's tone indicated a wise woman would reconsider her brazen insubordination.

Wisdom had never been her strong suit. Plowing straight ahead was the only way out. "Goldie wants a . . . special piece."

"Special piece?" Modyne's mustache twitched.

Sensing this conversation was spiraling out of control, Leona's gaze skittered to Ivan's empty desk and back. Her boss was not here. What should she do?

Shoring up the bulky file slipping out from under her arm, she realized the situation called for one of her tried and true diversion tactics. Maxine Davis loved to pump the preacher's wife for inside information, but Leona had always managed to point the nosy woman in another direction by simply changing the subject.

Praying the feeble ploy would work yet again, Leona smiled, "Should I keep these forms or do you want them back?"

"Special piece?" Apparently, Modyne was not so easily distracted. "What do you mean, special piece?"

"It's complicated." Leona's body heat was rising toward lethal levels inside her heavy winter coat. It would serve her right if the ratty thing burst into flames and took her out in a fiery ball of shame. "Where's Ivan?" She unfastened the buttons.

"He went out to get some pictures of the snow. Won't be back until after lunch."

Maybe if she begged for mercy, Modyne would understand how she had been thrown to the dogs . . . cat . . . on her very first assignment. "I tried to explain that this was my first day, but Mrs. Pond insisted I write Owen's obituary."

Gaze steady, features calm, Modyne said, "Guess you better get started." Lightning quick, the seasoned reporter's fingers returned to the keyboard, zipping across the keys, sparks flying every which way. "You don't want to miss your first deadline." Her tone parceled each word and wrapped the curt package with enough rope for Leona to hang herself.

But Leona knew reverse psychology when she heard it, having fed her kids a steady diet of the tricky stuff for years. She strode to her corner desk and tore out of her coat, grateful for the burst of cool air. The dark computer monitor presented a minor problem. From the corner of her eye, she could see Modyne pecking away like a crazed banty rooster. No way was she asking that small-town-rag diva for help.

Draping her coat across the back of the chair, Leona wished she'd paid closer attention to J.D.'s navigation of the techno-monster when he opened Word at home.

She swiveled the chair around and plopped down on the fake leather seat. Remembering her husband working the mouse, she thought, how hard could it be? She gave the ladybug-shaped contraption a nudge and the screen came to life. A sense of triumph bolstered Leona's confidence.

She recognized the Word icon, dragged the arrow across the blue background, and clicked. No change. After a sneaked glance in Modyne's direction, she clicked the mouse button frantically. To her amazement, the program opened . . . several times.

Look out, publishing world, Leona Harper is in business!

Success straightened her spine and realigned her courage. Maybe she did belong here. She cracked her knuckles. Flexed her fingers. Held her readied hands over the keyboard. She studied the unfamiliar symbols on the excessive rows. Well, maybe not.

She opted to take a moment to . . . pray . . . sift through her messages . . . anything to put off touching the wrong key and destroying her progress.

The first was from David. He'd managed to book a flight out of London on Saturday. Good boy.

The next was from Maddie. She had a surprise for her momma. What in the world? Those messages out of the way, Leona finally looked at the last pink slip Modyne had given her.

Mt. Hope Rehabilitation Center. Call immediately.

Leona relegated the rehab center's message to the bottom of the stack and skewered the slips on the wire message holder. She rooted through the compartments of her extravagant handbag until she located Mrs. Pond's papers. Running a smoothing hand over the wrinkles, Leona wished removing the creases grief had pressed into her once perfect life could be as simple.

* * * * *

"Had . . . the . . . first . . . nickel . . . he . . . ever made." Squeezing the phone between her ear and shoulder, Leona jotted Councilman Clark's words. Pleased that years of taking notes during J.D.'s sermons had honed her dictation skills, Leona risked asking the respected local official a follow-up question. "Would you care to elaborate, sir?"

Councilman Clark cleared his throat. "Off the record?"

A burst of unexpected pleasure surged through Leona's veins. This influential man considered her a reporter. Her? Leona Harper? A working professional? Leona lifted her shoulders and summoned her most competent voice. "Absolutely, Councilman."

"Tighter than a tick." The unprintable quote whirled in Leona's mind. Maybe she had misunderstood. Forcing her gaping jaw to operate, she sputtered, "Could you repeat that for me?"

"Owen Pond was a stingy son of a—"

Leona dropped the phone. She scrambled to grab the line and reel in the dangling receiver. "I'm so sorry . . . Councilman

Clark, did you say . . . hello?"

The upstanding civic leader had hung up. Leona replaced the phone. Heavy-handed, she drew a black line through the last name on Goldie Pond's lengthy list.

She laid her ballpoint pen on top of her notes and rubbed her pounding temples. The comments had all been the same:

"Owen Pond grew up in the Depression. Managed his financial affairs like another Dust Bowl was imminent."

"The man thought his hearse would pull a U-Haul trailer."

"Penny-Pinching Pond."

Looking over the scathing commentaries, the sinking feeling intensified in Leona's stomach. What am I going to do? She'd contacted every source, worked every angle she could think of, even backtracked Owen's education all the way to his high school shop teacher, and she still didn't have a column's worth of printable copy. Knee-deep in troubled thoughts, Leona snapped to attention at the tap on her shoulder.

"You going to lunch?" Modyne's eyes covertly surfed Leona's notes.

Leona flipped over her lined yellow tablet. "Already?"

"It's noon."

Leona checked her watch. "The time just flew by."

"Always does when you're having fun."

Fun? Listening to a bunch of old geezers bad-mouth one of

their own sounded too much like church for Leona's comfort. At least Owen Pond was spared hearing the disparaging comments. Leona's ears, on the other hand, were permanently singed from the remarks of well-intentioned members rehashing her failings. But if these political dragons thought she would back down just because people had criticisms, they obviously had never chaired a Ladies Retreat Committee.

"I do need to run by and check on Mother." Leona scooped up her notes and stuffed them into her large handbag. "Maybe I'll eat at the rehab center."

"You got one hour. Make the most of it."

Leona scooted her chair away from the desk and grabbed her coat. Some fresh air would help sort out Owen's life and frame the ugly picture into some form of respectability, hopefully without aggravating Goldie with flowery, worn-out phrases. This experience had given Leona a much deeper appreciation for J.D. and all the funerals he performed when the record of the departed's life left him without one decent thing to say.

Wait a minute. Maybe J.D. still had some of those funeral sermons. Leona's pulse raced as she basked in her stroke of brilliance. She could run by the office after visiting Mother, find out what Shirley wanted, and search her husband's old files for some fresh ideas . . . eliminate several dirty birds with one stone, so to speak.

* * * * *

Tracking the smell of meat loaf, Leona located the rehab dining room. She stopped outside the closed double doors and looked through the rectangular glass. Across the bustling room, Roberta's wheelchair was wedged between two other chariot-bound patients. While the frown on her mother's face gave Leona pause, the old girl's soured expression seemed to have very little effect upon the chatty army lined up on either side of the long brown Formica table.

"Look at you, out of bed and dressed," Leona chirped as she breezed into the cafeteria. She gave her mother a quick peck on the cheek. "I've heard the first time up is rough."

"Hurts like—"

"I'm sure it does." Leona spotted a chair against the wall and hurriedly retrieved it. "Did you call this morning, Mother?"

"Would it have done any good?"

Ignoring the jab, Leona placed the chair at an empty space between two wheelchairs opposite her mother. "I got a message to call the rehab center. Have you been causing trouble?"

"If wanting to go home is causing trouble, then, yes, I have."

Before Leona could delve into her mother's reasons, the stubble-faced man on her mother's right interrupted. "Hey, who's the looker?"

"Hooker?" The gray-haired lady on her mother's left scowled. "Looks like a horse who's been rode hard and put up wet. I hate to say it, but she ain't gonna be a big moneymaker."

The woman's candor tickled Leona, but her mother snapped, "You're bad-mouthing my daughter, you old fool."

Surprise silenced Leona's levity. Had her mother just jumped to her defense? Did her mother desire a truce in their rocky relationship? Oh, what she wouldn't give not to have to share the doctor's report. Leona took a deep breath. "You probably won't go straight home, Mother."

The square-jawed woman leaned forward in her wheelchair, pounding the table with her index finger. "What do you mean?"

"The doctor won't let you go home until you can function on your own."

"Won't happen here."

"Rehab is designed to get you started. But after you finish here, you're still going to need help for a bit. I thought you could come stay with me."

"In that hovel?" Her mother stiffened ramrod-straight, crossing her hands in her lap. "Certainly not. I can afford a personal therapist in the privacy of my own home."

Feeling as misunderstood as the Wicked Witch of the West, Leona rested her elbows on the table, propped her chin with clasped hands, and prayed she wouldn't melt from the cold water Mother had tossed on her offer. "Who are your new friends, Mother?"

"Don't ask—"

"Hi. My name is Eleanor." The paper-thin artifact beside Mother flashed a toothless grin.

"Eleanor." Leona smiled at the small wisp of a woman. "Nice to meet you. Have you—"

"Hi. My name is Eleanor."

"Here we go again." Mother glowered. "Just got the wacko quiet. Why did you have to go and be all preacher's-wife friendly and pull her string?"

"Hi. My name is Eleanor."

Mother rolled her eyes and snorted. "See what I mean."

"Sorry. I didn't know. Surely she'll wear out eventually." Leona noticed the woman next to her struggling with a milk carton. She reached over and popped the waxy cardboard seal and stuck a straw through the triangle-shaped opening. "So, Mother, who's the gentleman who thinks I'm so cute?"

Mother shrugged. How could she blatantly ignore the man's intent rearranging of the food on his plate?

"Come on, Mother. What's his name?" Eyeing the man warily, Mother cupped her mouth and whispered, "Bob."

Hearing his name, Bob lit up like someone flipped his power

switch. "So who's the looker?" He winked at Leona.

"I'm Leona Harper, Bertie's daughter." Leona offered her hand around the plastic daisy stuck in a glass bud vase, but Bob had returned to positioning the half-eaten hunk of meat loaf and depleted mound of mashed potatoes.

"I've got a lovely plate of food for sale." Bob held up his melamine dinnerware. "Who'll give me five dollars? Five dollars? Do I hear four?"

"Bob was an auctioneer." The lady with the milk carton took a tiny sip on the bent straw. "Won't quit until somebody buys it."

"Who'll give me three? Did I hear three?"

"Hi. My name is Eleanor." Gumming mashed potatoes, the old woman leaned in close to Mother. "Hi. My name is—"

Mother put her hands over her ears. "Leave me alone, you decrepit bag of bones."

"Two? Anybody two? How about you, lovely lady?" Bob set the plate on the table and shoved it in Leona's direction. "One-fifty, and I'll throw in a helping of corn."

"Sold!" Leona shouted. "I'm starving." Smiling, she reached inside her purse and retrieved the money and slid it across the table. Focusing on a person who took joy in selling his lunch felt good, almost normal.

Mother slapped a veined hand over the currency. "Have you lost your mind? Don't pay him."

"Security. We've got a shady lady." Bob pushed his chair back from the table. "Security."

"Hush, you idiot." Mother snatched her fork and aimed the tines toward Bob's face.

"Mother, can't you see the man has a problem?"

"You bet he does . . . and it's me." Roberta stabbed the untouched potatoes on her plate and flicked the stiff mound right between Bob's frantic eyes.

"Food fight." Eleanor made boxer fists and jabbed the air.

Leona's mother took her glass of iced tea and dumped it in Eleanor's lap. "Shut up."

"Mother! What on earth do you think you're doing?"

"Get me out of this place, Leona, or I swear I'll tear these dingy walls down one cinder block at a time."

"No. You have to stay here. Complete your therapy." Leona yanked a cloth napkin free of the silverware it bundled. "Here, Eleanor. I'm so sorry."

"Nurse! Nurse!" Mother pounded her fork. "Nurse!"

Leona pressed her hands to the table and leaned across. "Mother, stop."

The receptionist ran into the dining room carrying a pitcher of tea. "What's going on?"

Blood flushed Leona's cheeks. Not Penny. How could she ever sign in again after this humiliation?

The aide rotated her head slowly, eagle-eyeing the cafeteria like a teacher who had stepped out of the classroom, but was confident her return would stop the chaos.

"Nurse." Mother banged the table. "Can I get some service here?"

Penny's reckoning stare landed directly on Leona's mother. She started to say something ugly, but caught herself. "Did you say please?"

Mother's unpenciled brow twitched. "Either get me out of here—" she pointed her fork in Leona's direction—"or get her out of here . . . puh-leez."

"Mother, you can't leave until you're better."

"I guess you'll be the one leaving." Leona's mother plucked a handful of meatloaf off her plate and threw it.

Ketchup and hamburger dripped from the lapel of Leona's new suit. "Mother. What on earth—"

"Roberta Worthington." Cotton stepped beside Leona. "That is enough."

Leona wanted to throw her arms around the janitor's thick neck and never let go. "Cotton. How long have you been here?"

"Long enough." He pointed at the napkin tucked into the blouse of the lady licking ketchup off her milk carton. "May I?"

Her eyes were wide over the top of her straw. "Ain't doing me any good."

"Thank you, madam." Cotton handed Leona the cloth, the brush of his touch comforting. "Clean yourself up and get back to your job, Leona. I've got it from here."

Mother straightened her back. "Oh, do you?"

"I do." Cotton squared his shoulders and marched around the table. "And you'll watch your mouth in the presence of a lady." He wrapped his large hands around Mother's wheelchair handles and spun her around on the back wheels. "Leona, Shirley needs you to drop by the church before you head back to the paper."

Leona nodded, numbly blotting the red glob spreading across her heart. Mother's aim has certainly improved since this morning. Watching Cotton push the unrepentant rabble-rouser down the hall, Leona wished there was a cliff at the end of the corridor. Then it hit her . . . Father had never, not once, silenced Mother with two words.

* * * * *

Leona knocked on the varnished door frame of the church office. "Hey, Shirley."

The secretary's head popped up from the bulletins she was folding. Salt-and-pepper tendrils framed her startled face. "You scared me to death." Color draining from her normally rosy cheeks, she clutched her sagging chest.

Leona was afraid her stealthy entrance had reduced

Shirley's chances of outliving the next pastor by at least a year. "Sorry. I used my office key to let myself in the side door. I tried making noise on my way through the building, but I guess you didn't hear me."

Shirley waved off Leona's explanation. "I've been a little spooked here by myself now that J.D. is . . ." Her voice trailed as she yanked a tissue from the box beside the office phone and dabbed at her reddened eyes.

A twinge of compassion shot through Leona. Why hadn't it dawned on her that she wasn't the only one feeling the void J.D.'s death had left? Nobody had the pastor's back like his secretary, and without a boss to guard, what would the faithful woman do?

Shirley sniffed. "Why do you smell like a meat loaf sandwich?"

"Don't ask." Covering the stain like a grade-school kid saying the pledge of allegiance, Leona massaged the ache in her heart. Standing in the very spot where J.D. greeted his secretary every morning was harder than she had expected. "Modyne said you stopped by the paper. You didn't need to drive downtown for me."

"I needed to talk to you." Shirley lowered her voice. "In person."

"About what?"

The secretary's darting gaze surveyed the office like she was James Bond and the place was bugged. "Howard asked me to get in touch with you."

On the one hand, Shirley's tendency to make everything a matter of national security irritated Leona, but on the other, she appreciated the woman's tight-lipped nature. Gossip never got a leg up on the keeper of all church secrets.

"What did our fearless leader want?"

"He wants to know when you can get J.D.'s office packed up."

The muscles in Leona's neck raised the tiny hairs that refused to stay tethered in her bun. "You mean, can I have my husband moved out by Sunday?"

Shirley gave a rueful nod. "Howard thinks the church will show better with J.D.'s things removed."

"He's afraid the kid will think this place could kill him prematurely." Leona dropped into the chair beside Shirley's desk, her mind drifting back to that tiny grad school apartment she and J.D. shared right after they married.

Seminary had been a priority once her new husband made the decision to forsake law. She loved cuddling next to him late at night, listening to his insights, watching his faith grow, and dreaming of the lost souls they'd reach once he got through Greek. Had she known those cherished moments, along with their dreams, would vanish so quickly, never to return, she would have clung to each one.

The cut-glass treat dish appeared under Leona's nose, the smell of chocolate making her painfully aware of the present. Leona refused Shirley's offered candy.

She and J.D. had been robbed. It wasn't fair. The lifetime they'd planned of doing the Lord's work together had been denied them. Everything they'd worked for was over in the blink of an eye. Suddenly, she felt tired. Old. Used up. Real mad.

Leona took a paper clip from the plastic desk holder. "Who is this kid coming to try out?" She tugged on the flimsy silver wire until the curves disappeared.

Shirley opened a file marked Résumés and took out the sheet on top. "Ted Postier. From Florida."

"Wife blonde?" Leona thrust her hastily fashioned sword in the direction of the embossed missive.

Shirley's brow crinkled. "You know them?"

"Just a guess." Leona stabbed one of the foil-covered chocolates. "Two-point-five children?" She unwrapped the skewered prize. Caramel oozed from the wound in the dark, creamy temptation.

"How did you know they had one on the way?"

"Experience."

Shirley stuffed the résumé back into the folder and picked

up her phone. "Want to call Howard yourself?" She held out the receiver, awaiting Leona's decision.

Leona contemplated touching the foundation-covered phone, shook her head, and popped the candy in her mouth. "David's coming home on Saturday." The harder she chewed, the gummier the mess became in her mouth. "I'm not moving a single box until my son gets here." One final swallow and the sweet disappeared for good. "If Howard Davis has a problem with that, tell him I'll see to it that Reverend Postier gets a welcome packet, complete with Mt. Hope's board meeting minutes for the past eighteen years."

A sly grin crossed Shirley's lipstick-feathered lips. "Have them right here." She hung up the phone and pointed at the large cardboard box marked Confidential sitting beside her desk.

Warmth buzzed along Leona's veins like a caffeine boost. "You'd do that for me?"

Shirley nodded. "In a heartbeat."

"You're a peach."

"You're tougher than you think." Shirley nudged the treat bowl closer. "And don't forget it."

Taking another decadent goodie, Leona wondered why God opted for fire when it came to shaping his children. Why pain and suffering? It didn't seem fair. It wasn't fair. If she were in charge of the world, the good guys would be dipped in chocolate and the bad ones covered in meat loaf.

When she got to heaven, Leona expected the Lord to address his confounded decision, and if he didn't, she intended to bring it up. But first she would pin J.D. to the wall for throwing her into the furnace and telling God she was ready for the heat.

Chapter Twenty

Maddie hoisted her bulging suitcase off the conveyor belt. She scanned the crowded baggage claim area. Her friend's height and mop of curly hair should make him easy to spot. No Parker. Maybe he was circling the terminal waiting for her to pop out of the automated doors.

Pushing through fretful passengers, Maddie was thankful her flight had not been cancelled. The forecast called for worsening weather conditions. Several inches of snow were expected during the afternoon and evening.

She was relieved Parker didn't have to make the drive into the city for nothing. This was not the weather to inconvenience friends.

Friends?

Twice, in a matter of minutes, Parker's ambiguous word had bullied its way into her thoughts. Maybe her subconscious needed reassuring this arrangement was not open to interpretation. Limits had to be set and maintained or someone could get hurt. Maddie zipped her parka. Friends suited her fine.

Maddie popped the handle of her wheeled bag and stepped into the biting cold. Snow whipped under the covered pick-up area. She checked the line of idling cars. No Parker. Where was he? And why was she so disappointed he wasn't here?

An arctic blast swooped in from the north and nipped that last ridiculous thought in the bud. Whew! What she meant was, nobody likes to be stranded at an airport during the holidays. Maddie hustled back into the terminal. She found an empty place along the cinder block wall and slid to the floor. She dug out her cell phone and punched in Parker's number.

"Maddie?" The tenseness in his voice aroused Maddie's concern. "Guessing you landed safely."

"Yeah. You all right?"

"Roads are awful. But I'm almost there. Give me a few minutes. Stay inside where it's warm. I'll pull up to baggage claim and call you."

Envisioning Parker's large white knuckles gripping the wheel accelerated Maddie's heart rate. "Don't hurry. I'm fine."

Just because she didn't want harm to come to Parker didn't imply he was more than a friend. Friends worried about friends, and there wasn't a thing wrong with that. Right? Why did knowing Parker was on his way make her feel . . . safe? You're still raw from everything. Get hold of yourself, girl. She went to the snack counter, bought a cappuccino, a bag of trail mix, and the last piece of pecan pie. Parker loved pie.

Maddie dismissed the self-condemnation for acting upon her unsettling impulse. Friends eat pie. It was a considerate gesture. No more.

Someone had nabbed her spot along the wall, but a seat had been abandoned in front of the windows. One eye on her phone and one on the cars inching past, she munched raisins and cashews. The minutes dragged on.

Finally, Parker called.

She quickly gathered her belongings, balancing the cellophane-wrapped dessert on her wheeled suitcase. Parker waited on the other side of the automated doors. Black curls peeked out from under a red stocking cap pulled over his ears, and a Santa Claus grin crinkled the corners of his eyes. She couldn't help but smile. She stepped on the activator, and the doors parted.

"You look great, Maddie." Exhaust fumes polluted swirls of white precipitation.

"You're quite the sight yourself." Resisting the urge to hug him, Maddie unlocked her gaze from his and searched her pockets for gloves. "It's cold here. Has it been like this all day?"

"It's getting worse." They stood for an awkward moment, avoiding each other's eyes, their breath forming overlapping vapor clouds in the frigid air.

"Pie?" Parker pointed at the snow-dusted plate. "For me?"

"I usually leave Santa milk and cookies, but this is all they had."

"If you've been a good girl, Santa is not too picky." He picked up the plate, his warm breath fogged the cellophane. "The way to the heart is through the stomach."

"I'm glad you're not operating on me." Maddie shivered and crossed her arms over her chest.

"You may not know this, but I wield a mean spading fork. A flick of the wrist and I could pluck your heart out like a new potato." He held the pie under his nose and inhaled as if he could smell the caramelized filling right through the wrapper. "I'm starving."

Maddie laughed for the first time in several days. To her surprise, warmth surged through the veins Justin had proclaimed clogged with ice. The shards crept away from her heart like an early spring thaw.

"Hey, mister. You born in a barn?" a man holding a crying baby shouted, waving his fist as he paced inside the waiting area. "Get off the door sensor."

"Sorry, sir." Parker took Maddie's elbow and gently guided her off the automated door pad. "I'd hoped we could stop and grab a bite to eat, but the roads are deteriorating faster than predicted. Once it gets dark, they'll be slick as glass."

"We better get going." Maddie's gaze locked with Parker's intent creamy brown eyes. "Parker?"

Red flushed his cheeks. "Oh. Right. Let me get that." He opened the truck door, stepped aside and helped Maddie in. He handed over the pie. "Guard this with your life."

While Parker tossed the suitcase into the truck bed, Maddie searched the littered floorboard for an empty spot to put her feet. Seed catalogues, weather reports, and Farmers' Almanacs were tumbled amongst the remnant smells of seed corn and fertilizer.

Parker climbed into the cab. "Sorry for the mess. I thought I'd have time to clean up a bit, but—"

"Let me guess. The Storys had a cucumber emergency."

"How did you know?" Parker grinned, shifting into drive. As the wheels spun on the wet pavement, the back of the truck swayed back and forth.

"Whoa, Santa." Maddie clutched the shoulder strap holding her against the seat. "Little slick for the sleigh?"

Concern creased Parker's brow. "Maybe we should stay at your grandmother's place."

"No way." Maybe she wasn't the risk taker Justin was, but she had too much rebel in her to turn back now. Besides, in her needy state of mind, spending the night with Parker in the same house was riskier than slick roads. "Let's do this."

"Okay, it's Mt. Hope or bust." He nudged the gas pedal, and they crawled away from the curb. "On Cupid. On Dasher."

Inching down the interstate ramp, Parker eased the large vehicle into the first opening in the slow-flowing traffic.

The hum of the heater filled the silence. Maddie noticed her chauffeur didn't seem bothered by the lull in conversation. Why should he? They'd known each other for years. In fact, their parents played spades every Friday night.

As kids, they'd been dragged to those boring card tournaments and expected to entertain each other. Parker read farm magazines while Maddie operated on stuffed animals. Once in a while Parker would show her a tractor picture he admired, and if Maddie needed help stitching up her stuffed Batchy Bear, Parker willingly held the furry patient steady.

Watching him now, she decided that either Parker felt the same familiar comfort they'd known when they were young, or keeping the truck on the road demanded every ounce of his concentration. And no one concentrated with Parker's intensity. The year he and Maddie were assigned to the same Bible Bowl team, he carried the study guide with him wherever he went, poring over the many kings of Israel. But Parker's dedication paid off at the contest. He laid bare one dirty royal deed after another, and their team won the trophy. Near as she could tell, he was clueless that it had been his persistence that carried the day then, or how she was counting on him now.

"So, did I forget to shave or something?" Parker's question dislodged Maddie from the sticky web of their entangled lives.

What is wrong with me? Maddie felt her face flush like it used to when she pronounced Batchy Bear a goner, but Parker insisted she perform mouth to mouth. "Busted."

"Busted staring at me or thinking about something else?"

Maddie struggled with the shoulder harness to get at the zipper on her coat. She wished she'd spent less time traipsing down memory lane and more time making herself comfortable before belting herself into this predicament. "I was wondering why you'd do this for me."

"You'd do it for me, right?"

Would I? Maddie bristled against the pat-answer training of her youth. Somewhere along the line she'd outgrown her willingness to follow suit and give the desired answers without question. She was a grown-up, determined to be free of duty. But despite her progress, the odds of ignoring Momma's years of continual guilt transfusions were slim to none.

Listening to the rhythmic swipe of the wipers pushing snow into heaps on the windshield, Maddie wished her conflicted state could be so easily obliterated. She looked at Parker, wanting to say she'd climb a mountain if he needed her to, but instead she shrugged.

"You'd leave me stranded at the airport in a blizzard?" Doubt flickered in his eyes.

"Maybe."

Parker shook his head. "Anybody who'd sweat through four years of medical school, with plans to dedicate her life to saving the world, would never leave a friend stuck in a snowdrift." He lifted a bushy brow. "I doubt Batchy would be pleased."

"Who?" How in the world did Parker do it? How did he read her mind as easily as he read farm magazines?

"What would that scruffy little fellow say concerning your sudden bout of hard-heartedness . . . and after he sacrificed his furry, poly-filled body to advance your ability to save the world?"

A smile tugged at the corner of Maddie's mouth as she remembered Momma stitching her favorite teddy bear back together after an emergency appendectomy or reattaching button eyes after a cataract removal. "What makes you think I want to save the world?"

"Friend to friend? Saving the world is part of the Harper DNA."

"What makes you think we're friends?"

"Why did you call?"

Maddie cocked her head and stared at the straightforward man awaiting her answer. "I needed a ride."

Parker cranked the radio dial and the twang of the country-western station filled the cab. "You could have called Melvin." He drummed his fingers on the steering wheel to the beat rattling Maddie's nerves. "Things have been a little slow for him since Bertie's been laid up."

Maddie flipped the knob to a classical station. "I don't want anything from my grandmother."

"You don't want anything from anybody."

"Everything is black-and-white for you, isn't it, Parker? No gray matter. How easy life must be when all major decisions are color-coded." Maddie could not restrain the sarcasm creeping into her rising voice. "Don't know what to do with your life? Pick a card and there the perfect answer will be written out in nice, neat penmanship. Need to know where a relationship is going? No problem. Either you marry or you break up. It's all in the cards. Just pick one."

"Is that why you called? Something happen between you and Justin?"

Maddie's jaw tightened. "A cucumber expert *and* a relationship counselor. Talented guy, aren't you?"

"You said it, not me." Parker flipped the radio station back to country. "Knight in shining armor gets to pick the music."

Large, wet flakes covered the windshield faster than the wipers could keep up. Maddie turned toward the passenger window, her hot breath forming a foggy little cloud on the glass. Next to Momma, no one could get her riled like this. She didn't need psychoanalysis; she just needed a ride home. That's it. Nothing more. Just a ride.

Drifting snow blurred the edges of the road. A blizzard warning interrupted the country song. Maddie inhaled slowly, fortifying her brain with fresh oxygen and hoping she could regain control of her emotions. She curled one leg up under her, bumping into something hard.

She pulled out the paperback book wedged under her foot. "What's this?"

"Spanish."

"I can see that it's Spanish, but why do you have it?"

"Can't a man be bilingual if he is so inclined?" Parker's tone had an icy edge Maddie was sure the weather had not put there.

"Certainly, but why do *you* want to learn Spanish?"

"You're bilingual."

Maddie straightened in the bucket seat. "What does that have to do with anything?"

He took his eyes off the road for a second and stared straight at her. "Okay, you've got me."

If it was not his directness that disturbed her, why did Maddie feel she had broken the seal on a Christmas present for an early peek . . . a forbidden thrill she had no right to demand?

Parker continued, his face all serious. "I want to be able to read the menu at a Mexican restaurant."

Hoping to cover her disappointment at his refusal to let her trespass beyond the fence she'd erected between them, Maddie laughed. "Parker, don't tease."

Immediately he returned his focus to the indiscernible line between pavement and sky, the muscle in his clenched square jaw twitching.

Maddie reached out and touched his jacket. She could feel the heat beneath the wool surface but he did not pull away. He never had. "Why Spanish, Parker?"

"Okay. If you really must know." Again, he looked into her eyes. "I plan to work in South America."

"You're leaving?" The words constricted Maddie's airway. Served her right for being such an inquiring mind. Now her persistence had paid off. He'd answered her question. Why wasn't she more pleased at hitting pay dirt?

"Yes."

"When?" she managed to cough out.

He shrugged. "After I save enough money."

Brake lights glowed up ahead. Parker lightly touched the brakes and the truck bed fishtailed back and forth before sliding to a stop.

Maddie exhaled slowly, squeezing the paper dictionary tight. "What are you going to do down there?"

"You said Third World countries are crying for folks who know agriculture."

"I didn't say that."

"You did."

"When?"

"The summer you came home from Guatemala." Parker lifted his foot from the brake and touched the gas. "Here we go. Hang on."

"You're going to give up your job in the States because of something a naïve college girl said years ago?"

"I'm going because I feel called." Voice firm, knuckles white, Parker steered the truck through the rutted tracks left by the few fearless morons still on the road.

"Who called?"

"God."

"You sure?"

"I'm positive."

Maddie could not believe what she was hearing from this grown, seemingly levelheaded man. Who, besides her parents, actually believed God spoke to them? "I know a pastor who thought the same thing, and look what that foolishness did to him."

"I saw what it did to him. Accepting God's call made your father one of the happiest men on the planet."

Maddie chewed on the barbs of truth. Parker was right. Her father was one of the most fulfilled people she'd ever known. The Reverend Harper looked for the good in every circumstance, from a drop in contributions to the Storys dropping in. "Count it all joy," he would say. How had Parker known her father so much better than she? Maddie's curiosity refused to let the discussion end. "So what does this call include?"

"I intend to go down there, teach poor people how to feed their families and, more importantly, how to feed their souls."

"Parker, look out!" Maddie screamed.

Her warning came too late. The sound of metal impacting metal pierced the storm. Then silence.

* * * * *

Leona picked up her cell and scrolled to the number of her mother's chauffeur.

"Melvin, how are the roads?"

"Pretty rough, but I'm almost to the city."

"I just wanted to let you know, David has been delayed. He said they diverted his flight to Atlanta."

"I'm not surprised. This weather is worsening."

"Why don't you go on to Mother's and wait there? I'll call when I hear from him."

"Anything else I can do while I'm in town?"

"Pick up Mother's mail. Oh, and see if Sophie can pack a few things for the old girl's rehab stay."

"I'll take care of it, Mrs. Harper."

Mrs. Harper? The title she'd cherished all these years now plucked the taut strings of her raw nerves. "Leona."

"Excuse me?" Melvin sounded confused.

"Call me Leona." Or Naomi, for I am bitter. A hammering pain echoed in the hollow cavity where her sense of purpose had resided since the day she'd said I do.

"I've got to go, but if it looks too bad, don't try to bring David home tonight. Just ride out the storm at Mother's. And Melvin . . . be careful."

* * * * *

Maddie fumbled with her seat belt. "Parker?"

His head was plastered against the headrest, his eyes closed. Blood gushed from a gash on his forehead. She peeled the glove from her trembling hand and firmly pressed the leather into the wound. She placed two fingers against the pulse point in his neck and counted. The steady beat slowed the gallop of her own racing heart. Thank God, he's alive.

"Parker?" Maddie kissed his closed eyes, tamping down her

sense of foreboding when he did not respond. "I'll be right back."

She kicked open the passenger door and stumbled out into the blinding snow. Leaving an unconscious patient was not her first choice, but someone might be injured in the other car, and moving Parker was out of the question until his spinal cord could be protected. Stepping over pieces of torn metal, Maddie made her way past the accordion-shaped hood of their truck and peeked inside the shattered driver's side window of the crumpled SUV.

Maddie pushed the air bag away from the stranger's face. A pungent white safety powder filled the air and choked her words. "Are you hurt?"

"I don't know. I don't think so." The bloodied man removed his broken glasses and wiped his eyes.

"I'm going to see if I can get you out." Maddie tugged on the mutilated latch. She breathed a sigh of relief when the door sprang open. "Before you move, let me check your injuries."

"I'm good." The middle-aged man unsnapped his seat belt. With Maddie's help he was able to slide out from under the air bag. Other than being a bit wobbly on his feet, the shaken fellow seemed fine. His teeth chattered as he rubbed his arms. "I saw your headlights, but I couldn't stop."

"None of us could." Maddie reached out to steady him,

checking the cut on the bridge of his nose. "You're not bleeding anywhere else, but you might have internal injuries. I don't want you to move around too much. Do you have a coat?"

A puzzled look clouded his face. "Yeah. Somewhere."

"Better put it on. If we keep your body heat up, that will help stave off shock."

He opened the door to the backseat and pulled out a parka. "You a doctor?"

"More or less."

"Anybody hurt in your truck?"

"My friend. He's unconscious."

Maddie shifted under his wary gaze. She wondered which part the dazed man didn't believe—that Parker was knocked out cold or that she and Parker were just friends.

In a few seconds, he turned and reached under the driver's seat. "I have a blanket. You need it?"

"That would be great." The man freed a bundle of red wool. "What else can I do? You want me to help you get your boyfriend out of that mess?"

"No. We shouldn't move him . . . unless we have no choice." Maddie looked at the man's shaken expression, amazed he could think so clearly. "Try to stay warm until help gets here. You have another blanket or anything else you can put on?"

"Was on my way up north, so I've got some stuff in the back.

How about you, lady?"

"I'm good." Maddie took the blanket. "I'll call for help, but it could be a while before anyone can get to us."

"What else can I do?"

"Are you a praying man?"

"Yes."

"Climb in your backseat, wrap up, and get to it."

Chapter Twenty-One

Pacing the airline gate, David thumped his watch and checked the departure screen. Cancelled had not appeared beside his flight number. That he might still make it home tonight should have offered some consolation, but diverting from New York to Atlanta had put him in a very non-conciliatory mood.

Keeping an eye on the serious-faced TV weatherman pointing at a swath of white in the middle of the country, he dialed his mother's cell. Still no answer. Not answering at home either. What if Momma was stranded on an icy, dark road?

David dropped into the slick vinyl seating. Momma was the one who jumped to worst-case scenarios. He'd always tried to think more like Dad. If only he could give his father a call.

From cars to girls, his father had always been a trusted sounding board . . . until they differed on what David should do with his life. Regret for the way he'd handled that conversation had haunted David for the past four years. Why had he hardened his heart and stormed out of his father's office? Why had he let his pride get the better of him and not called to apologize?

David Googled the number for the Mt. Hope Messenger. "Modyne? David Harper. Is Momma in the office?"

"No," Modyne said. "Don't expect her to come in today. I'm the only one works on Saturdays."

David fought to dismiss worse-case scenarios. "I can't get Momma to answer her phone. Just wondered if she might have come by the office."

"Most people are staying off the roads."

"It's that bad?"

"One pileup after another. You'd think these yokels had never seen snow before."

The image of Momma making him and Maddie Texas snow boots popped into his head. She'd wanted them to experience the fun of making snow angels so she spent thirty minutes duct taping plastic bags over their shoes. Growing up where there was no need to own a heavy winter coat, he knew even the smallest amount of frozen precipitation had the potential to turn Southern traffic upside down. Hopefully, Momma was not one of those brake-happy motorists spinning out of control.

David raked his fingers through his hair. "If she comes in, can you tell her that I'm still in Atlanta, but my flight is due to leave any time now?"

"Sure."

He'd pressed the tight-lipped guardian of the local news this far—might as well ask one more question. "Do you know if she was sending Melvin to get me?"

"Nope."

"Will I be able to make it to Mt. Hope tonight?"

"I doubt it. Ivan just got back with photos. Place is iced over. Looks slicker than snot."

Click.

Helplessness swirled like the wintry images on the overhead TV screens. David slid his phone in his pocket and dropped his head into his hands.

An unfamiliar hand tapped his shoulder. "Excuse me."

David lifted his throbbing head. "Can I help you?"

The well-dressed thirty-something man offered a sheepish smile. "I didn't mean to eavesdrop, but did you say you were going to Mt. Hope this evening?"

"Yes."

"Mt. Hope, Texas?"

David shifted uneasily in his seat. "Yes."

"That's where we're headed." The cheeky fellow did a half turn, panning the immaculately groomed entourage seated on a row of airport vinyl. A breathtaking blonde with a small pregnancy bump smiled while nudging the angelic children nestled on either side of her to do the same. The kids promptly obeyed.

David studied the foursome. They appeared to be ripped from the perfect pages of Facebook. "Well, let's hope we get there."

"You from Mt. Hope?" Optimism shone from the man's unduly impressed face.

"Grew up there." David intended his terse answer to end the maddening interrogation. All his life he'd been obliged to answer when people pried into his business, but not anymore. He was his own man. From now on he would divulge nothing and let the nosy world guess.

"Nice place?" The man offered a hopeful smile. Despite his unseasonable tan, pleated chinos, and Bruno Magli slip-ons, something about the inquisitive guy seemed . . . genuine.

"Nice enough." Chafed by his interrogator's ability to upset the indifference he had struggled to cultivate, David seized the opportunity to step down from the witness stand. He straightened in his seat, determined to take over the line of questioning. "Your first visit?"

"Yes, we're from Florida." The man pointed at the menacing weather map filling the television screen. "Weather in your part of the country always that . . .severe?" White lines of apprehension creased his bronze face.

He felt a little shady employing his mother's tactics. Momma was an expert at throwing the curious off the trail by appearing interested in them, inquiring into their lives. Before the busybodies knew what hit them, they'd spill their guts, forgetting the original purpose of their fishing expedition. But something about this family drove him on.

"Mt. Hope might be a little less tropical than you're used to. What brings you to town?" David leaned forward, invading the man's personal space . . . another trick Momma had taught him. "Visiting family for the holidays?"

The stranger shook his stylishly mussed head. "Going to look at a new work."

David's ears perked at the unusual phrasing. "Work?" Comprehension knotted his innards. Pausing, he weighed whether or not he wanted the answer to the next question perched on the tip of his tongue. "What do you do?"

"I'm a pastor." The man offered his hand. "Forgive my manners. Let me introduce myself. Ted Postier. This is my wife, Bridget."

David stared at the callous-free palm. What were the odds he'd end up on the same plane as the man coming to replace his father? Even Momma couldn't have fathomed this worse-case scenario. David sputtered incoherent sounds, unable to force completed thoughts past the constriction in his chest. He fell back in the chair, grateful for the solid back breaking his fall.

"Are you all right?" Concern crinkled the flawless features of the blonde Barbie who had joined her husband, as if on cue. "Apparently the last guy died, so the congregation is looking for someone young and full of energy." She gazed adoringly at her Ken doll, ignoring the stranger spinning in the airport seat.

Gulping air, David spit out, "Reverend Harper always struck me as a pretty active fellow."

"There comes a time when everyone has to face their limitations. Some guys are never willing to retire." Bridget's perfect smile would be minus its synthetic dazzle once Momma wiped it off her face.

"Even fewer are willing to die with the name of Jesus on their lips." David picked up his bag. "I believe they're boarding our flight."

Trudging down the narrow gateway, the sticky hot breath of the replacement preacher and his perfect family scorched the back of David's neck.

Fly or remain stranded. Whatever he chose, David realized this time that running was not an option.

Chapter Twenty-Two

Leona dropped her keys into the ceramic bowl on the kitchen counter and tossed her coat into the hall closet. She turned on a lamp and collapsed into J.D.'s recliner. Tater jumped up and wiggled in beside her, his furry body a warm comfort against the freezing winds rattling the parsonage windows.

Letting out a long, exhausted breath, Leona stroked the dog's silky coat. "I should start a fire, but I'm too tired to carry in the wood."

Memories of many nights sitting in front of a roaring fire, wrapped in J.D.'s strong arms, flickered in her mind. Tears trickled down her cheeks. Ignoring the pity-filled gazes she encountered everywhere she went was the only way she managed to hold back. Relief swept over her as she unlocked the bulging floodgates. "Tater, we made it through the week . . . and I thought church work was rough," she blubbered.

The cocker heaved a sympathetic sigh and rested his hairy chin on Leona's lap.

She was talking to a dog. What choice did she have? It was

either the dog, the wall, or heaven forbid, herself. She pulled a tissue from her pocket and blew her nose.

Kindling the flames of her neglected creativity this week had required so much effort that Leona did not have a minute to stew over the uncertain future. Forcing words to flow from her head, through her fingers, and onto the page had given her an amazing sense of accomplishment. But most importantly, the hard work had temporarily stunted the growth rate of the bitterness choking the arteries to her heart.

Lord, help me accept your will for my future.

Was it circumstance or choice that had shortchanged her time with the Lord these past few days? She'd told herself that once things settled down, she'd get back into the swing of a regular devotional time. But the truth was, for the first time in her life, she understood Jonah's desire to run one way while God waited in the opposite direction. When she was ready to resume her conversations with the Almighty, he had some serious explaining to do.

The ring of the phone startled Leona from her argument with God.

With a sigh, she lowered the recliner footrest. "Tater, I'm going to have to teach you how to pull your weight around here." Hopscotching over the dog, she made it to the kitchen phone before the answering machine clicked on.

Leona held on to the counter while the agitated woman on the other end of the line ranted. When she took a breath, Leona cut in. "What do you mean you're kicking my mother out of rehab?"

"We're evicting her immediately."

"Penny, let me see if I'm understanding you correctly. You want me to come get Mother now?"

"Right now."

"Have you seen the weather?"

Penny cleared her throat. "Mrs. Harper, your mother pulled the fire alarm. To make matters worse, she tried to escape while Charlie and his volunteers had the back door open. She would have made it, too, had she been able to get her wheels over their fire hose."

"I'm sure—"

"Mrs. Worthington is a liability the rehab center cannot afford. She's got to go! Tonight!"

"Well, can't you tie her to the bed or something?"

"And get sued?" Penny's snappish tone didn't offer much room for negotiation, but Leona refused to be deterred.

"I don't have a bedroom downstairs, and I'm sure I can't get her up the stairs by myself."

"We'll loan you a hospital bed . . . free of charge. Set it up in your living room, the garage, or the sidewalk. But you've got to get that woman out of here tonight."

"Okay, okay. Give me a minute to think." Leona cupped her pounding forehead while slogging through her limited options. "I guess I can send Cotton over with the truck to get the bed, and I'll come with the van to load up Mother."

"She'll be packed and ready to go. Just pull in under the drive-through and we'll shove her out the front door."

"It will take me a few minutes with the roads like they are. Could you at least wait until you see my headlights before you toss an old lady out in the cold?"

"Very well." Penny sounded put out. "Oh, and Mrs. Harper, I'm afraid we'll have to charge extra to paint over the pickle juice."

"Put it on her bill." Leona slammed down the receiver. "Could this week get any worse, Tater?" She yanked her coat from the hanger, grabbed her purse and keys, and headed out into the storm.

* * * * *

Leona scurried around J.D.'s tiny home office, helping Cotton toss books and bric-a-brac into a box. "Tater, get off the couch."

The dog sighed and jumped down.

"You expect me to convalesce in this hole?" Mother clucked from her wheelchair, blocking the doorway.

Anger pulsed against the top of Leona's skull like a pressure cooker lid ready to blow. "So help me, I'm going to kill her and tell God she died," she mumbled to Cotton as she thrust the heavy box at him.

"It's so small in here that if I got bit by a mosquito, I wouldn't have room to swell."

"Maybe you should have considered the possibility of second-rate accommodations before you threw pickles, caused a food fight, and pulled the fire alarm." In one clean sweep, Leona cleared the top of J.D.'s desk into another box she'd dug out of the chilly garage. "Would it be too much to ask if, for once, you thought of someone besides yourself?"

"You're one to talk."

"So help me, Mother—"

"Ladies. This isn't helping." Cotton eased past Leona with hide-a-bed cushions stacked on top of his sturdy arms. "Bertie, you're gonna have to back that chair up so I can get this couch out of here."

"Why can't I go home?"

"Because your broom is unavailable." Leona shoved J.D.'s desk into the tight corner. "In case you haven't noticed, we're having a blizzard. I barely got us back to the house. I doubt Melvin will be able to get David here, let alone turn around and take you back to the city."

"Bertie, move that chair or I'll do it for you." Cotton's tone meant business, and his glare over the cushions said he was the man to complete the transaction.

Leona's mother cocked her head defiantly. "You don't have to get testy, mister." She released the brake and slowly backed away from the door, allowing Cotton just enough room to squeeze out. "I missed dinner. I don't suppose you could make me something to eat, Leona."

"None of us have eaten, Mother. Your stomach is going to have to wait. Cotton and I have to get that bed off his truck before it's covered over with snow." Leona stepped past her mother and gave the wheelchair a jarring shove down the hall. "Now, stay out of the way while we get this room cleared. Tater, keep her out of here."

The dog obediently dropped in front of Mother's feet. "Move it, mutt, before I have you made into a throw rug." Leona's mother nudged him with her good foot.

Tater growled, the hair on the back of his neck standing at attention.

"Stay, Tater." Leona flattened her palm toward the cocker's snarling face. "If she tries to get past you, boy . . . bite her."

Her mother's granite gaze morphed into the picture of composure regained. "I believe the law allows prisoners bread and water." Roberta Worthington would have made an amazing trial lawyer, no question about it.

"You want supper? Open a can of soup." Leona stormed back into the study and started throwing more books into a box. The flames of her temper flared with each item of memorabilia she cleared from the shelves.

Cotton returned to the room, remaining wisely silent. Arms crossed, the longtime family friend rubbed his gray chin stubble, giving the impression he was as stumped as Rodin's Thinker. In a few minutes, he cleared his throat. "Leona, maybe you could grab one end of this couch while I take the other."

"I'm so mad right now, Cotton, I think I could spin this old parsonage until the front door opened to the backyard."

"Well, how about we put your muscle where your mouth is?" Cotton winked and Leona felt her heat index drop a notch from steaming to a rolling simmer.

She picked an end, braced her feet, placed two hands under the ratty arm of the couch, and prepared to lift with her legs. Cotton took the other end. Together, they pulled and tugged until they wrestled the heavy monstrosity from the room. Once in the deserted hall, they set it down and slid it out of the way.

"Whew! Not so cold any more, is it?" Leona dropped onto the couch arm and caught her breath. No sign of Mother. "Hunger must have driven the lioness to prowl the kitchen."

Cotton chuckled. He took out his hanky and mopped his

forehead. "Sure wish Parker was in town. I would have asked him to come give us a hand."

"Where is he?"

"Uh . . ." Cotton stuffed his hanky into his back pocket.

Something didn't feel right. Maybe this sense of foreboding was her pesky hypersensitive feelers kicking in again, but more likely it was the uncharacteristic shade of red on Cotton's face. "Where is Parker?"

"In the city to pick up . . . a package."

"The city?" Leona jumped up. "Oh no. I hope he isn't still on the road."

"Parker's smarter than that." Cotton wiped the dust from his hands, brushing away Leona's unfounded fears with the nonchalant action. "Why don't you run the vacuum over that carpet while I bring in the mattress. I'll let you help me unload the bed frame. Once we get that hospital bed set up, we'll slip the old girl a couple of pain pills and things will settle down." His eyes twinkled reassurance, melting Leona's visions of icy catastrophe.

"Cotton, you're a prince."

"Just a servant, kiddo."

Tater barked and bolted from the kitchen. He raced through the hall, and headed for the living room.

"Girlfriend." The familiar Southern alto called from the front room.

Leona whirled. "Roxie? What are you doing out in this weather?" She glanced at Cotton. "Did you call her?"

Cotton shook his head, confusion and denial creasing his face.

"How did you know we needed help?" Leona fell into her friend's arms and wrapped herself in the comfort. "I don't care how you knew; I'm just so glad to see you."

Roxie pried herself loose. "Leona, you better sit down."

Leona stepped back and studied Roxie's face. Only someone who had been Roxie's labor and delivery coach for her change-of-life surprise bundle would have recognized the revealing twitch of angst in the corner of the perfectly lined lips.

Fear seized Leona. "What's going on?"

Roxie's eyes became liquid. "There's been an accident."

"David?"

Mother poked her head out of the kitchen. "Accident?" Bony arms pumping, her wheelchair sped down the hall. "Is it Marvin?"

"Melvin! Your driver's name is MELVIN, Roberta!" Roxie freed herself from Mother's white-knuckled grip and guided Leona to the hide-a-bed. "Sit down, girlfriend."

Leona waved her off. "Just tell me, Roxie."

"It's Parker."

"Oh, no."

"And Maddie." The walls of the crowded little hall closed in. "That can't be right." She struggled to breathe. "Maddie's in Denver."

Roxie shook her head. "She was coming home early . . . to surprise you."

The empty place in Leona's womb quivered. "Surprise me?"

"For Christmas. Help you decorate. Make things as normal as possible."

"Maddie wanted to come home?" Leona could not hold back the tears. J.D.'s death had accomplished the reconciliation nothing else could. Her Maddie had wanted to come home. "What happened?"

"Parker went to get her. His truck slid off the road. Bounced off a guardrail," Roxie paused, obviously what was next wasn't good. "They spun into oncoming traffic. An SUV hit them head-on."

A scream started to form in the pit of Leona's belly. She clamped her hand over her mouth. Afraid to ask, but desperate to know, she squeezed her daughter's name past the barrier guarding her trembling lips. "Maddie. Have I lost my Maddie?"

Roxie shot a worried glance at Cotton, who gave her the nod to continue. "Maddie's cut up, but she's all right."

"Praise God." Leona slumped onto the couch like a

pinpricked balloon. She dragged the back of her hand under her nose, relief bolstering her willingness to risk one more question. "What about Parker?"

"He's alive, but unconscious."

"How do you know?"

"Maddie called."

Leona jumped to her feet. "Why didn't Maddie call me?"

"Because she did not want you to hear this bad news alone."

Alone. Alone. Alone. The terrifying word clanged in Leona's head like the rusty bell in the church steeple. Where was J.D. when she needed him? Or God, for that matter? *Don't fall apart. You don't have the luxury of falling apart. If you do, who will rescue your girl?*

Leona paced. She had to think. Think fast. She swiped frantically at the tears cascading down her face. "What can we do? How can I get to my baby?"

"You can't." Mother wheeled her chair into Leona's path and grabbed her flailing hands. "That van of yours would never make it."

Leona jerked free. "If you think I'm the kind of mother who would sit here while her daughter is—"

"Melvin's got the limo. It's a heavy vehicle. Send him for Maddie and Parker." Compassion softened the decisive edge in her mother's rapid-fire commands.

Leona stopped. "Mother, that's brilliant." She kissed her mother's cheek. "David should have landed. Between the two of them, surely they can get to Maddie. I'll try to call." She ran to her purse and dug out her cell phone. "God, let Melvin have David. And please God, forget I asked for Nineveh. My kids need you on the interstate."

Chapter Twenty-Three

David avoided eye contact with the pensive Postiers as they circled their mound of matching luggage. Had the tanned interlopers been clad in Western attire rather than those ridiculous matching windbreakers, they would have resembled a wagon train party on the lookout for warring natives. If they joined hands and prayed before the baggage turnstile, he'd lose it.

David adjusted the heavy bag strap slung over his shoulder. Ted—the name the reverend insisted David call him—had mentioned during their rough flight that the church was sending an elder to meet his family at the airport. David hadn't said anything, including giving away who he was, but he knew there was no way Howard would take one of his shiny Caddies out on salted roads. And Harold and Horace were too chicken to come alone. The Postiers didn't know it yet, but they were stranded.

"Uh . . . Ted?" David tapped the shivering man on the back of his lightweight jacket. "You folks need a ride?"

"We aren't sure what to do." Uncertainty lined Ted's brow.

"Maybe we should just get a hotel room."

David cast a wave over the sea of stranded travelers. "You think they'd be sleeping on the floor if there were rooms left in the city?"

Ted zipped his windbreaker. "I'm sure the Lord will provide."

"He just did." David pointed to the black shiny limo gliding to a stop outside the baggage claim windows.

Bridget peered over Ted's shoulder. Her blue eyes grew saucer-sized. "Yours?"

"So to speak. Look, I've got plenty of room and—" David's cell vibrated in his pocket. Momma's number was on the caller ID. "Excuse me, I need to get this. Take your stuff on out there and Melvin will load you up."

Ted shook his head. "We hate to inconvenience—"

David held up his hand and stopped Ted's protests. He poked his finger in his free ear, blocking out the airport noise. "Momma, I've landed and Mel . . . What? . . .When? . . . How bad? . . . Where are they? . . . We're on our way. . . . Yes, as soon as I know anything. . . . I promise. We'll be careful. . . . I love you, too, Momma."

"Is there a problem?" Ted's commiserating expression must have garnered an A-plus in Ministry 101, Crisis Management.

"My sister and a friend were involved in a car accident between here and Mt. Hope."

"We can help." Bridget placed a confident hand on David's arm. "We're trained in crisis management."

David almost voiced his objection to counting hospital visits as medical training. But at this moment, he did not have the luxury of cross-examining them. He grabbed two pieces of Postier luggage off the pile. "Let's move."

* * * * *

The anxious eyes of the Postiers followed every fidgety move David made on the limo's slippery seats. David rapped a knuckle on the half-lowered window separating passengers and driver. "Melvin, can't you go any faster?"

"Not if you want to avoid the ditches, sir."

Ted rubbed his reddened hands together as if the friction would return them to their original sun-kissed state. "Would you like us to pray?"

"No."

"Do you mind if I use your phone? Mine seems to lack service in this part of the country."

David pointed to the phone on the car wall. "Be my guest."

"I just need to let Elder Davis know that we have secured transportation." Ted stopped his frantic hand warm-up and blew between his cupped palms.

"We wouldn't want the good elder worrying about your health and well-being." David tapped on the window. "Melvin, could you turn up the heat? Our guests are a little chilly."

The chauffeur glanced into the mirror and rolled his eyes.

Bridget pried apart her blue lips and offered what reminded David of Momma's stock grateful smile.

The reverend extracted a tiny slip of paper from his pocket and began punching the phone's black buttons. He cleared his throat as he waited with the phone to his ear. "Brother Davis? Ted Postier . . . Oh, yes, sir. Not a scratch on us. . . . Had a few delays, but we've made it to the city. . . . Of course, you couldn't risk these roads. . . . No hotel rooms available, but God provided. We're on our way to Mt. Hope now. . . . Nice fellow offered us his limo. . . . His name?" Red-faced, Ted put his hand over the receiver. "Forgive me, but I haven't even asked your name."

"David."

"Says his name is David. . . . Well, I guess it could be Harper, but I didn't ask. He mentioned he grew up in Mt. Hope. Maybe you know him. . . . Sir? . . . Hello, sir?" Ted stared at the buzzing phone and shrugged. "The storm must have broken our connection."

David suppressed a guilty chuckle, knowing full well weather was not the culprit. Howard's lightbulb-shaped head had shorted out when the little snake realized Momma had called in legal reinforcements. David's only regret: he wasn't there to see the elder squirm.

"What was your little sister doing out in this weather?" Bridget's question interrupted David's mental revelry.

"Coming home from med school."

"Your parents are probably worried sick." Her portrait-perfect face was a masterpiece of concern. This girl was good.

Parents?

He and Maddie had been blessed to grow up in a house where the father loved the mother and both adored their children. Why had he taken that blessing for granted? What he wouldn't give to right that wrong, along with several others gnawing at his guilty conscience.

"Momma's a tough cookie."

"And your father?"

"Recently deceased."

"Oh." Bridget blushed. "I'm so sorry. How did it happen?"

"Work-related incident."

"What kind of work did your father do?"

"Pastored a miserable little church."

* * * * *

Maddie huddled as close to Parker's slumped body as she dared. It seemed they'd been frozen that way for hours, but when she checked the time on her phone, only a few minutes had passed since she called Aunt Roxie. She adjusted the blanket. Hoping to slow the escape of their body heat, she wrapped her arms around Parker.

Resting her head on Parker's shoulder, she felt the comforting rise and fall of his chest. Wake up, Parker. Please wake up. The snow whipped through their mangled vehicle. If the storm kept up this pace, before long they would be buried. Finding them would *be impossible. Lord, please. I know I have no right to ask, but please, for Parker's sake, send help.*

The vibration of her cell phone against her gloveless hand startled Maddie. That was the fastest answer God had ever sent. She looked at the caller ID. "Momma?" Grateful tears stung her cold nose.

"Maddie, are you all right?" Conviction that she would not be otherwise rang in her mother's voice.

"I wanted to surprise you."

"You surprised me, sweetheart."

Maddie remembered the time she wanted to make breakfast in bed for her mother. She'd planned the menu for days. Toast, cereal, and orange juice. On the fateful morning, she dropped the orange juice jug, cereal went everywhere but the bowl, and the toast burned. But Momma acted like she was still asleep when Maddie stumbled into her bedroom with the tray. Momma had her faults, but ruining a surprise wasn't one of them, even if she had to fake it.

"And Parker?"

The question brought Maddie back to the dire situation. She glanced at his still face. "I'm not sure."

"Is it safe for you to stay put?"

Maddie closed her eyes against the darkening sky. She could fib too, if necessary. "Truck's probably totaled. But we're out of the snow. The man that hit us gave us a blanket."

"Great. Here's what I want you to do. Can you hear me, Maddie?"

"Yes, Momma."

"Stay right where you are. Melvin and David are not far behind you. They should be there any minute. I've checked with the Highway Patrol. They're trying to get help there."

"Good. I'd hate to move Parker without a board."

"Hopefully you won't have to. Now, see if you can get the truck flashers to come on; that will make it easier for David to spot you."

"David?"

"He's on his way from the airport."

"I hope he doesn't wreck." Maddie searched the crumpled dash and found the emergency button. She pushed and miraculously an orange glow from the truck's lights cut through the snow. "They work."

"Of course they do." Momma's confidence transcended the

airwaves, warming Maddie's numb extremities. "I've been praying."

"Momma, can you stay on the line until David gets here?"

"I won't leave you, Maddie. I promise." The words covered Maddie with a blanket of comfort.

"I know, Momma."

Momma cleared her throat. "Why don't you tell me what you're doing in the truck with Parker Kemp."

"I needed to come home."

"It's okay, baby." Momma's small talk drifted in and out of Maddie's prayers that the flashers would be enough.

* * * * *

Sirens and lights cut through the deepening darkness, arousing Maddie's numb limbs. "I think help is here, Momma . . . Momma? Oh no, my battery is dead." She dropped her phone and wiggled out from under the blanket.

Parker opened his eyes. "What happened?"

"Don't move." Maddie touched the glove stuck to his forehead. "We need to fix that gash on your hard head."

"I remember spinning around, but—" A hooded paramedic pounded on the passenger side of the truck. "Anybody hurt?"

Maddie pointed toward the SUV. "There's a man in the backseat of that vehicle who appears fine, but he might have internal injuries."

Parker cut Maddie a sideways glance. "Looks like I slept through all the fun." He lifted his hand and brushed snow from Maddie's hair. "But I'm sure the good doctor didn't need any help."

"When you get a chance, we need to cuff this man's neck and tape his ungrateful mouth," Maddie informed the paramedic before he disappeared in the snow.

Headlights pierced the freezing curtain of white and pulled alongside the flashing lights.

"Maddie!" David's voice cut through the wind. He reached inside the cab. "Oh, thank God, you're alive." He drew her into his arms and squeezed tight. "You're not hurt, are you?"

"I wasn't until you broke my ribs." Maddie cocked her head back and looked into David's moist eyes.

"Sorry, I—"

She put a finger over her brother's trembling lips. "Thought I died?"

David hugged her again. "Thank God you didn't."

"Hey, in case anyone was wondering, I didn't die either." Parker's head rested on the seat.

Releasing Maddie, David asked, "Is he going to be all right?"

Maddie lifted the bloody glove stuck to Parker's forehead. "He's destined to be a knot head, but I think he'll live."

Parker flashed a smile as crooked as his truck bumper. "I

dreamed an angel was kissing me, begging me to open my eyes."

"Kissing angels, Dr. Harper?" David grinned.

"He's delirious." Maddie felt her cheeks flush. "Totally unaware of what he's saying."

"No, I'm sure an angel kissed me," Parker insisted, a wry grin activating his charming dimples.

Maddie turned to David. "See what's keeping that medic. This guy is worse than I thought."

Chapter Twenty-Four

Leona dropped onto the plaid couch, the silent phone clenched in her hand. "I lost her."

"Maybe her battery died." Cotton placed a firm hand on Leona's shoulder. "Try calling David."

"Sounds like a plan." Roxie fished her phone out of her shirt and handed it to Leona. "Use mine. You're probably about out of battery too."

Balancing the sleek device between her jittery hands, Leona forced her mind to bring forth David's number. She moved her thumb deliberately over the keypad, punching in the proper sequence and praying the storm had not cut off David's signal. The doorbell rang, jolting every nerve in Leona's heightened-alert body. "Who would get out in this weather?"

Roxie shrugged. Cotton and Leona looked at each other.

"Well, is everybody just going to stand here or am I going to have to get it?" Leona's mother flipped her brake lever and rolled toward the door.

"Park it, Bertie. I'll go." Cotton grabbed the handle on the wheelchair. "Leona, you call David and see what you can find out."

Leona stepped into the hall and dialed David's number again. While she waited, the familiar voices of the Storys filtered through the walls and drowned out his voice mail greeting. Leona returned to the living room. "Etta May and Nola Gay, what on earth are you doing here?"

"Grab this, would you?" Nola Gay handed Leona a heavy towel-wrapped parcel. "That's our famous chili and sweet pickles. So be careful with it, dear."

Etta May wiped her feet on the mat and followed Nola Gay inside. "Shirley activated the prayer phone tree after she got Roxie's call. Sister and I are first responders."

"But—"

"Once I get this Crock-Pot plugged in, you'll have something hot in your belly in nothing flat." Nola Gay took the bundle from Leona's frozen grip. "Sister, see if you can't talk Cotton into laying a fire in the fireplace. It's freezing in here." Nola Gay marched toward the kitchen. She stopped at Leona's mother's wheelchair and kicked the tire. "Bertie, I could use your help."

"Well, I'm a little preoccupied at the moment."

"I can see that. But taking up space isn't accomplishing a thing. Grate the cheese and that'll give Leona some help she can sink her teeth into."

Etta May draped her coat over the back of the couch and winked at Leona. "God's in control." She shuffled over to Mother's wheelchair. "Why don't I give you a little push in the right direction, Bertie?"

Listening to her mother's protests disappear into the kitchen, Leona opened her clasped hand and looked at the phone. She had more important things to do than referee squabbles between a gaggle of puffed-up old women. God may be in control, but he obviously needed her help to get her children home safely. She entered David's number a third time, but the doorbell rang before she could push Send.

"Who else in the world would be out in this weather?" Leona stomped to the door and jerked it open.

There stood her boss, wood stacked up to his chin. "Ivan?"

Cotton stepped up and took a couple of pieces off the top of the bundle. "Thanks, Ivan. I was just on my way out to stock her bin."

"Didn't smell any smoke when I drove up, so I figured Leona hadn't got around to starting a fire this evening. Any word?"

"Shirley called the press?" Leona couldn't help checking the porch for any signs of her kids before she closed the door.

"She called your brother in Christ." Ivan's abbreviated statement communicated his conviction just as strongly as his hard-hitting editorials. "Now, where do you want this wood?"

"I'll show you." Roxie took Ivan's elbow and guided him to the box by the hearth.

Leona watched helplessly as Cotton and Roxie unloaded Ivan's arms. Here she was again, up to her neck in hot water, when suddenly, out of nowhere, unexpected floatation devices splashed into her stew from every direction.

Grab hold.

Leona glanced at the friends gathered around her hearth, but none of them had spoken to her. The explicit words had come from someplace deep within her drained soul, wrapping her weary shoulders in a peace as comforting as a Story-crocheted shawl. She rubbed her eyes. This had been a very long day. She was tired, and her imagination was running amuck. Hearing things would be just the ammunition Maxine Davis needed to have the pastor's widow committed.

The doorbell jangled Leona from her thoughts. Using her pointed forefinger, she parted the window curtain. Bette Bob McDonald shivered under the front porch light, holding two foil-covered pans. Leona opened the door. "That better be chocolate."

Bette Bob grinned. "Prayer warriors need their strength." She bustled past Leona and headed straight for the kitchen, shouting over her shoulder, "Amy called. The hospital is on standby. They're all set to patch up Parker and Maddie."

The doorbell buzzed yet again, jarring Leona from the bloody images assaulting her peace. Why was she worrying? Maddie had assured her she and Parker were not lying in a blood-soaked snowdrift. Her daughter had promised, leaving Leona no choice but to trust her. J.D. had always claimed her overactive imagination was Satan's greatest tool. If the king of darkness could keep her fears bigger than the truth, he'd win every time.

Leona yanked the door open. "Ruthie?"

The café proprietor thrust two large paper grocery sacks at her. "Heard there was an emergency over here. Maybe these sandwiches will help."

Cold swirled around Leona's dropped jaw as she stared at the rosy-cheeked woman. "Oh, my. I don't know what to say. You didn't have to—"

Ruthie held up a hand. "Don't get all mushy, Leona. I'm just doing my civic duty."

Roxie appeared at Leona's side. "Ruthie, you look absolutely frozen. Did you walk?"

She nodded. "Didn't want to block Leona's driveway, so I parked down the street." Ruthie jerked her head in the direction of the lone streetlight.

"Come on in and have some coffee." Roxie took the old girl's hand, obviously ignoring Ruthie's ingenious reference to Leona's parking problems. "Sit by the fire."

"It is pretty slick out there." Ruthie cast a wary look in Leona's direction. "I don't want to tie up your parking if your kids make it home."

"I insist you stay, at least until the weather clears." Leona patted J.D.'s chair. "Sit here. It's a recliner. Put your feet up."

A surprised look crossed Ruthie's face. "Well, I have been on my feet all day."

Leona helped Ruthie remove her coat and dropped it over the pile of coats growing at the same rate as her anxiety level.

"This is real Christian of you, Leona."

Christian? Maybe that was stretching things a bit, especially since it was Ruthie who had come to her to make amends rather than the other way around. If she dared claim her thoughts and actions had been anywhere near Christ-like when it came to Ruthie Crouch the Lord would raise an eyebrow for sure.

Ruthie sank into the cracked vinyl and pulled the lever, lifting her fallen arches perpendicular to the floor. "A cup of coffee, when you get a chance, would hit the spot." She closed her eyes and exhaled slowly.

"Sure, Ruthie." Leona flashed Roxie an I'll-get-even glare. "Make yourself at home."

The doorbell rang again.

"Bad news travels fast," Ruthie said.

Roxie laid a calming hand on Leona's arm. "Why don't you try to complete that call to David." She pointed to the phone still in Leona's clutches. "Let me get the door."

"You're a doll." Leona turned her back to the door and punched in David's number.

A swoosh of cold air blasted the room.

"Well, if it isn't et tu, Brute and the missus," Roxie growled. "Leona, that chicken-livered traitor and his bossy wife are here."

Leona wheeled.

Howard flicked snow from his hat brim. "Mrs. Brewer, if you don't mind, I need to speak to Leona."

"Before or after you stab her in the back?" Roxie crossed her arms over her chest, blocking their entrance into the parsonage.

Maxine brushed the snow from her shoulders. "This is private church business, between us and Leona."

Leona stepped forward. "What can I do for you, Howard?" Her icy tone could have frozen the melting snow sliding down the slope of the elder's nose.

"May we come in?"

"I'd pat 'em down first." Roxie hadn't budged from her barricade. "Maybe run them through a metal detector."

"Roxie." Leona pulled an imaginary zipper across her taut lips and Roxie reluctantly followed suit and clamped her mouth shut. "Of course, Howard. Come in. Get out of this weather."

"Thank you." Howard wiped his feet on the mat. With each scuff of his heavy all-weather boot across the rubber mat, Leona couldn't shake the feeling that she was the mat face down on the porch. Howard and Maxine scooted past Roxie with record speed.

Howard took out a hanky and buffed his head dry while Maxine fiddled with the buttons on her coat. "The new pastor candidate and his family are . . ." The stammering elder paused. He lowered his hanky and caught the drop hanging from the end of his snout. "As I was saying, the new pastor candidate is . . ."

Glancing from Maxine to Howard, Leona zeroed her gaze on the nervous board chairman. "Spit it out, Howard."

Volkswagen Beetle red crept up the slick sides of the elder's bald head. "With David."

"Hell's bells." Roxie's eyes flashed fire. "You sorry little snake."

"Roxie, please." Leona stepped between them. "What do you mean?"

"I talked to Ted earlier and he told me they'd caught a ride to Mt. Hope with a guy named David in a limo."

Leona squeezed the cell phone. "And?"

Waving his hanky as if it were a white flag, Howard continued, "And, so . . . I'm going to have to ask you if the Postiers can spend the night here in the parsonage."

"Hell's bells!" Roxie flew around Leona, hands thrashing the air. "Have you lost your mind, Howard Davis?"

"Roxanne!" Leona pulled her back.

Hands on hips, Maxine launched a rescue missile, aiming for the blank space on Leona's shocked face. "The Double D is chock-full and you're the only one with enough room to put them up, Leona. Besides, it seems logical that if they're going to live in the parsonage, they should check it out. See what changes they'd like to have made before they move in."

"Changes?" Leona's blood boiled.

"You know, new carpet, paint, whatever it takes to make this place presentable."

"How about I stick your pointed head in that firetrap oven you've stuck my friend with for the past eighteen years and let you check that out, Maxine Davis!" Roxie struggled to break free of Leona's hold.

Pressure pounded in Leona's ears. Every stick of wallpaper holding this dilapidated old house together had been lovingly chosen and applied with her very own hands. Not once had the board offered to hire any of the work done. She'd spent hours, and tons of her own elbow grease, increasing the value of this property, and for what? For the next pastor, that's what. But she'd die before she'd give Maxine Davis the pleasure of knowing her comment had skewered her heart like a meat kabob.

Leona squared her shoulders and shook her friend. "Roxie, I'm going to send you to the kitchen if you don't settle down." She blinked back gathering storm clouds and conjured her Christian-hospitality voice. "The Postiers are welcome to stay here."

Roxie's jaw dropped. "That's all you've got to say about it?"

"What do you want me to do? Throw a fit? Make them sleep in a snowdrift?"

"How about you let me stuff this used car salesman in a snowdrift?" Ruthie lowered the recliner footrest and came to stand by Leona, hands planted on her hips.

"Now, Ruthie, you aren't even a Christian—"

"You just wait one cotton-pickin' minute, Howard Davis." Anger spewed from Leona's mouth. "How dare you declare who is and who is not a Christian. Who made you the Almighty's judge and jury?"

"I'll tell you who," Maxine said. "The members of Mt. Hope Community Church, that's who."

Leona balled her fist and reared back. But in mid-swing, a

hand came out of nowhere and clamped down hard around her wrist. The phone shot out of her hand and sailed through the air. Tater Tot jumped off the couch and scurried after the shiny silver projectile clattering across the wooden floor.

"If anybody is going to hit him—" Cotton released Leona's wrist and stepped between her and Howard—"it's going to be me."

"I'd like a round or two in the ring myself." Ruthie whipped a spatula out of her pocket and assumed a battle position beside Cotton.

"Well, if she gets to flip him, I think I should get to tighten his loose screws." Roxie grabbed the screwdriver on the hospital bed and lined up beside Ruthie to create a unified wall of hostility.

"I can run over his foot and make him a cripple for life." Leona's mother pushed her way between Cotton and Ruthie.

"Mother. What on earth?" Leona said.

"If it bleeds, it leads." Ivan reached in his shirt pocket and snatched his notepad. He propped one foot up on the hearth, flipped to a blank page, and began scribbling notable quotes.

Nola Gay, Etta May, and Bette Bob burst into the room.

"What's all the commotion—" Nola surveyed the tense faces. "What's going on here?"

"Howard's being ugly to my girl," Mother snapped.

"That true, Howard?"

"Of course not, Nola Gay," Maxine spat out.

"That's good, because I would hate to think that one of our leaders and his dear wife willfully added another ounce of grief to our dear, sweet, overloaded pastor's wife." Nola Gay came and put both hands on Leona's mother's wheelchair. "If my friend Bertie says you're being ugly, you're being ugly. May you choke on sweet pickles if it's so, Howard."

Bette Bob stuck her head between the Storys. "If you're up to no good, Howard, your church dinners will never see another brownie."

"And good luck meeting the budget if Sister and I are forced to withdraw our tithes." Etta May shook an accusing finger in the elder's face. "And you call yourself a servant of the Lord."

Howard and Maxine inched closer together, simultaneously slinking toward the door.

Grab hold. Leona heard the command distinctly. Grab hold to these friends who love you, and know that I am God.

Chapter Twenty-Five

Within moments after their arrival, the rescue team had Parker's neck stabilized. Satisfied her patient could be safely moved, Maddie directed his transfer to the backseat of the limo. "We'll take him to Mt. Hope. It's closer," she shouted over the howling winds at the serious-faced EMT on the other end of the board.

The paramedic scowled at Maddie's demands. "That's a nasty bump on his head. You sure he'll be fine, Doc?"

"I don't want to take any chances. We'll run him by the hospital and let them check him out."

They slid the board across the backseat of the limo. "I'm fine." Parker nearly upset the rig trying to right himself.

Maddie gently pushed him down. "Are you a doctor, Parker?"

"If your corn has weevils." His lips curled into a goofy grin.

"Well, right now you're a few bushels short of a load, so I guess you'll have to trust my professional judgment. And, for future reference, I don't plant corn." She hopped into the limo. She had to squeeze in between David and her mother's blonde replacement on the opposite seat. Her brother had introduced his passengers when the tanned strangers wearing inappropriate outerwear swarmed the truck and started praying.

"He's all yours." The paramedic winked. "You folks take it easy." He shut the door and Melvin slowly pulled away from the accident scene.

"David, have you called Momma?"

"Yeah, while you were helping them load that other guy in the ambulance. How did you know he was in worse shape than Parker?"

"Four long years with my nose in the books, Brother." Maddie rubbed her hands together, trying to return some feeling to her numb fingers and hoping to delay forced small talk with the curious new pastor's family smiling at her. "How was Momma?"

"Thrilled to know you're alive. Said the house was crammed with people praying until we get home."

Parker opened and closed his fists in front of his face. "If my neck is broken, why can I move my fingers and toes?"

"I'm going to tighten that neck collar several notches if you don't cooperate and lay still, Parker Kemp." Maddie reached over and tucked her patient's arms under the blanket.

Parker frowned. "Your bedside manner could use some

work."

"Why don't you try to rest?" Maddie used the palm of her hand to apply firm pressure to the glove stuck to Parker's forehead.

"Ouch!" He pulled his head away. "That hurt. Aren't you supposed to keep me talking? Keep me awake? Not try to knock me out. I could lapse into a coma or something."

"I doubt it. Your mouth hasn't closed since you opened your eyes."

"I have things to say and one of them is praise God, glory hallelujah, I'm alive." He looked at Maddie. "We should thank God I'm alive, don't you think?"

Maddie wrinkled her nose, and the grin disappeared from Parker's face.

David chuckled. "So is he going to make it?"

"Not if I kill him." Maddie fell back on the seat, happy to lean upon her brother's strong shoulder.

Too much had happened, too fast. She needed a minute to plow through the rubble, put things in some sort of order, and dissect each incredible development. But with the crisis under control, the adrenaline rush had quickly dissipated, leaving a sinking exhaustion in its wake. If her current state was any indication of how she'd hold up under pressure, she'd count it a blessing she wasn't interested in emergency room medicine.

She studied Parker stretched out on the opposite seat. His eyes were focused on the limo sunroof like it was a portal to heaven. His lips moved slightly, probably offering the prayers she had just pooh-poohed. Why did his unshakable faith fly all over her? She watched the lines of Parker's pained expression soften with each word he whispered, as if doses of peace were administered with every utterance of his praise.

Maybe the bump on the head had knocked him cuckoo for a bit, but she had to admit the man still possessed the uncanny gift of discernment. He was right. They had been fortunate . . . no, they had been miraculously protected to escape that twisted mess of steel with only scratches and bruises. Blessed no one had died. Blessed they could get in out of the snow. Blessed David and Melvin were right behind them. And blessed they had been rescued so quickly. No doubt about it, their salvation had only one explanation . . . God.

Shame washed over Maddie. Stiff-necked and strong-willed, she'd put her back to the blizzard and hung on, but for what? In the end, she had been unable to change their dire situation or do a thing for the injured on her own. Prayer had been her only option. And in her darkest hour, God had answered.

How could I have been so arrogant? So self-assured? So dependent upon my own limited and frail abilities? Didn't

Daddy's death teach me anything?

Life was fragile and could be snuffed in an instant. Nothing in this world was permanent. Insecurity ruled. And what did this insecurity leave in its wake? Nothing but the one thing her father had preached for years: the hope of life eternal. The promise had sustained her father through the peaks and valleys of church work. Momma's head was above water right now because she held on to God's guarantee, as if it were a life raft. And Parker was so convinced of that hope that he had packed every egg of his future in faith's fragile basket and pointed his ship toward a foreign country.

Bridget touched Maddie's arm, compassion oozing out from under her heavy mascara like too much mayo on a club sandwich. "I'm sure your mother offered prayers of thanksgiving."

Maddie swiped at her wet cheeks. "Momma's an expert in crisis management."

"So are we!" the blonde said proudly.

"You're gonna need it to survive living on Hobo Highway." David elbowed Maddie and flashed the play-along-with-me look they had used on the many occasions questionable antics in the sanctuary had to be explained to Momma.

Just as she was never certain of the course David's discourse would take, Maddie wasn't sure what her brother was up to now, but she dutifully assumed her supportive role. "Never knew from day to day what would happen next."

"Hobo Highway?" Bridget's voice cracked.

"Vagrants." David leaned around Maddie. "The parsonage porch is always littered with them."

"Littered?" Bridget pursed her lips, fear clouding her blue eyes. "Why?"

From the pleased look on David's face, Maddie realized her brother was trying to scare these trespassers right back to Florida. Brilliant.

Rallying to the cause, Maddie charged full-speed ahead. "Because the parsonage is so close to the highway, the rumble of eighteen-wheelers rattles our windows day and night."

"To make the hairpin curve, they have to slow down. That's when the hobos fall off and land in our yard," David said.

"But that's only during the hobo migration." Parker proved remarkably quick on the uptake for one suffering from a head injury.

Maddie fought the urge to leap across the car and plant a kiss of gratitude on the less-bloody side of his noggin.

"Migration?" Bridget's brow furrowed unattractively.

"In early spring and late fall, the hobos migrate, following the trail of the silver bullets." Parker's expression was so serious, Maddie checked for signs of cucumber rot on the Postiers' frozen faces.

Ted swallowed, his eyes wide. "Silver bullets?"

"Retirees pulling silver camper trailers head south to escape the cold of winter. Don't worry, they turn around and head north to escape the heat of summer." Parker could not have sounded more convincing if he had ripped the information from the pages of the Farmers' Almanac.

"Exactly what do you mean by . . . hobo?" Bridget obviously was the kind of person who needed things spelled out . . . several times.

David jumped on this flaw. "I remember the time this strung-out, gypsy-looking lady pounded on the front door demanding Momma open the screen and feed her chicken-fried steak."

Determined to help Bridget see the light, Maddie said, "Remember the time that drunk fellow rammed the door in the middle of the night demanding to be let into his own house?"

"Scared me almost as bad as the night someone set off the alarm in the church building and Dad went tearing across the parking lot in his underwear?"

"Thank goodness Momma had the presence of mind to call the police and stop him before he charged in on the thieves stealing the church's only computer."

Ted's face clouded with concern. "The church only has one computer?"

"Technically, the computer belongs to Momma," David said. "She bought it with her grocery coupon money."

"How about the guy Dad found taking a bath in the baptistry?"

"He was miffed that the church didn't supply shampoo," David added.

Maddie leaned forward. "But my all-time favorite was the night we woke up and our house was completely surrounded by flashing blue lights."

"Cops everywhere, shouting, 'Freeze!'" David shaped his right hand into a gun and slapped it into his left to steady his aim at the Postiers.

"Next thing we knew, three armed robbers were facedown and spread-eagle in our backyard."

David beamed. "The show those crooks put on was better than Law & Order."

"Did they ever find the sawed-off shotgun they used to hold up the liquor store on the corner? I can't remember." Maddie chewed on the corner of her lip for added effect.

"Shotgun?" Bridget's voice squeaked.

"Crooks?" Ted added.

Maddie and David nodded their heads slowly.

Parker picked up the lull in the conversation. "And if you think this snowstorm is bad, you haven't seen anything. By New

Year's Eve, the wind will peel paint."

David put on a somber face and leaned forward. He waited until he had the full attention of all four Postiers. Next to their father, no one was better at the dramatic pause. "I remember the time it snowed so bad, semitrucks skidded off the interstate and drifts of white buried their overturned rigs."

The Postiers gasped. Ted cast a worried glance out the foggy windows, wrapped an arm around each child and pulled them close. Bridget crossed her arms over her chest and rubbed her hands frantically over her windbreaker, shivering like she'd suddenly contracted an uncontrollable chill.

Going in for the kill, Maddie heaved a sigh. "Yeah, we had truckers sleeping on every inch of floor space in the parsonage . . . for days and days and days."

"Days?" Bridget's eyes were liquid.

David and Maddie turned to each other. "Breaker, breaker, good buddy," they said while executing a unified high-five.

Melvin cleared his throat. "Miss Madison. Should I proceed to the hospital as planned?"

Maddie scanned the ashen faces of the Postiers. "Absolutely, Melvin. I believe we have a medical emergency back here."

Chapter Twenty-Six

"Leona, it's about time you let yourself cry, or you're going to drown in all those tears you're holding back," Roxie said.

Stretched out on her bed, Leona stroked Tater's head as she considered Roxie's advice. Even her best friend didn't know how often she'd wept in private. Getting away from the serious faces huddled around her fireplace was the only way she could maintain her strong front. Holding herself together in the face of prying eyes didn't mean she was in danger of drowning. Dammed-up tears had ample room in her hollow chest.

"The Harper replacements are waltzing in here at any moment and there isn't a thing I can do about it . . . except try to thin the crowd downstairs and get the place tidied up." Leona sat up and swung her legs over the edge of her bed. "Maybe this dark night will pass faster if I get up and get busy."

"Hold on, girlfriend. Give me a minute to think."

Tater bounded off the bed. He barked and pawed at the

closed door.

"No time." Leona's heart skipped a beat. "They're here."

"So are your kids." Roxie offered Leona her hand. "Isn't that what we prayed for?"

"Remind me to be more specific in the future."

"Leona, David and Maddie are home!" Nola Gay shouted from the bottom of the stairs.

Roxie smoothed Leona's mussed hair. "Look on the bright side."

"And what's that?" Leona placed her hand across her heart, willing it to slow its beat.

"Maybe they won't like the place when they find out the Storys come with it."

Leona laughed out loud. "What would I do without you?" She kissed Roxie's cheek.

Roxie's eyes lit up. "That's it, Leona." She raced over to the bedroom window, yanked on the yellowed shade. Dust flew everywhere. She pried open the window. A blustery draft swept through the room.

Shivers rippled along Leona's spine. "What in the world are you doing, Roxie?"

"Beating Howard at his own game." Roxie darted to the next window and repeated her madness.

"What are you talking about?"

Breathing hard, Roxie brushed the dust from her hands. "Let's say the Postiers meet the Story sisters in all their splendor, spend a night in this drafty old house, and try to shower while the dishwasher is running."

"Have you lost your mind? They'd hate—" Leona stopped midsentence. "Roxanne Brewer. You have sunk to deplorable depths, even for you. And I refuse to be dragged into yet another of your evil schemes."

"You want to live with Bertie?" Roxie parked her hands on her hips. "I didn't think so."

"But—"

"Here's what we'll do. You will go down there and give your children a hero's welcome. Then you will turn on your best charm."

"And then what?"

"You will leave the rest to me. That way you can sleep tonight with a completely clear conscience."

"Momma?" The urgent sound of Maddie's voice tugged Leona toward the door.

"I don't think this is—"

Roxie opened the door and Tater bolted out, yapping all the way down the stairs. "Even Christ tossed a few gold diggers out on their ears." She pushed Leona in the direction of the steps. "Now, go."

"But the parsonage is hardly a Temple."

"Momma!" Maddie stood at the bottom of the stairs.

Her girl was home. Nothing else mattered.

Leona raced toward Maddie's open arms. She threw herself into the embrace of the child the Lord had graciously spared. They pulled each other close, and Leona buried her nose in Maddie's tumbling hair. "Thank you, God. Thank you, God."

Maddie sobbed, "I'm all right, Momma. I'm all right."

"Praise God." Leona clasped Maddie's cheeks between her hands and kissed her forehead. "Praise God."

"Hey, Momma." David stepped into the hall.

"Son." Leona grabbed his neck. She drank in the smell of him. The family she feared she'd lost had been restored to her. Thank you, God. She pulled back and looked into the watery eyes that resembled her husband's. Her boy was whole, well, and wonderful. "Wouldn't your daddy get a kick out of seeing my worries proved all for naught yet again."

David chuckled and kissed her cheek. "So many worries, so little time."

Leona straightened with a start. "And Parker? Where's Parker?"

"Right here, Mrs. Harper." Parker's forehead sported a few Steri-Strips plastered along a jagged, dark line. But other than the railroad track crease in his brow, he looked no worse for wear. He ran a finger over his wound. "Just a little bump on the head. Your girl took good care of me."

"His hard head is what saved him." Maddie beamed.

David loosened the grip Leona had upon his arm. "Momma, I brought some folks with me that you need to meet."

Leona smoothed her hair, and straightened her blouse. "Our replacements?"

David nodded.

"Give me a minute, will you?"

David and Maddie reluctantly left her in the hall.

She could hear laughter coming from the living room where she'd raised her family. Howard and Maxine liked the Postiers. "Don't ask me to do this, too, Lord," she whispered. But no one answered. The battle was hers alone to fight.

Leona stepped into the room.

There, seated on her plaid couch, were the Postiers, hands clasped in their laps. Surrounded by the backbone of the congregation, they eagerly answered questions about their perilous journey to Mt. Hope.

A wry smile curved Leona's lips. The greenhorns had no idea one bald, backstabbing weasel rested his hands upon their shoulders while the other served them hot coffee. But stay in ministry long enough and they would learn . . . all too quickly. And hopefully, like her, someday they would discover that true servants of the Lord survive no matter what kind of vermin attacks the henhouse.

Mr. Postier noticed Leona's entrance and stood respectfully. "Mrs. Harper, Ted Postier."

"Reverend." Leona shook his outstretched hand, warmed by his firm and sure grip. "A pleasure."

She turned her attention to the pastor's beautiful blonde wife. The woman's young, unlined face made the perfect backdrop for those incredible sparkling blue eyes. Leona studied their glitter and realized she had seen this expectant look before.

The same conviction had illumined the soul of the man she loved every time he took the pulpit, as if today would be the day the whole world claimed Christ.

Leona backpedaled, trying to escape the heart-piercing gaze.

"The Lord your God is with you, Leona Harper. He is mighty to save."

"J.D.? Is that you?" Leona scanned the room, searching for the source of her husband's voice. Did the kids have an old home video in the VCR?

"He delights in you, Leona."

"Don't you tease me, J.D. Harper. You know I'm nothing but a cheap Popsicle. Besides, I'm not speaking to you at the moment." Leona crossed her arms, unwilling to continue the argument, desperate for the contact to never end.

"He quiets you with his love."

Immediately a sweet-smelling peace poured over Leona, as if someone had broken open a hot oil treatment. She closed her eyes and allowed the soothing warmth to course down her body, kneading the panic from her knotted soul. She inhaled deeply, her first deep breath in weeks. When she opened her eyes, there stood before her a man in dazzling white. She took a moment to admire the way the iridescent light captured the silver strands traipsing across his well-trained waves.

"You remind me of a pastor I knew."

He smiled and offered her his hand, and she took it. He led her from the living room, out the front door, down the porch steps, along the sidewalk, past Roxie's, and around the corner.

There, high on a grassy green hill, sat a beautiful house. On the shady wraparound porch a crowd had gathered. They had welcoming grins, and what appeared to be pitchers and pitchers of ice-cold lemonade. Leona followed her guide up the steps and through the throng.

They stopped before an ivory door and he motioned for her to come forward, indicating she should read the etched inscription gracing the front of the golden mailbox. How could she have lived in Mt. Hope all these years and not noticed this lovely home? Leona was dying to know who lived there. She stepped forward and began to read.

"The home of Leona Harper . . . a woman of worth."

A huge lump lodged in her throat, but Leona managed to turn toward her guide and choke out, "For me? All of this for me?"

He smiled and nodded and finished the verse. "The Lord rejoices over you with singing, Leona Harper."

And in a blink of an eye, her knight in shining armor was gone.

Once again, Leona stood in the middle of the living room the Lord had loaned her for eighteen years.

Through the front door glass she could see the glimmer of snowflakes swirling under the porch light. She glanced at the Harper replacements seated on the threadbare couch, their feet planted firmly on the worn carpet, and she thought, Maxine Davis, you can have this place. The Lord's got something better for me. How I'm going, I don't know. When I'm going? It's anybody's guess. What I'm going to do until I go? Lord only knows. But whether or not I'm going is my choice, and it is nonnegotiable.

Leona turned, looked into those hopeful blue eyes, and clasped the young woman's hand in hers. "Mrs. Postier, welcome home."

Chapter Twenty-Seven

Sunday morning dawned bright and sparkly, the stormy dark streets washed white with peaceful drifts of snow. Leona bustled through the living room, humming "Joy to the World," her heart lighter than it had been since the Sunday before Thanksgiving. "Etta May, would you mind cranking up that stereo a bit?"

"How long has *he* been in that shower?" Nola Gay wrenched the lever on J.D.'s recliner. Her thick ankles shot out in front of her.

"I don't know—a while, I guess."

"Do you think this Postier fellow knows what time church starts?" Etta May held the jar of her latest pickle offering up to the light for careful examination.

"I went over everything last night," Leona said. "They're probably just taking a little extra care with their appearance. Meeting a new congregation can be a tad intimidating."

"Our brother had an old coon dog that bayed off-key like that." Nola Gay reached for her coffee mug.

Etta May set the pickles on the coffee table. She pushed

herself up from the couch. "Sister, you keep it down. We don't want the new pastor to feel anything but completely welcome." She turned the knob on the CD player and smiled. "Perhaps he's making music to the Lord . . . in his heart."

"Perhaps Leona ought to start that dishwasher." Nola sipped her coffee.

"I'm not going to do that, so just get that out of your devious little head."

Leona's mother wheeled into the living room. "I'll start it myself, if he doesn't shut up."

"Well, look who's up and about." A wry grin crossed Nola Gay's dentures. "If you're feeling so perky, Bertie, how about you serve us some of those cinnamon rolls I've been smellin'?"

Leona kissed her mother's cheek. "Wait here, Mother. I'll see if they're done." She turned to the Storys. "In the meantime, I'm counting on you two to hold the fort."

Nola Gay waved Leona on. "Don't we always?"

Leona raced to the kitchen and opened the oven door, enjoying the delicious blast of smells as if her senses had been awakened from a deep sleep. She and the kids were dressed, but she hadn't seen hide nor hair of the Postier family all morning. Maybe Bridget awoke naturally gorgeous, free of the laborious effort Leona's presentable appearance required. Leona dismissed that catty thought from her mind and concentrated on setting out the cups and saucers and arranging the company napkins. Suddenly, screams erupted from the direction of the living room.

Leona dropped the napkins. "What has Mother done now?" She tore down the hall and burst into the living room. "What in the world happened?" She gasped for breath.

"Pastor Postier walked by." Etta May's dentures clacked faster than her words, the woman clearly shaken.

"So? He has to get to his bedroom."

"He was naked, Leona." Her mother shook her head.

"Except for your best monogrammed towel wrapped around his very tanned middle." Nola Gay turned her mug bottoms-up and polished off the contents, dribbles escaping onto her blouse.

David and Maddie bounded down the stairs. "What's going on?" David flew to his mother's side.

Maddie joined him on the other. "What was that ruckus?"

Nola Gay dabbed at the spots on her blouse. "That new pastor paraded past us in his birthday suit."

David bristled. "What?"

"He was wearing a towel, David." Leona took Nola's empty mug. "Pastor Postier probably was not expecting company so early this morning. I think the rolls should be done by now. Why don't we all have a bite to eat? Give our guests a little privacy?"

Voices and a loud clamoring upstairs stayed Leona's intended progress toward the kitchen.

"David, would you mind checking on our guests?"

"Sure." David started up the stairs, stopped midflight by bundled-up Postiers on their way down. Each toted a heavy piece of luggage. "Morning. You folks going somewhere?" David reached for the wife's overnight bag, but she held up her hand.

"I think we've got it." Bridget shifted the strap to her shoulder, the pleased-to-be-here warmth missing from her voice.

"There's really no hurry to pack up before church." Leona came to the foot of the stairs. "I'm sure the elders will have a committee who'll want to visit with you this afternoon."

Bridget pointed an acrylic nail at the sisters. "Are *they* here every Sunday morning?"

"You better bet we are." Nola Gay shifted the footrest lever and brought herself to an upright position.

"Like clockwork," Etta May added.

"Then I'm afraid we won't be." Ted pushed past David. "I'm not interested in displaying my private wares for the congregants."

"Just as well, they weren't that impressive," Mother chirped.

"You're all a bunch of backwoods bumpkins." Bridget

stormed down the stairs.

"Yes, we are." Leona's mother wheeled up alongside her. "And proud of it."

Leona hugged her mother as the Postiers stalked past. "Wait. You can't leave before church."

"Watch us." Bridget snatched the hands of her children.

"Maddie, can't you give them a sedative or something?" Nola Gay crossed her arms over her sagging chest.

Maddie shook her head.

David jumped into the fray. "But you don't have transportation."

Ted staggered under the weight of several suitcases. "We'll call a cab."

"Don't bother." Leona's mother wheeled herself in front of the door. "I insist you let my chauffeur return you to the shallow hole from which you have slithered or I'll be *fixin' to* do it myself."

"You tell 'em, Bertie." Nola Gay beamed.

"Melvin. Fetch the limo."

"Mother, you remembered his name." Leona fought the urge to jump up and down.

"I'm not a total waste of effort."

"I never thought you were." Leona blew her mother a kiss.

Within minutes Melvin had the car warmed, the Postiers

loaded, and the parsonage back to normal.

"Good riddance." Leona's mother shut the front door. "Now, who's going to preach?" She looked directly at David. "Seems to me there is only one plausible choice."

"Don't look at me." David backed toward the hall.

"Young man, you wait right there. Don't think I don't know why you've put off taking your place at the firm." Leona's mother flashed a look that dared David to defy her.

"Grandmother—"

She held up a stiff hand. "I'm looking at a man who will never be a lawyer."

Peace came over David's face. "I'll be right back." He turned and shot up the stairs. He returned carrying his father's black Sunday shoes. "Figured this would be the best way to start." He sat in his father's chair, removed his own boots, and slipped on the scuffed black Florsheims. "A little big."

Leona smiled. "You'll grow into them." If David could take such a bold step, hadn't the time come for her to do the same? "Wait right here, son."

Leona ran upstairs and found the shipping box in the back of her closet. Swift kicks sent her Sunday flats flying. She lifted the red shoes from the wrapping and carefully slid her feet inside. She fastened the ankle straps and stood before the row of suits hanging in the closet.

"You're right, J.D. Harper. Living in the parsonage is not for sissies." Leona Harper closed the closet door and took her most daring step yet.

Aren't the people of Mt. Hope fun? If you enjoyed escaping into the community of Mt. Hope, you'll be happy to know your adventure doesn't have to end with **WALKING SHOES.**

There are three more books in the Mt. Hope Southern Adventures series: **SHOES TO FILL, DANCING SHOES,** and **BABY SHOES.**

Subscribe to Lynne's JOIN THE ADVENTURE Newsletter. Subscribers receive updates on new releases, special offers, and ACT 1 of Lynne's audio performance of this story. www.lynnegentry.com

Your REVIEWS are so important to me. Taking the time to put up a REVIEW is a helpful encouragement to me and a wonderful source of info for other readers.

Want to continue our conversation?

I've traveled the country performing Leona's story as a one-woman-show. Some have asked how I could infuse such a sad time in someone's life with humor. Having faced several tragic losses of my own, I found two things sustained me. My faith in God and sharing laughter with good friends.

I hope you'll gather a few friends for a few laughs and a closer look into your own heart. Invite me to join you via FaceTime at www.lynnegentry.com. Here are a few ideas to get our conversation going:

Book Discussion Questions

1. J.D. declares, "If want to wear fancy red shoes, wear 'em." Leona's reluctance demonstrates her unwillingness to do anything that might bring shame upon her. Does this statement define someone you know? Why does shame hold us back?

2. Leona's struggle with the elder's wife, Maxine Davis, is one of the major conflicts in the story. Hierarchical relationships are tricky. Have you ever had to navigate the thorny line between boss and friend? Explain how this person's ability to hire and fire you made sustaining a friendship with them impossible.

3. When Leona slides next to her pastor husband during the song service, she feels this incredible sense of security and purpose. But within a few short paragraphs, everything that defines and sustains this woman vanishes. Compare Leona's losses to any losses you've

suffered. What happened to your self-worth? Was your faith shaken?

4. While Leona is defined by her fear of what people think, her children are defined by their anger at having to grow up in the public eye. Growing up inside a "glass house" makes David and Maddie desperate for privacy, or at the very least, the freedom to make mistakes without judgment. A traumatic past can set us up to believe a lie that creates our deepest fear. What event in Leona's past shaped her, caused her to believe the lie that she must be perfect, and contributed to her fears? What happened in your past that created your fears?

5. I believe fear hinders the reinvention process. For years I worried that we could lose our ministry job. And then we did. Amazingly, we survived. What is your biggest fear? What if the worst thing that could happen happened? Tell how Leona survived an unexpected realization of her worst fear. What are some adjustments you would have to make to your life to survive a course redirection?

6. Strained family relationships take a toll on Leona. How does the theme of starting over affect Leona's thoughts and actions toward her mother? Her children? Consider your relationships: marriage, children, friends, neighbors, co-workers. What relationship do you long to reinvent? What would it take to accomplish restoration in these relationships?

7. The Story sisters are two of the first people Leona meets when she moves to Mt. Hope. Her impression of these wrinkled busybodies is based on what she perceives as their unfavorable impression of her. Discuss the dangers of first impressions; and the

difficulty of reinventing someone's incorrect impression of you. Should we even want to change another's opinion of us? How was Leona's relationship with the Storys reinvented?

8. Leona has poured herself into the career of being a wife, mother, and pastor's wife. In this paradigm she feels confident and comfortable. Maybe you, too, are well-established in your chosen profession and feel defined by your occupation. In today's economy, people who have invested time, money, and long years in a certain career field are finding themselves tossed aside, cut loose, and released from their jobs. Unable to find comparable employment, not only is their financial security lost; the walls of their paradigm have been bulldozed. How do you reinvent yourself for a second career so late in the game? Discuss Leona's return to some of her former dreams. How did she capitalize on those desires God put in her heart? What unfulfilled dream lurks in the back of your mind?

9. When Leona realizes life will have to change for her, do you think she had to compromise to find happiness? If so, how?

10. Change, the theme repeated over and over, comes to several of the characters in this book. Who do you think had to change the most? Why are we so resistant to change?

11. One of the beauties of "the church" is the family it can potentially create. A unique group of people with absolutely nothing in common are bound together by the blood of Christ. But just like any family, there are the crazy uncles or no-good cousins. Conflict is inevitable.

When Leona chooses to seek a confidant outside of this body, it doesn't set well with Maxine. Why?

12. If you suffer a tragic set back or serious change in life plans, will you get up or curl up?

About the Author

Lynne Gentry knew marrying a pastor might change her plans. She didn't know how ministry would change her life. This author of numerous short stories and dramatic works travels the country as a professional acting coach and inspirational speaker. Lynne allows her imagination to run wild and also writes in the fantasy/science fiction genre of time travel and in the fast-paced romantic suspense genre. You can find out more about these adventures into historical worlds at www.lynnegentry.com. Lynne lives in Texas with her husband and medical therapy dog. She counts spending time with her two grown children and their families her greatest joy.

Insider Chat with the Author

Where did you find Leona Harper?

I watched three of my older friends lose their husbands. Two of them regrouped, rebuilt, and reinvented their lives. One shriveled up and died in a nursing home. Observing their experiences made me ask, what if tragedy struck me? What would I do? Do I have the spiritual chops to pick myself up and start over? Could I trust God to lead me through a dark valley? So I guess part of Leona Harper was found inside of me.

Tell us how much of yourself you write into your characters.

Every author brings a little bit of themselves to their characters. It can't be helped. Drawing upon life experiences is a great starting point. But for my characters to leap from the page, their personalities have to be far bigger and their circumstances far more dire than anything I've experienced.

Humor is tough to write, but you did a spectacular job. Any writing secrets you'd like to share?

In a way, everyone lives in a glass house, so to speak. With the advent of social media and cameras on every phone we are all at risk of having our failings replayed on a constant loop. Shame is one of our greatest fears.

Learning to laugh, especially at myself, has helped me cope with the scrutiny that comes with vulnerability. But as a minister's wife, it was not always appropriate for me to say what I was thinking, let alone laugh out loud. So, with the quirky cast in Mt. Hope, I get to say and do all sorts of things a good pastor's wife would never say or do, but I often thought. I'm happy to report that laughter is good for the soul.

Tell us, what brings protagonist Leona to the point of changing?

Circumstances beyond her control. Like many of us, Leona doesn't like change. But none of us escape the twists and turns of life. Whether it is the loss of a spouse or the loss of a thirty-year career, nothing stays the same.

What does the future hold for the Harpers?

David and Maddie are slipping on shoes that will take them on different paths. The zany cast of Mt. Hope will dog them every step of the way. Find out what happens next in David's story: **SHOES TO FILL.**

What is your greatest shame?

Sooner or later everyone encounters setback or tragedy. When then bottom fell out of the ministry we'd worked so hard to build, it made me ask: Why do some thrive in conflict while others struggle to survive? And which one will I be?

Years of ministry had afforded me the opportunity to observe people undergoing identical difficulties (divorce, loss of a spouse, illness, financial ruin, etc.) Some remained faithful, even emerged more committed to their faith. Others floundered and fell away?

I've pondered the reasons and come to believe, those who make it are those who prepared ahead of time. The survivors grounded themselves in God's word, surrounded themselves with a strong support system, and regularly yielded their will to the Father **before** the storm hit. Thus, when life spins out of control, they rock on the waves, but eventually they grab hold of the Hand they knew well and allow Him to bring them to safe harbor.

This is the assurance I craved, and the comfort I achieved by writing this book. I was prepared and that is why when it was my turn to sink or swim, I made it safely to the shore.

You can too!

Tell us the kinds of books you enjoy reading and writing.

I'm an eclectic reader. I read everything from serious scholarly research books on the Roman Empire to issue-driven fiction by Jodi Picoult to time travel by Diana Gabaldon. I haven't traveled as much as I'd like so I'm drawn to foreign settings with rich characters in unusual circumstances in places I'd love to visit.

The excitement that comes with escaping into another world is why I'm also an eclectic writer. As a shade-tree historian, I often stumble across unique incidents in history. **The Carthage Chronicles** were written after I learned about a third-century plague that nearly wiped out the Roman Empire. Learning about the Plague of Cyprian spurred my imagination. What if a twenty-first century doctor dropped into the troubled times of the third century?

If you enjoy adventure, romance, and a glimpse into history, you'll love reading **The Carthage Chronicles.**

I'd love to have you escape into another world with me at www.lynnegentry.com.

Let's connect
Facebook
Instagram
Twitter

Thanks for joining the Harper family on the first leg of their Mt. Hope Adventure. I hope you'll take the next leg with David in SHOES TO FILL, available on Amazon.

Download for only $4.99

Find out what happens next in Mt. Hope …

Add SHOES TO FILL to your library now @ www.lynnegentry.com

Subscribe to Lynne's **JOIN THE ADVENTURE** Newsletter
and get your FREE download of ACT 1 of Lynne's audio
performance
of this story. Read the series and collect all three audio acts for
FREE.
**Subscribers also receive exclusive news on latest releases
and limited time offers.
www.lynnegentry.com**

If you enjoy southern series, you'll also want to grab the first
book in my newest series set in the Texas Hill Country. The story of
the Slocum women is an emotionally packed inter-generational tale
that will warm your heart.

BUY FLYING FOSSILS now @ www.lynnegentry.com:

Made in the USA
Monee, IL
29 August 2020

40370321R00216